Storm of the Magi
A Cornish Fantasy

Chris Vick

ISBN **978 185022 208 8**

Published by Truran, Croft Prince, Mount Hawke,
Truro, Cornwall TR4 8EE
www.truranbooks.co.uk

Truran is an imprint of Truran Books Ltd

Acknowledgements: With heartfelt and warm thanks to Ivan and
Heather Corbett of Truran for their faith and invaluable advice.
Thanks also to Linda Garland for her wonderful cover art, to
Donald Rawe for his counsel on Cornish folklore and history and
to Sarah, my first reader. The sources of inspiration are too
numerous to list, but special mention must be made of George
Ewart Evans and David Thomson's book: *The Leaping Hare* and of
Kit Williams' *Masquerade*.

Printed and bound in Cornwall by R. Booth Ltd,
Antron Hill, Mabe, Penryn, TR10 9HH

For Lamorna

Prologue

Dearest Abi, beloved great-granddaughter,

Providing my solicitors have followed my instructions correctly, you will have received this letter shortly after my funeral. Further to those instructions, you should now be alone with the box in which this letter arrived and will have some time during which you will not be disturbed. Should you not be alone then I must ask that you get rid of whomever it is you are with, lock the door, take the phone off the hook and settle down for a few hours.

You see, I have much to tell and my story is for you, and you alone.

Along with this letter, you should now have in your possession two items. The first is a large key. Don't worry about its use for now, but keep it safe about your person. The second is a leather bound book. I want you to read this book, but before you start I have some news for you... I hope you are sitting down!

I am leaving the responsibility for Lyonesse House in your hands. The fate of the house... and so much more besides... is entrusted to you. This will come as a shock I know (and to all the family) and you will no doubt question why such a great responsibility should fall upon such young shoulders. More than that, you may question why indeed you should inherit such a mantle, when the problems of the estate are not of your making; and all for a house that you have never even visited! But please believe me when I say there are very, very good reasons for this. No doubt there will be many that will say this act was the final proof of madness of an old man of already questionable sanity. If they do say this- and they will – ignore them, they are fools. I know exactly what I am doing!

Now, to the book. You will recall me telling you of your great uncles, Anthony and Meredith Tregenza and of mine and your great-Aunt Elsa's holiday with them when we were young, and of the great storm that swept across Penwith that summer, the likes of which has never been seen before or since. Well, this is an account of that time, but as you will discover, what you know is but a fragment of the whole story. Other than the bare bones of the tale – my uncles, Lyonesse House, the great storm – you must forget what you know… or think you know.

Rid yourself of the shackles of reason; cast out logic, expel rational thought. In their place I am going to ask that you entertain a host of magi, elemental spirits, mermaids, monsters, smugglers and pirate ghosts, characters all, of a tale never told. I ask that you employ all the instruments and faculties of your imagination to give those characters shape and voice once more, to breathe life into the pages of the book, and in so doing, draw from them my memories.

Do this for me Abi. It will make sense of my strange legacy. Besides that, I suspect it will answer questions for you, questions that you have never dared to ask another living soul. I suspect you see, that you will find some of the tale's elements unnervingly familiar, that you will hear echoes of a world un-named, a world you believed that you alone knew of; a world that lurks behind the fabric of your waking life; a world you know in your dreams Abi… and perhaps… your nightmares…

But do not be afraid, you see the isle of which you dream, (yes, I do know it *is* an island) is full of noises, songs and… well, I shall say no more. If there are answers for you then they lie within the pages of the book.

Yours, always, and with much love.
Your great-grandfather,

William Smith

PART 1

FAR WEST
CORNWALL 1916

'… to see a hare near a Cornish seaport meant
that a storm was coming.'

George Ewart Evans and David Thomson: *The Leaping Hare*

Chapter 1

Elsa and I arrived at Penzance that summer tired and blinking off the London train, in the late afternoon of a still, hot, cloudless day. We were met by an elderly man wearing a well-worn black suit. In spite of the strong sun he wore a jumper under his suit and a cap on his head. In his large, weather-beaten hands he held a roughly painted sign, bearing the words 'William and Elspeth.'

'We're Bill and Elsa,' I said holding out my hand. The man didn't move, he just looked back at me with large forlorn eyes.

'Bill and Elsa. I mean, William and Elspeth… like your sign.' The man nodded. He tucked the sign under his arm, picked up our luggage and walked briskly out of the station without saying a word.

'Where are our uncles? Aren't they supposed to meet us?' asked Elsa.

'How should I know?' I replied, grabbing her hand and pulling her after the man.

Outside the station was a rickety old cart and horse. The man swung our cases on to the back of the cart, climbed on to the driver's seat and sat in silence, staring straight ahead until we'd climbed clumsily aboard. Without warning the horse urged forward.

'Where are our uncles?' said Elsa to the man. The driver said nothing. We looked at each other, bemused. Elsa shrugged her shoulders.

'Excuse me,' said Elsa in as clear and authoritative voice as an eleven year old can command, 'would you mind telling us where our uncles are? Have they sent you?' The man didn't reply, in fact he gave no indication he had heard Elsa at all. She tugged at his sleeve. But this elicited no response either. Elsa 'humphed' with disappointment and sat down.

'What do you suppose they're like?' she said to me in a loud voice. I shrugged.

We knew little about our uncles. Our mother was estranged from her Cornish family. She had married a man who suffered, in the eyes of the Tregenza family, from being both a 'commoner' and from 'up-country'. She had had to run away from home to marry him, and at a very tender age. My grandmother, whom we had never met, had disowned her and ensured that the family followed suit, though her brothers sent Christmas cards and, secretly, the odd letter. Now, a few months after our Grandmother's death, my sister and I were sent to Cornwall for a holiday, to help 'mend the rift.' Our mother had rarely spoken about her brothers and then only when pressed by the ever-curious Elsa. Perhaps she had never really forgiven them for siding with their mother. When she put us on the train in London she had said that 'one's quite eccentric and the other quite sensible,' but had enigmatically replied, 'you'll find out soon enough,' when Elsa had pushed for more information.

We drove along the promenade, through the fishing village of Newlyn and up the hill away from Penzance. To either side of us were green fields and stonewalls overflowing with wild flowers. The countryside was charming, but what held my gaze as we climbed higher through the lanes was the huge crescent of the bay stretching out behind us. In the heart of the bay, perhaps half a mile off shore was an island, on top of which, was a castle. It looked to have come straight out of a fairy tale. The sun pierced the turquoise waters around the island, which were so still, so clear, that every reef, sandbank and garden of seaweed were illuminated. Further out the blues, greens and shadows of the deep merged into one sheet of brilliant blue, stretching out to a crisp line where the sky met the water. It was the most beautiful sight I had ever seen, and though I have travelled far and wide in my life I have never recaptured the sense of wonder I felt on seeing the ocean for the first time.

Slowly the lanes began to twist and turn to cope with the undulating hills, and Penzance disappeared from view. We passed through several hamlets of houses and farms, making frequent turns. Whenever the path took us to any height we would get a sudden, unbroken view of the distant sea.

I meant to ask the man if we were nearing our uncles' house, thinking perhaps that his silence was a response to Elsa's impolite manner rather than a particular rudeness of his own. I opened my mouth to speak but my attention was caught by the barking of dogs.

In a field a little way ahead of us stood a circle of ancient stones. At one end of the circle a pair of the stones were set closely together, with another flat rock placed on top. These rocks sat against the hillside and seemed to be an entrance to a cave, or perhaps, I thought, an ancient burial chamber. The whole circle reminded me of the stones at Avebury or Stonehenge that I had seen in history books. In the centre of this circle stood a man. He was quite tall and well built, with long, unkempt black hair. He wasn't wearing a shirt, and by his brown, toned body I thought he must be a farm worker. He looked very fit, though he must have been in his forties or even fifties. Two large and hairy Irish wolfhounds lay at his feet. The man was holding a large wooden staff and was staring into the sky. A group of hunting dogs were prowling around the edge of the circle, barking madly. The dogs belonged to ten or more men, several of which had large staffs of their own. It was a curious scene, but what struck me as particularly odd was that there were no horses. Then I saw that the master huntsman was carrying a large, dead hare. This must have been their quarry. He strode through the circle and threw the hare at the man's feet.

'Is this your work?' demanded the huntsman, barely audible above the dogs' barks. The man gave no response. In fact he didn't appear to have even noticed the men or their dogs.

'We opened it up. It's got no 'eart!' said the man angrily.

'Witchcraft!' came a voice from the band of huntsmen.

'Don't be daft, the dog's 'ad it already,' said another. The man stared levelly at the huntsman.

'Stop, please stop,' I pleaded with our driver. We were much closer now and without the horse's hooves clattering on the road I could clearly hear what was being said. The man slowly placed his staff on the ground and picked up the hare in both arms.

'You can't kill that which cannot die,' he said to the huntsmen. With that he turned away and walked to the cave entrance. He placed the hare in the mouth of the cave and stood back.

'You got our quarry, give it back,' shouted one of the huntsmen. ''Tis no use to you.'

'No Christian use. He's for the pot! Let's 'ave 'im,' said another man. For all their bravado, none of the men or dogs - other than their leader - seemed willing to step within the circle. The strange man smiled.

'If 'e's for the pot, you'll have to catch 'im first'!' he gestured to the cave mouth. Where he had lain the hare's body there was nothing but a small patch of dried blood. Then, from the darkness beyond appeared a small twitching nose, followed by the face and body of a hare. The hare made a beeline to where the man stood and sat down, pawing the air in front of him. The two dogs leapt up from where they lay and trotted over to the hare. I waited for the hare to run, expecting the dogs to give chase. Instead, the dogs and the hare sniffed each other's noses by way of greeting and proceeded to roll and chase as if they were lifelong friends. The man picked up his staff and pointed it at the playful animals. At that precise moment the hare and the dogs stopped their playing. The dogs returned to the man. The hare reared on his hind legs for a moment before bounding off over the far boundary of the field and out of sight. Our horse, as though knowing the drama had come to the end, set off, pulling our cart slowly behind him.

'What was that all about?' said Elsa excitedly. 'Did you see that Bill?'

I didn't answer; I was still watching the hunt's master, who was shouting and waving his arms.

The man in the field gave no indication that he had seen us and as we drew off the huntsman continued to argue with him, encouraged by jeers from his fellows. As we departed this strange scene Elsa said 'They ought to leave him alone!' She drew herself to her knees and cupped her hands to shout out. Just in time I grabbed her arm. There was something about the man, something familiar. His unruly black hair, his square jaw and large nose were not unlike our mother's.

'Elsa, I think that might be one of our uncles.' I said.

'Really?' said Elsa, twisting her position to get a better look as we passed the field.

Not long afterwards we reached the top of the hill, and were met by a gentle, salty breeze. From there we could see a great deal of the north coast of the peninsula and Land's End to our left, as well as the bay and the strange island behind us.

The northern coast of Penwith was markedly different to the south. Though the hedgerows, walls and flowers were similar there were not so many flowers and fewer trees. Looking up the coast we could see a vast tableau of moorland, broken by the chimney stacks of mines near the cliff tops and further inland, peaks of exposed rock, worn by centuries of Atlantic rain and gales.

We descended steeply until we turned on to a lane running parallel to the coast. In the late afternoon as the sun began casting shadows and filling the fields and moors with a burnt orange light, we arrived at our uncles' house. The gateway to the house was flanked by stone pillars and high stone walls. But the years and weather had broken down the walls and the pillars were covered with moss. On one pillar, carved into the stone were the words 'Lyonesse House'. Had we not turned off the lane we would not have noticed the gateway or the small wooded valley to which it served as an entrance.

A pitted, uneven track led through a copse of gnarled and twisted trees to a clearing, and then the house. Though past its heyday the house was very grand, square and tall, built of large, uneven granite stones with deep-set windows. Unkempt and overgrown grounds were hedged by the woods on two sides and a steep hill to the right. Its garden overflowed with flowers of purple, scarlet and sun yellow, spreading over the lawns and climbing up the walls of the house. Exotic plants struggled through the weeds and grasses, spreading into the woods. The house and its gardens nestled perfectly in the little valley and seemed a natural part of it, an ancient, weatherworn part, steadily being claimed back by the land on which it stood. An adult might have seen this run down old house in an ill light, but to us, surrounded as it was by the woods, birdsong, and the gentle whistling wind, it seemed both adventure and romance distilled.

'Lor!' cried Elsa standing in the cart to fully appreciate the glorious scene. 'It's fantastic – I'll bet it's haunted too,' she added with uncontrolled glee. 'I certainly hope so.'

I wondered if she'd be so eager in the middle of the night. The house was certainly pretty. But there was something indefinable about it that was not wholly welcoming. Perhaps its remote location, run down façade, or perhaps the still, blackness of the windows that suggested something altogether darker, something that would show itself better on a cold winter's night than on a summer's afternoon.

The cart pulled up in front of the door, which had an overhanging stone porch with thick stone pillars to support it. The man offered no more help than when he had met us and simply waited whilst we unloaded our heavy suitcases and bags. The moment we were on the ground he cracked the whip that had hung harmlessly over the horse for our entire journey. The same horse that had pulled us so lazily to our destination now cantered off at great speed, taking the man with him. I tried the bell. There was no sound and no response.

'I think it's broken,' said Elsa.

I knocked on the door. There was no answer. We were alone with the house, with no-one to guide, comfort or welcome us.

Chapter 2

I knocked on the door once more, louder this time. We tried to look in the windows but as the sun was now behind the house, the rooms we could see into were very dark. The little of what we could see of the grand dining and drawing rooms, showed no sign of life.

'Well?' said Elsa, shrugging her shoulders and wiping her sandy, shoulder length hair from her face. 'I wish they'd hurry up and welcome us, I could do with a wash and some food.' Being three years older, and I daresay, wiser than my sister, I was more worried that we were to be welcomed at all, let alone fed or bathed. I sat on the flagstone doorstep whilst Elsa tried around the back.

'It's fantastic,' she said when she reappeared moments later. 'There's more garden, and you can see the sea from there too, and there are more woods, and…'

'Any sign of anyone?'

'No.'

'And a back door?'

'Locked.'

'You shouldn't have tried.'

'Why not? What choice do we have?' said Elsa, trying the great front door too. It eased open without a creak, and more easily than its imposing size and thickness suggested. We paused for a moment before Elsa cautiously stepped inside, peering into the dark. I followed. The hallway was considerably cooler than outside. Heavy oak panelling and ornate, sombre furniture gave it an austere, absorbing atmosphere.

'It's like a church,' whispered Elsa. A huge grandfather clock ticked away, governing the silence. Suddenly, there was a heavy clatter of something being dropped nearby, metal by the sound of it and onto a stone floor.

'Oh my God, look at the time… those kids!' A loud, gruff voice boomed from some distant part of the house. There was a commotion of clattering and scraping of chairs. From a doorway off the hall a man appeared.

He was quite tall, though he stooped and shuffled as he walked towards us. He was dressed in a black frock coat and matching trousers and would have been quite smart had his clothing not been so awry and crumpled. In one hand he held a bottle. The moment he saw us, he pulled himself upright and whipped the bottle behind his back.

'What the devil?' the man cried out, a look of shock on his face.

'We knocked, but there was no answer. So we t…tried the door,' I stuttered, pointing to the open doorway. Elsa had slipped invisibly into the shadows, as was her way when trouble was afoot.

'Right, right, well. Never mind that. Are you them?' he said eagerly, trying in a rather comic fashion to tuck his shirt in with one hand whilst holding the bottle out of sight with the other.

'Them?' we replied in unison.

'Yes, 'them'. The children.'

'We are children,' said Elsa, needlessly.

'Well surely, but you know! You must be, judging by your looks, especially you boy. The children, erm, erm,' and he waved his free hand in the air to conjure up something he had forgotten 'Elizabeth and….'

'Elspeth and William?' I offered.

'Yes! Well, thank God for that!' He made towards us, a look of great relief on his face, then stopped still as though shocked. 'How did you get here?' He looked genuinely surprised and more than a little suspicious; his eyes darted back and forth between Elsa and me.

'A man, in a cart,' said Elsa.

'What man?' His eyes narrowed.

'An old man. He didn't say who he was.'

'He didn't?' The man's eyes narrowed further 'What *did* he say?'

'Not a word. I thought he was rude,' said Elsa.

'Oh I see. You told him who you were hoping to meet and he brought you here. The man. Quite right.' He nodded for a moment, rubbing his chin, then added, 'Yes, I sent him.' I had the distinct feeling that he was lying. 'I'm er, glad he found you all right. Good journey, I trust?' he enquired. The bottle had vanished, and he was rubbing his hands together. He looked rather pleased with himself. 'In fact you must be tired, and hungry and thirsty. Would you like some lemonade?'

'Yes please!' said Elsa, emerging from the shadows. 'You're not our uncle, are you?'

'No, I'm Stephen, the butler.'

'Is that what you do? I've been wondering,' came a voice from behind us. We spun round. The source of this voice was a man; very like the one we had seen in the field, except that he was younger and wore a smart, beige linen suit. His hair was also black and curly though most of it was tidily tucked under a straw hat. I was struck by conflicting thought and emotion. This man seemed familiar and yet he was a total stranger. He too looked like my mother, and as our eyes locked a thrill of recognition went through me and I suspect him too. There was no denying it, my uncle Anthony looked a great deal like me.

'Well I never,' he said. He stood for a moment stroking his chin and smiling as though in thought before making towards us with arms outstretched. At the last moment he changed his mind about hugging us and instead patted us rather awkwardly on our shoulders.

'I'm sorry I'm late. It's the pony trap I use. Keeps getting stuck in potholes. I take it Stephen found you all right then?'

'I sent a man, so I could get on with polishing the silver,' said Stephen.

'You sure you weren't polishing off our cellar?' he asked,

sniffing the air, which held a trace of stale alcohol.

'Oh no sir, certainly not. In fact I must get back to it. Um, the polishing that is, not the cellar,' Stephen, laughed nervously as he backed away and turned to disappear down the hall.

'What about our lemonade?' said Elsa, almost to herself. She was not inclined to let someone forget a promise where food or drink was concerned. Stephen either didn't hear or pretended not to.

'Never mind, I'll get us some lemonade, and cake too, and later I'll show you your rooms. Oh don't worry about the bags, they won't go anywhere. I'm your Uncle Anthony, by the way, and needless to say you're Elspeth and William'.

'Actually we're always known as Bill and Elsa at home,' lied Elsa.

Anthony led us to the back of the house and the kitchen, which had an adjoining conservatory. The back of the house was considerably lighter than the front, lit as it was in the glow of the late afternoon sun. We sat in the conservatory whilst our uncle stood in the kitchen shouting questions to us concerning our mother. It was warm and comfortable with a view of the hill directly in front and to our right, and a view of the sea to the left. The uneasy feelings I'd had about the dark, lonely façade of the house soon faded.

Over lemonade and cakes Anthony tried to ask further questions about our mother. Unfortunately most of his questions were met by short, incomplete answers and a barrage of our own questions regarding the precise number and walking distance of coves, caves, woods and beaches in the nearby vicinity. He did his best to answer and tried not to get too carried away with promises to dive, swim, walk, fish, go horse riding and various other activities.

'We'll see, we'll see, we'll see, I'm a very busy man,' he said laughing and holding his hands up as though to hold back our enthusiasm, 'I'm glad you're so keen. I must admit I was rather worried that you'd be bored here.'

'Oh no, not us,' said Elsa confidently.

'My brother and I aren't used to keeping children you see. In fact this house hasn't seen children for many a long year. It's a good thing you're here. We could do with a little joy,' he smiled, but for a brief second a shadow of worry passed over his face.

'You're not used to keeping children,' Elsa repeated his words to ensure she had understood him correctly and sat back in her wicker chair smiling, somewhat like a cat who had got some cream. 'Don't worry, we know how to behave,' she said kindly. Behind her pale green eyes I could see her mind working. These uncles would not know what our bedtime should be, nor what activity would be considered too dangerous by adults but fun by us, nor how much cake or bacon and eggs was 'good' for us.

'Well, you'll need to. In fact, finding time to entertain you might be tougher than I'd thought. I expect Meredith will have plans for you.'

'We've seen him Uncle Anthony. He was up on the hill. In the stone circle,' said Elsa.

'Really. In the stone circle you say?'

'Yes, He was talking to some huntsmen. He brought a hare back to life,' said Elsa, clearly impressed.

'Really.' Anthony looked slightly embarrassed. He looked to me for explanation.

'I'm not sure the hare was dead,' I said.

'No… I don't think it could have been. Meredith's got a very active imagination, no matter what he told you…'

'He didn't tell us anything Uncle Anthony. We just saw it,' said Elsa. A look of confusion passed over Anthony's face for a second. Then he clapped his hands together and forced a smile.

'Now, I tell you what,' he said in a jolly tone. 'Elsa, Stephen can show you your room. It has a wonderful view!'

'All right,' said Elsa in a resigned voice, aware that Anthony was trying to find time alone with me. He stood up and entered the kitchen to shout for Stephen. Elsa gave me a rather intense glare to let me know that anything discussed in her absence was to be memorised and later divulged, word for word. Stephen arrived to let us know our bags were in our rooms. Elsa reluctantly went with him.

'Now, Bill,' he assumed a serious tone the moment Stephen and Elsa were out of earshot, 'you're older than your sister so perhaps you will understand a little more of what's going on.' He said these words with great care. 'Did Meredith welcome you when he was engaged in this…this game?'

'No, I'm not sure he even saw us. If he did he didn't let us know.'

'Bill, I didn't really want to talk to you about this, not yet. But given what you've seen, perhaps I'd better.' He waited a moment before taking a large breath. 'This is an ancient and large Estate. It needs a lot of thought and energy to run it. When our mother died that responsibility fell on Meredith's shoulders. Now Meredith is a very clever man but he has always suffered from having his head either in a book or in the clouds, without bothering to see if there was anything much between. That doesn't help when you have to run an estate like this one. Also, the fish catches have not been good these past months, and early signs are for a very poor harvest though there is no obvious reason as to why this should be so. What business we have managed has been run with a skeleton staff, most of the men having gone off to fight the Germans. Rightly or wrongly, some of the locals blame Meredith for this state of affairs. That, and our mother's death… well, I think he's been affected more than he will admit to himself.' There was a long pause. Then he said 'You saw what he was up to, up on the moor, amongst the stones?' his eyes narrowed.

'Not exactly, I think he was interrupted by the hunt.'

'There are certain… customs, um… local to Penwith, that are as old as those stones, some say even older. Meredith's got wrapped up in them of late, and he's paid more attention to this nonsense, than to the Estate. He's been keeping strange company too.'

'What sort of customs?' I asked.

'Fertility rites, customs to secure good harvest. It's almost mid-summer, the Festival of Lyonesse. You'll find out soon enough.' He said with a sigh; 'I have tried everything I can to make him forget about these delusions and get back to the real business of wages, sales and bills. Unfortunately he will have none of it; he seems intent on pursuing this nonsense, which he believes in heart and soul. I've had to take over the running of most of the Estate, which as you can imagine has caused some friction between us. I do however, consider it my duty to rescue what is left of the Estate, before it is too late… ' He stared intensely into my eyes and then looked away with what may have been a tear in his eye. 'I'm sorry my boy, I've probably told you far too much. I just thought it important that you knew and once I'd started… well.'

He smiled weakly. To this day I am not sure why he confided in me so fully. Perhaps it was because I was family; perhaps it was because he had no one else to talk to. I don't know, but in spite of my years and lack of experience I was glad he had confided in me, and I told him so.

'Wiser than your years boy!' he said squeezing my shoulder. 'Please don't let on to your sister all that I have told you.'

'All right. I won't,' I said, and I meant it, though I knew Elsa would interrogate me mercilessly.

'Good lad. Now, you'll want to see your room.'

There was a landing half way up the stairs with a stained glass window, which poured incandescent light into the dark, gloomy hallway as the sun began its descent. The upstairs of the house had not been decorated, or even cleaned for some time, possibly years. Yet it still exuded a grand and noble character, in spite of the fading wallpaper and gathering dust. There was a large open floor with more stained glass windows and a longer, narrow passage from which I could see doors leading to a dozen or more rooms. Mine was right at the end of the corridor, facing the front of the house. A large window overlooked the garden, woods and the crooked lane from which we had first seen the house. There was an enormous double bed, washbasin, dresser and a cupboard, which dwarfed the meagre collection of clothes that I put in it. All the furniture was solid and old with ornate, subtle patterns carved into it. I was surprised to see a log fire as it was nearly mid-summer, but Uncle Anthony explained that the room was a little damp and it would help with the airing.

Directly opposite, I soon discovered, was Elsa's room. It was much smaller with a single bed covered by a brand new pink quilt. The best feature was a bay window in which Elsa comfortably sat, overlooking a path leading down to the cliff.

'Divine,' she said dreamily, a huge smile on her face. Anthony left us, promising dinner within the hour. As predicted Elsa quizzed me, getting angry when I told her that I had promised not to say too much. Luckily for me her curiosity concerning mine and Anthony's conversation, was nothing by comparison with her interest in Penwith itself.

'Stephen told me there's a beach a mile or two west Bill. We can do it easily after breakfast tomorrow. Did you pack your costume? There's a harbour there and they've got boats for fishing and catching lobsters, and one day we can go out if the weather's alright! Bill, Bill, did you imagine it would be this good?' Out of the window I could see a blue eternity of sea, sky and adventure.

'No, Elsa,' I smiled, 'I didn't.'

Growing up in the war years, we had become accustomed to meagre rations. So it was no small treat to be served fresh fish, vegetables and new potatoes with butter and a sauce of herbs and cream. I have no doubt that a long tiring day and sea air sharpen the appetite also, but I am sure it was quite rude of us to eat with so much gusto. There was little conversation, so concentrated were we on filling our bellies with the delicious meal.

'Well, I'm glad you like the food,' said Anthony, picking at his own half-empty plate as we tucked into a second helping.

We enjoyed the dinner, but not as comfortably as we might

have. One of the places at the table had been set with a cover on it and a full, open bottle of red wine. Clearly it was for our Uncle Meredith, and as the meal drew on his absence began to feel like a dour presence at the table. I was a little nervous about meeting him and the longer the moment was put off the more nervous I became. It was after a long silence that I thought it wise to ask.

'Will Uncle Meredith be joining us?' As though in answer, we heard the clunk of the front door opening. Barks and the sound of paws on stone shattered the silence. Within a second the door to the dining room flew open and two dogs, or rather hounds, all shaggy and lolling tongues, bounded up to sniff and lick us, charging around our feet and under the table almost sending the plates flying as the table jolted and jumped. Elsa screamed, though more in excitement than fear.

'Meredith Tregenza! I have told you this dining room is no place for dogs!' shouted Uncle Anthony.

The man we had seen in the field strode in. He was simply dressed in a thick cotton, navy blue shirt and canvas trousers, with a large leather bag slung over his shoulder and onto his hip. He wore no shoes and had hair almost down to his shoulders. In those days, both of these were unthinkable for a man, let alone a supposed gentleman at the dinner table. Uncle Meredith was almost identical to his brother, but his skin was well tanned, and he had an earthy smell on him. He kissed us both on our heads, sat down and poured himself a glass of red wine which he held aloft.

'Welcome Bill and Elsa!' he said and downed the wine in one gulp. 'I trust my servant met you at the station and my brother has provided for your needs?' he attacked his meal with at least as much gusto as Elsa and I had. We sat there, with mouths open, unsure of how to react to this strange character.

'What's the matter, cat got your tongue?' he muffled, his mouth full of fish. Had he seen us on the moor? Was he pretending that he hadn't?

In front of him even Elsa was shy, or like me, a little nervous. So we said nothing.

Without any apparent cause or encouragement he began a story about a rendezvous with a young mermaid that he had planned. The mermaid, he told us, had promised to bring him a sea serpent's egg. She had however, failed to appear at the allotted time and he was late for dinner as he had been searching for her amongst the rocks and pools at Sennen Cove. He had a low, soft, yet clear voice, which was both calm and commanding. As we listened to him tell us his tale between mouthfuls of food and wine, we slowly relaxed, laughing at his impossible story one moment, listening intently with anticipation the next. Unwittingly we put ourselves entirely in his thrall. Meredith seemed so full of life, so warm, that within minutes any nerves we had evaporated. He finished his comical tale, by saying that the mermaid must have taken full human form to deliver the egg to him and he expected her to arrive any moment.

'Do you think she'll come?' asked Elsa in wide-eyed wonder.

'Perhaps she already has,' he replied, leaning forward and covering Elsa's mouth with one of his large rough hands. She gave a little cough. Though my eyes were clearly deceiving me, he appeared to pull a large, blue and green coloured egg from her mouth. Elsa looked stunned.

'You can do magic,' she said, more as a statement than a question. He closed his fingers around the egg and squeezed. We heard the crunch of the shell being crushed, but when he opened his fist, he showed us only an empty palm.

I forget the details of the rest of the evening's conversation, with one notable exception. As Stephen was clearing away the dessert dishes, Anthony saw fit to ask how Meredith had sent a 'servant' to meet us, when Stephen had professed to doing the same thing.

'Oh, the man I asked must have spoken with Master Meredith's man and didn't need to go,' flustered Stephen.

'You lie. You were drunk and you fell asleep,' said Meredith in a voice as quiet as it was serious.

'Not so, not so. How could you tell that? Even if it were true that is. Besides, Master Meredith doesn't have any servants does he? Apart from me that is,' said Stephen, appealing to Anthony.

'Well, no,' said Anthony looking confused.

'O, I have servants, Stephen…' said Meredith, grabbing Stephen's arm as he leant over to retrieve a dessert bowl. He lowered his voice to a whisper, but I could still hear, '… and one day soon they will attend you'. He let go of the butler's arm and Stephen hastily made a retreat for the kitchen. Although the table had not been fully cleared we didn't see him again that night.

The remainder of the evening was spent chatting and laughing. We stayed up much later than we should have considering Elsa's age and our long journey. We slowly sunk into a hazy tiredness, comforted by full stomachs, a journey ended and a comfortable bed nearby. Even after a few hours we began to truly feel at home in the house.

We were more than ready for our beds when we were sent upstairs but we still managed to steal a few moments whispering in Elsa's room. Of course we discussed our mysterious Uncle Meredith. Our mother had said he was 'eccentric'. He was boisterous and energetic, youthful in spite of his years, eccentric certainly, but there was nothing about him that led me to believe he was anything other than in full command of his faculties. In fact, quite the opposite. Another thing that struck me was that he was not at all bookish as I had expected from Anthony's description. His clothing and brown, weathered skin suggested more time at sea or in the field than in a library. This strange, charismatic man had kept us entertained, enthralled and (I almost hesitate to write this) under his spell. So hypnotic was his story telling, so strong his control of the conversation that I had never thought to ask him how he knew we liked to be called Elsa and Bill, who his wordless 'servant' was, or exactly what he had been doing up on the moor.

These questions still burning in my mind I retired to my

own room. The fire had gone out and the window was still open. I sat down on the bed to undress, but lay down and was asleep before I had even unbuttoned my shirt.

I slept heavily, but in the morning recalled a vivid dream. I dreamt that I awoke, roused by the sound of voices whispering my name. In my dream I went to the window to discover where the voices were coming from. But I recoiled. The world outside the window was markedly different. The night sky, though cloudless, was moving. The blackness of the night shifted and rocked like a stormy sea, as though the stars and moon were lanterns on a seabed, covered by invisible raging waves. It made me dizzy to look at it. Gasping in horror, unaware that I was dreaming, I grabbed the sill of the open window to steady myself. My knuckles immediately felt wet and cold, as though plunged into ice cold water. The voices called my name ever louder, and with increasing urgency. I was becoming dizzier, but could not tear my eyes away from the turbulent sky. Amongst the shifting tides of the night sky holes were appearing, almost imperceptible patches of sky that were, somehow, different to the pitch background of endless night. It was like storm clouds breaking to reveal patches of the sky behind. The broken patches were the shape, or silhouette, of a great hare, bounding through the night sky. I ventured my head out of the window to get a better look. Now, the air was full of noise and commotion, rain, wind and the sound of crashing waves. I gasped, feeling a sudden, sickening roll of my stomach. The house reeled, lurching like a boat on a tempestuous sea. I looked at the ground, gripping the sill with all my might. My name was no longer whispered, but shouted by many voices. They did not cry in unison, but came from all directions, like sailors drowning in a stormy sea. Now long, haunted and far away…

'Williaaaaaaammmmmm.' Now quiet, near and urgent. 'William, William, William, William.' The house creaked and groaned. I feared it would be dragged from its moorings and pulled into the storm of the night. Then suddenly, a wave of invisible water hit me, cold and cruel, causing me to gasp a desperate breath of air. I grabbed the shutters of the window, and pulled them inwards, though it took some effort, so strong were the invisible forces of the storm.

Silence. The sky through the window was still and quiet. I was dry.

On the lawn, casting a long shadow from the light of the moon, was the hare we had seen in the field with Meredith that day. He stood on his haunches, still as a statue. But around him his shadow jumped and played in the moonlight.

Chapter 3

'I trust you slept well?' I awoke to the sound of Meredith's voice and a flood of light as he opened the curtains. At first my mind was blank and heavy, but as my eyes adjusted to the light I remembered where I was and our arrival at the house the previous day. It all seemed very distant, as though I had slept for days rather than hours. Then I remembered the dream and the window. Though I was woozy with sleep I knew I hadn't drawn the curtains the previous night.

'The window,' I mumbled.

'I came in during the night to check on you. I heard a noise. You were asleep on top of the bed and you'd shut the window. You don't want to do that at this time of year, it's too hot,' he said, showing me the now open window. Meredith left me with a cup of tea, saying there'd be a jug of hot water for me in the bathroom and bacon and eggs waiting for me downstairs, but not to hurry. I took a few moments to wake properly and gather my thoughts, enjoying the quiet sunny atmosphere and time alone. I let my mind wander, imagining what we might do for the day, but wasn't allowed to daydream for long. The door to my room flew open. Someone already seemed to have my day perfectly well mapped out.

'Morning, Bill. I've been up ages, and I've been down to the cliff top, so I know where the path is to the beach. You have packed your costume haven't you?' Elsa scowled at me. 'Hurry up. I can't wait for breakfast any longer, I'm starving'. She stood on her tiptoes and stuck her head and shoulders dangerously far out of the window. 'Your view's nowhere near as good as mine.'

'Good morning Elsa. Did you sleep well?'

'Like a log. Funny dreams though.'

'Really, what about?'

'That's just it,' she said turning to look at me 'I sort of know I had odd dreams, but can't remember any of them. That ever happen to you?'

'Sometimes.' I got rid of Elsa, promising that the sooner she left me alone the sooner I'd be downstairs.

The long journey and a night in my clothes had left me feeling stiff and dirty. Washing both invigorated and relaxed me. Afterwards I changed into shorts and a light shirt and headed downstairs.

Breakfast was a more informal arrangement than our dinner the previous night. A small buffet had been laid out on the kitchen table. Once we'd collected our plates of bacon, eggs, tomatoes and mushrooms we were ushered by our Uncle Meredith into the conservatory where a small table and wicker chairs had been set out, with a rack full of toast, a steaming teapot and a jug of fresh, frothy milk.

Though we had eaten well the previous night, we still had ravenous appetites. Uncle Meredith joined us, though he hardly seemed dressed for breakfast. He was wearing a long nightshirt. By contrast our Uncle Anthony, who did not eat with us, was pacing around the ground floor of the house wearing a formal, dark suit. His clothing and mood seemed rather heavy and sombre for what promised to be a beautiful day. He barely spoke to us and bit his nails, occasionally glancing at the clock on the wall.

'Don't make any more of a mess than you have to,' he said to Meredith. 'We have guests coming, you know.'

'What about these two?' said Uncle Meredith from his chair, pointing at us with a slice of toast.

'Ah yes. Could you take them Meredith? Though frankly I would rather you put on some decent clothes and welcomed our guests yourself!' he said. I was surprised to see Anthony in this state. He had been so warm and welcoming the day before.

'Don't worry,' said Meredith quietly, noticing the

exchange of glances between Elsa and me, 'it's only a bit of business.'

'Important business?' I asked.

'No Bill, I take care of the important business,' he smiled and winked at us.

Anthony disappeared to another part of the house whilst we finished our breakfast and planned our trip to the beach. Meredith informed us that we were no more than two miles away from the beaches of Gwynvor and Sennen. To find them all we had to do was head down from the back of the house towards the sea and follow the cliff top westward. Meredith had his own business to attend to, but after that he promised he and his dogs would meet us on the beach.

Eager with anticipation we tore away from the breakfast table. I was about to run up the stairs after Elsa when there was a loud knock at the front door. I hesitated, waiting for Stephen to appear. But neither he nor one of our uncles appeared. After a second burst of insistent knocks I went to answer it myself.

The man at the door wore a plain black suit and bowler hat. Behind him in the driveway was a large black car. It was very grand; I think it might have been a Rolls Royce. On its bonnet stood a large crow, making an aggressive 'caw-caw' sound and flapping its wings. The bird was staring straight at me. The man raised his hat, bade me a good morning and headed back to the car where he opened the rear door. Another man climbed out, dressed like the first, but taller and with the addition of a walking cane. This man turned to the crow and spoke to it, though I couldn't hear what he said. Whatever it was, the bird stopped its racket and stood still with its head cocked, as if listening to the man. He pointed into the sky with his cane. The bird flew off.

He walked up to the door followed by the first man, who now held a briefcase pulled from the trunk of the grand car. Other than his rather formal dress, there was nothing of particular note about Lord Pendrogeth. He had plain features, short, straight dark hair and was neat and formal. Unlike our uncles he had very pale skin.

'Good morning,' he said politely, raising his bowler hat.

'Good morning,' I replied. 'Who should I say is calling?' I peered back into the house hoping someone would come. As if on cue Meredith appeared, still attired in his cotton nightgown. He walked straight up to the door and shut it, without so much as a nod towards the callers.

'Now then Bill, hurry up and get ready, your sister will be waiting.'

The man, or his servant, knocked again, but Meredith ignored it. I froze, not knowing if I should obey Meredith or answer the door. Then Stephen appeared, running to the door.

'Lord Pendrogeth, forgive me, the bell has recently been broken. Please come in,' said the butler, backing away from the door and bowing. 'Such a lovely day, not too hot for you I trust? Perhaps you would like some tea, or some other refreshment?'

'Tea would be fine,' said Lord Pendrogeth.

I looked back and forth from Meredith to the two visitors. Neither party seemed to think the other existed. Meredith beckoned me to follow him up the stairs.

'Who's he?' I whispered.

'That… is a vulture, Bill, hovering over its prey, waiting for its death,' he answered curtly. Behind us I could hear Anthony greeting the guests and apologising for his brother's lack of manners.

I told Elsa about the guests. Despite her insistence that we should stay and spy on them I managed to sneak us out of the house without being seen, which I thought was how Anthony would prefer it.

The cliff path was slight and narrow, roller coasting over small headlands with steep valleys in between, the most severe of which had almost vertical drops to the sea below. Several times we mistook a sheep trail for the true path, and found ourselves breathlessly climbing rocks or stumbling through leg lacerating heather and gorse to get back to the path.

After some time we came to a final low-lying headland

where the path descended rapidly to the sea. We could see the two beaches Meredith had promised. The first was enclosed by steep hills and a further rocky headland. Beyond it lay Sennen, a mile or more of white, golden sand leading to a small village and its harbour. The moment we saw it, we knew that if we did nothing in our holiday other than visit this place, we should have a wonderful time.

And so it proved, that for a week or more it became our daily habit to visit the two beaches, sometimes accompanied by Uncle Meredith, but more often than not left to our own devices. For those first few days we were more than content with the riches and secrets of our cliff top walk and the two beaches at its end.

As the days rolled into each other we changed; we became browner, leaner, the skin on our feet grew tougher, our limbs became used to lengthy swims and strenuous climbs. Gradually, we became accustomed to this light and windswept world and our time became ruled not by hours or minutes but by the ancient timekeepers of the tides and the ceaseless sun in the sky. We passed our time with paddles in the fearsome surf, and swims when the swell was calmer. Yet as the days passed we would spend ever longer periods in silence, sunbathing or making solitary explorations of the rock pools at low tide. I would spend hours watching the wind-broken surf roll in, unaware of the hour, or even which day it was.

It was at such a time that my attention was caught by what I took to be birds bobbing and diving in a choppy, peaking sea. One bird, or what I thought to be a bird, seemed to be diving then resurfacing in a regular pattern, moving swiftly along and below the surface. Then I noticed several more, behaving in exactly the same way.

'Elsa, look at those birds… ' I stopped midway through my sentence. I could now see they were not birds at all, but the arching, rolling backs of animals. A grey, muscular body flew from the water, slicing through the air and crashing back into the water with a mighty splash.

'Dolphins!' cried Elsa, standing and running to the shore. We watched, awe-struck as their sleek grey bodies cut the water, weaving effortlessly in and through the choppy sea. Every few seconds a finned back would arch, exhaling a plume of water from the animal's blowhole, making a 'foosh' exclamation of sound.

'Beautiful, aren't they?' said a soft, deep voice from behind us. There was Meredith, attired in his usual dress of brown jacket, canvas trousers and collarless shirt. Over his shoulder was slung the leather satchel he always carried. His two hounds were playing in the sand behind him.

'What are they doing?' asked Elsa.

'Looking for fish maybe, or like as not just playing. You know, some fishermen believe that dolphins and mermaids swim together,' he said.

'Is it true?' said Elsa, her eyes widening.

'Yes, in old times they were often the consort of the merpeople,' he said, in all seriousness.

'There's no such thing as mermaids,' I said.

'Of course there is if Uncle Meredith says there is!' Elsa said to me.

Meredith stood silently watching the dolphins until they crossed the bay and disappeared beyond the islands of rocks that jut out to sea beyond Sennen harbour.

'I'll tell you all about mermaids… whilst we eat our lunch!' he added, patting his satchel. Over a picnic of cheese sandwiches, boiled eggs and tomatoes Meredith told us all he knew – or pretended to know – about the merpeople. As was usual by then, we were enchanted and charmed by his story telling. So utterly did he himself seem to believe that it seemed rude and vulgar to point out to him, or Elsa, that none of what he said could have any possible basis in truth. So I let it go, convincing myself it could do no harm.

The merpeople, according to Meredith, had once lived beyond the reach of man in the blue, silent depths of the ocean.

The merpeople had rarely seen by humans. But in old times, if a sailor or fishermen should chance upon a mermaid he could fall instantly in love. Of the many men lost at sea, many were believed to have lost their hearts to mermaids. Some, it was said, were drowned, following a mermaid to the depths. But others, if blessed, were allowed to follow their beloved and join the race of sea people, never to return to the ways of men.

To illustrate his story telling Meredith had led us to the shoreline. As he spoke he worked his hands quickly in the firm sand, sweeping sand away here, curving a line there, to eventually reveal the form of a mermaid. The curious thing was, his hands appeared not to 'make' her at all, as you would make a model or a sandcastle. It was as though she were buried there and all he had to do was brush away the sand covering her. She was beautiful; voluptuous, with her hand outstretched and her tail curved, frozen in the act of swimming. For her hair he used straggles of thin seaweed, he used a shell to make the pattern of fish scales on her tail. He placed small, glistening green stones in her eyes and carefully carved out her nose and mouth, finishing at the very moment he completed his story.

'She's beautiful,' I said.

'But the tide,' cried Elsa pointing to the sea, which was slowly drawing in. 'It'll destroy her.'

'No,' he laughed 'It'll set her free. Now, enough of this. I've brought a kite for you.' From his large, leather satchel he pulled a kite roughly made from bamboo sticks and thick brown paper. When we tried it the stiff breeze could only just lift it, but once in the air, it flew well, tugging at our hands in an effort to be free.

We had been playing for an hour or more, when Elsa, who had been running with the kite, stopped in her tracks and pointed out to sea.

'It's the dolphins again!' she cried. This time they were closer. I rushed to the water's edge, running in till the water was up to my waist. There were three or more, it was hard to tell, as they ducked and dived in an irregular pattern, only occasionally breaking the surface together. At first they stayed in one place. Then, to our great delight they came even closer, following a bubbling mass of water.

'They're fishing!' I shouted. Sure enough, we could see the tails and the glint of fish scales thrashing around in the sea. The fish had been corralled into a tight ball by the dolphins who, Meredith told us, would be taking turns to swoop in at will and eat their fill.

'Look!' shouted Elsa, pointing to the mouth of Sennen harbour. Three boats had appeared in the bay, and with much shouting from the crew, were making a beeline for the dolphins. Two of the boats ran parallel to each other, the third headed further out into, and across, the bay. As they got closer the two boats split as if to go around the feeding dolphins, who still seemed unaware of them in spite of the noise and commotion.

'This isn't right,' said Meredith. Between the boats a net was being winched into the water. The fishermen's intention was obvious. They would surround the dolphins, and in so doing would net the fish. The dolphins' only escape lay towards Gwynvor beach, but the third boat had moved across the bay, blocking the dolphins between the boats and the shore. The dolphins were caught in a trap, as quick and deadly as the one they had laid for the fish.

I turned to Meredith in desperation. He wasn't even watching. He was rummaging in his bag. To my great surprise, he produced a book. With one hand holding the open book and the other in the air, he started to read aloud, though over the wind and the sound of the boats and the waves, I could not hear what was said.

I was about to shout out to him when the wind suddenly dropped. All was still in a moment. The sea, that had been so choppy only a moment before, was now as calm as a pond.

For a brief second I heard Meredith's words. He spoke in a language I had never heard before. His voice, though speaking, was something like the sound of water running over pebbles.

Then, just as suddenly, the wind started again, but with much greater force, and this time from the shore. The sea was brushed flat, but for the whisper of ripples caused by the off shore wind. The boats, which had moved through the water with such deadly speed, now bobbed harmlessly in the water, with their sails deflated and limp. The kite, which Elsa had been holding all the while, though she paid it no attention now, leapt into the air, as fast and as far, as it could, till it tugged at Elsa. She pulled it back, like an unruly dog on a lead. But the kite yanked and jerked, pulling at Elsa's slight frame. Its shadow swept across the beach first one way and then the other, weaving and swooping in great swathes.

Elsa looked confused; she did not seem to be in control of the kite. It swept through the sky, one way, then another until it hovered above the shoreline, directly over the sand-mermaid. Its shadow lingered, as the waves began to pour over the mermaid's form. I blinked and rubbed my eyes, unable to fathom what I was seeing. The shadow was changing shape, growing until it not only covered the mermaid, but was exactly the same size and shape. Now the shadow shook and wriggled, as if trying to break free from invisible bonds. With a final judder, it shot out to sea at great speed. The shadow passed within feet of where I stood and as it passed, it changed. It was no longer a shadow, but something light, blue and shimmering, racing through the azure sea.

For a frozen moment in time I saw – thought I saw – a face under the water. Whatever it was, it moved quickly out, straight towards the dolphins and the boats. I looked back to Elsa. The kite lay still on the sands. I looked for the sand mermaid. A wave retreated, revealing a hole slowly filling with sand and water. Elsa waded into the water to join me. In her eyes I could see fear and bewilderment. She grabbed my arm and pointed at the boats, which now began to list to one side. At first I thought the net must have been caught on the seabed, but as I watched it became obvious that something was pulling on the nets. Had they caught some of the dolphins I wondered. But no, the animals were already ahead of the boats making their way back to open water. The boats started to move towards each other, pulled by whatever force had hold of the nets, and as they moved they listed even further, causing the crew to sway and fall on the deck. My mind raced, desperate for a reason - any reason - to explain what I was seeing.

'Cut the nets, cut the nets,' cried a voice in panic.

'Drop anchor,' shouted another.

Large anchors were hastily thrown over the sides of the boats. As the anchors found the seabed so they slowed – but did not stop – the force that was steadily and surely pulling at the boats. A few more seconds and the sea would reach the deck, pouring over the men's feet and into the hold. But the men were quick with their knives, and had soon cut the ropes holding the nets to the boats. The nets disappeared. The boats righted themselves, rocking unevenly on the surface. Then, a metal object shot out of the water, three yards or more. In the brief moment it hung in the air I saw that it was an anchor. It crashed back into the water with a mighty splash.

'They're away,' shouted a man from the other boat. Sure enough, a mass of bubbling silvery water was moving away from the boats, followed by the dolphins. As they swam out to sea, they began to move rhythmically, their backs and tails arching and diving in a steady pattern. With a final wave of their tails they were gone.

Elsa and I waded back to shore, to the spot where the sand mermaid had been. I stood in the hole up to my ankles, staring blankly at the water and shifting sand around my feet. Elsa ran to Meredith.

'The dolphins! They're safe.' She was dancing ecstatically around him, waving her hands in the air.

'But how?' I said. Meredith shrugged.

'P'raps it was Lamorna of the Valley Cove. She saved them.' He was smiling and seemed content.

'Who is 'she'?' I asked, with mock naivety.

'The mermaid of course!' said Elsa.

'Mermaid. That's ridiculous. The boat must have got stuck.'

'You saw,' said Meredith, speaking directly to me.

'I... I... I don't know what I saw. There was a shape, maybe one of the dolphins... maybe one of the dolphins got caught in the net.'

'You saw,' said Meredith again, gazing into my eyes.

'I don't know... what I saw,' I repeated, unsure of what I had seen, even less sure of what I believed. The boat could have run aground, the shape I had seen could have been a dolphin; the 'face' could so easily have been a trick of the light. Dolphins were strong, perhaps one of them had thrown the anchor in the air. All of this seemed a lot more probable than a mermaid. Yet...

'Impossible!' I said. I felt angry, though I didn't know why.

'Who are you to say what is possible?' said Meredith calmly.

'I know there's no such thing as mermaids,' I scoffed.

'What you don't believe cannot exist, cannot happen?' Meredith countered.

'But mermaids... dug out of the sand!'

'You will believe in her one day, Bill. And more besides. I did not dig her up as you put it. I called her.'

'Called her! From where?'

'A place that... well, if I told you, you wouldn't believe me.' He seemed to be mocking me, though gently. I felt myself going red. I was infuriated by his trickery, his non-answers to my questions. I did not know if he had had anything to do with the dolphins' escape. Certainly I could not bring myself to believe it.

'The mermaid, Bill. You saw!' insisted Elsa, copying Meredith.

'There wasn't any mermaid, just sand, washed away by the tide.' Meredith didn't respond, he picked up his satchel and the kite and walked off down the beach, followed by Elsa and his dogs.

The village of Sennen was little more than a row of sea-front cottages leading to the small harbour. Behind the cottages was an inn and a few houses nestled amongst the bushes and granite boulders on the steep hillside. As we approached the harbour, we saw one of the boats was coming in. We watched the men disembark. They had reclaimed their nets from the sea and were hauling them on to shore (I noted they were torn and shredded) where they set about fixing them. Those that didn't work sat amongst the lobster pots passing around a stone bottle and smoking pipes.

Meredith walked over to them, followed by Elsa and me. His two hounds stood at his side.

'Did you see that, Mr Meredith? Dolphins… or somethin'… lost an anchor too, threw it in the air it did!' said one man by way of greeting. 'Didn't look right to me. More 'n just dolphins done that surely. 'Ow'd it look from the shore?' The man was short and muscular and had a fierce air about him, standing with his chest thrust out and his hands on his hips. He had blue eyes and a gaze that burned from a sun darkened face.

'I tell you what I saw, Mr Penrose. I saw men who've fished for our Estate many a year set upon dolphins.' Meredith's voice was lower and gruffer than usual and held more of an accent. ''Tis a strange way to catch fish, and a cause of bad luck.'

'I dunno 'bout that Mr Meredith, though sure it has brought us bad luck, now we got no anchor and no nets. But what we 'spected to do sir? There ain't been no fish for men to find and I should know. And them there is gets hunted by them animals. Why should they get fat, while we get thinner in stomach and pocket?' There was a murmur of agreement from the fishermen, some of whom held looks of ill disguised anger.

'Now you got men idle, while them that's gone over to Lord Pendrogeth… ' he pointed at the boats out to sea '… they'll come back with full nets. I can't explain that.'

'And did they teach you to set on dolphins to catch fish?'

'Mebbe they did, and mebbe we'd be stupid not to learn

from 'em. They got better boats and better nets – there's talk of boats with engines too – and 'ere's a surprise, better catches!' There was another murmur of approval from the men.

'Go that way Mr Penrose and soon enough there'll be no fish for any boat to catch.'

'With due respect sir I don't think thass why there's so few fish for us, but what I do know is that when there is so few we need any advantage we can take.'

'Any man setting on dolphins had better seek new employment and a new cottage,' said Meredith. This visibly angered the men, some of whom stood up. The dogs, hackles raised, began to growl and inched ever so slightly forward.

'Yeah, well them cottages won't be yours much longer, will they?' said one of the younger men, who was not much more than a boy, though too young to be called up for army service.

'They'll belong to Lord Pendrogeth 'cuz e'll be running things round 'ere. And 'e couldn't do much worse. I seen you on the beach with your books, and my Mam seen you on the moor with your staff and stones and all. King of Lyonesse is it? Well get us some fish then!' he shouted, keeping a careful eye on Meredith's dogs. Why, I wondered did he call Meredith King of Lyonesse? Lyonesse was the name of our uncles' house. And the Lord Pendrogeth, the man talked of, was that not the man who had visited Lyonesse House that very morning?

Some of the men cheered and laughed, but others, out of respect for Meredith, or perhaps what he stood for, bowed their heads. One man crossed himself. The man who had spoken looked around for encouragement.

'What? Don't be soft, you don't believe in that ol' rubbish di'ee?' He stepped forward. The dogs growled louder, crouching down and baring their teeth. I jumped, startled suddenly by the appearance of a man, right next to us. It was the man who had picked us up from the station when we had arrived in Cornwall a few days earlier. He was dressed in the same jumper, cap and old dark suit. I noticed he had a musty, almost fishy smell about him.

There was something about him that wasn't quite right, something that unnerved the men. Several of them looked down or away when he met their eyes. Some shuffled uneasily.

'Some do believe, some don't,' said Mr Penrose with his hands up, stepping forward and placing himself between the men and us. 'And some that do know 'ow it can be used too,' he said, looking straight at Meredith. He spoke quietly, more for our benefit than the men, I thought, and with a slight movement of his head and glance of his eyes, he gestured out to sea.

'Mr Meredith is still master 'ere, Jeff,' he said to the young man. 'You'd be wise to remember that.'

'I do,' said the young man 'and I dun' mean to speak out o' turn, but I also remember a time not long gone when the nets was full,' he said, more quietly. The wordless servant of our uncle turned and walked away. The men returned to their work.

'Come, Mr Penrose,' said Meredith. We followed, glad to be away from the fishermen. Mr Penrose talked to Meredith about fishing and boats, and more than once I heard him mention Lord Pendrogeth. It seemed, from what I overheard, that he was buying off fishermen and persuading them to fish outside of the Tregenza's traditional waters, that he had promised better catches to those that did. Meredith was also interested in whether or not the men had set on dolphins before, and how many they might have killed. Mr Penrose answered Meredith's questions honestly as far as I could tell, but with some discomfort.

'Don't be too harsh on the lads,' he said to Meredith, as we walked along the seafront. 'Times is not so good. I remember when these houses was full of women's gossip, and laundry and the street… well,' he turned to Elsa and me, '… it 'ad a smell about it. Baking, coal fire and the sea all mixed. It sounds odd but it was the sweetest smell. I misses that smell and they times and so does the lads.'

The horse and cart were waiting for us at the end of the road. Meredith's mute servant drove us home.

'That man at the harbour. Does he work for you?' asked

Elsa climbing aboard the cart.

'He's a Penrose, Elsa. They belong to themselves. But yes, he does work for me, as do most of his kin. There's quite a few of them too; the Penroses have been in Penwith as long as the land itself. They're loyal too, for the most part. There isn't anything of fishing, or farming, or hunting or game they don't know. They say that if you want to sink a mine, or find a shoal, or hunt the fox round here you're wasting your time if you don't have a Penrose with you. It's true too; they have the knowledge of this place, including where to find my trout!' He winked at us.

As the cart and horse tugged slowly up the hill to take the coast road home I pondered over the day we'd had, running over the afternoon's events in my mind. I couldn't entertain a belief in mythical creatures. If Uncle Meredith hadn't been telling us his fantastic stories we'd never even have dreamt of mermaids. And yet… in my mind's eye I saw a face. A pale, beautiful face beneath the waves.

Chapter 4

'**B**ill,' said Elsa's voice through the fog of sleep. She was knocking at my door. I awoke. It was the middle of the night.

'Yes, yes, come in.'

'Bill, you shouted.'

'I had… I had… a nightmare,' I grabbed my forehead, slowly bearing myself into the waking world.

'What about?'

'The mermaid… I don't know, I can't quite remember,' I said. In my dream I had been in the water with her, and I had been drowning.

'You're soaking!' she said. My nightshirt and my hair were indeed damp.

'And it's cold. The window's open. You'll catch your death.' My hair and nightshirt were damp, and I knew it was not with sweat, I could smell and feel the salt water. I felt as though my dream had been real, as though I had been in cold, deep water only seconds before waking.

'Are you okay?' said Elsa. She had a concerned look on her face. I must have been visibly shaken.

'Yes, I'm fine, really.'

'I've dreamt about her too since Sennen. But the dreams weren't nightmares; at least I don't think so. Do you remember uncle Meredith said the mermaid was called Lamorna of the Cove? Well, there is a place called Lamorna Cove, I've seen it on a map. Perhaps we could go there. Do you think?'

'Elsa, there was no mermaid at Sennen.'

'But your dream?'

'It was just a dream.'

'All right then, but what's the harm in going to this Lamorna place?' It had been some days since the incident at Sennen. We had avoided the beach since then and needed new places to explore, so I agreed, but only under the strict provision that we were not to go hunting for mermaids. Elsa beamed with delight. I sent her back to bed.

We explained our plans to our uncles over breakfast. Anthony described Lamorna as a pretty, hidden cove on the south coast, reached via a rough lane, at the end of a long green valley.

'How did you find out about Lamorna?' he enquired. I looked to Elsa to explain but she said nothing.

'Elsa saw it on a map,' I said.

'Oh, what map was that?' said Meredith.

'Erm, you know Bill,' she said after a moment's hesitation. Although her freckly face was getting quite brown by then, I noticed a flush of red. She stole a split second glare at me before finding something on her plate on which to concentrate.

I never was a good liar and I am sure this was quite obvious as I stumbled over my words 'Oh, er, yes. The map was… in Sennen. One of the fishermen showed us.'

'Telling you tales of treasure I suppose… '

'Treasure! What treasure?' interrupted Elsa.

'They didn't tell you? I'm surprised. The treasure of the *Seahawk*. A gang of smugglers are supposed to have hidden their horde somewhere near Lamorna Cove, more than forty years ago. It's quite a local legend! You know, we've got some maps around here somewhere, all kinds. Some really ancient ones our mother had that you might be interested in, though where they are I've no idea. Meredith?'

'A fisherman in Sennen you say?' Meredith spoke directly to me.

'Yes,' I said. My brain scrambled for more words, but none came.

I was rescued by the distant sound of knocking at the front

door. We could hear Stephen talking to someone. He was laughing and smiling when he came into the conservatory.

'It's the Lord Pendrogeth Master Anthony. He requires a meeting with the master of the house.' Stephen looked from Meredith to Anthony and back. He seemed pleased with himself.

Meredith busied himself with his breakfast without looking up. Anthony sighed and threw his napkin down.

'I'll meet with him shall I?' said Anthony.

'Good morning,' said a voice. Stephen stood aside with a slight, but fawning bow to beckon Lord Pendrogeth into the conservatory.

'Stephen, why did you not show Lord Pendrogeth to the drawing room, this is no place for our discussions?'

'Lord Pendrogeth required me to take him directly to you,' said Stephen, bending his tall frame even further and wiping his greasy hair from his forehead.

'You don't work for Lord Pendrogeth Stephen,' Anthony glared at him. 'Not yet at least,' he added quietly. For a fleeting moment, his face looked careworn and heartbreakingly sad.

Lord Pendrogeth was dressed in exactly the same fashion as the first time I'd seen him; a plain, dark suit and a bowler hat, which he raised on seeing Elsa and I.

'Ah, you must be the Tregenza children I've heard so much about?'

'Actually their name is Smith, these are our sister's children,' said Anthony.

'Well, Tregenza by blood perhaps, if not by name. After all it is blood that matters in family affairs,' he looked at me when he said this, 'I trust you are enjoying your holidays?'

'Yes, thank you,' we answered jointly.

'And what adventures have you planned for today?' His voice was mellifluous and polite, but there was the merest hint of sarcasm and something in the way he carried himself that I did not like.

'We're going to Lamorna Cove,' answered Elsa, as formally

as she dared without being rude. She had picked up on Meredith's obvious disregard for Pendrogeth.

'Lamorna? An enchanting, even enchanted, place,' said Lord Pendrogeth.

'I'm afraid Meredith won't be able to take you there today. He's going to be otherwise engaged,' Anthony said to Elsa and I.

'Perhaps my driver could take you? Or if you are prepared to wait a while I could accompany you, I have business there,' said Lord Pendrogeth. We didn't answer.

'That won't be necessary,' said Anthony, 'get yourselves ready children and go and see Mr Penrose in the garden. Tell him I said to take you.'

We left them to their business and went upstairs to prepare for our day.

As soon as we were out of earshot I turned on Elsa. 'What's this about a map! Why did you lie? What map?'

'It was on a table in one of the rooms, along with some books.' I struggled to think where she might mean. Though the house was large, we knew it well by now. The only rooms that were out of bounds were Stephen's quarters, our uncles' rooms and the room of our late Grandmother on the ground floor.

'Elsa! What table, what books?'

'Yes, a table with maps, and some books and… ' she noticed my disapproving look '… I had to Bill. You didn't see. You were in the water and if I'd said afterwards you wouldn't have believed me.'

'Didn't see what?'

'In Sennen that day. The book Meredith read from. It wasn't English he read, it was a language I've never heard, yet it wasn't like a language at all. It was like… '

'Water.'

'You heard him too! You know, I think he cast a spell of some kind, I think he brought that mermaid to life!'

We were on the stairs. I stopped by the stained glass window. Small shafts of light cut like swords through the dark and dusty hall. I held back from telling her she was being ridiculous, it would only make her ever surer of her conviction. Elsa could be very stubborn when she wanted to be. I sighed.

'And where did you find these books?' I said.

'They're in our Grandmother's room, and there's another room beyond, but I couldn't get in that one.' I didn't need to point out that we had been told not to go into our late Grandmother's room. I just raised my eyebrows, folded my arms and waited for Elsa to explain.

'After I'd seen him read from that book I just *had* to know Bill. I went for a search in the middle of the night.' Elsa seemed very proud of herself.

'Well why didn't you tell me?'

'"Cuz you wouldn't have come in any case, or tried to stop me.'

'Well I'm surprised it wasn't locked.'

'It was, I got the key from Stephen's quarters.'

'And how did you… Oh Elsa, don't tell me you sneaked into his room when he was asleep!' She shrugged and smiled.

'There's all kinds of books and maps and I reckon there's more in the room beyond her bedroom too. I checked from the outside too, but there's no windows.' Though I didn't admit it I was curious, and secretly wished to see these books myself.

'I'd make a good thief wouldn't I?' said Elsa. I just walked up the stairs to my room, making a 'humph' sound and assuming an air of disapproval. Secretly though, I admired her pluck, and admitted to myself that yes, she would no doubt make an excellent thief.

Mr Penrose (who was a relative of the Mr Penrose we had met at Sennen) had a pony and trap which, to our delight, he drove fast on account of needing to return to the house and finish his work. We sat at his side, bracing ourselves against the stiff breeze.

I remember that day was cloudier and colder than any before it though the sun still shone between the clouds. We had had to dress in light jumpers and longer trousers and a skirt. This felt quite alien to us as we were by now, used to running round in nothing more than shorts and swimming costumes. We were no longer the white and pasty children that had arrived on the afternoon train from London. Our skin was brown, our flesh had become sinewy and tight – the result of proper food and endless rounds of climbing, walking and swimming, and always under the constant glare of the summer sun. The skin on our feet had practically become our shoes; brown, leathery, thick-skinned and tough. Elsa's light brown hair had begun to bleach.

''Ow long're ye staying for?' asked Mr Penrose.

'We don't know exactly. I expect for a few weeks,' I said.

'Ye'll be 'ere for the festival then?'

'What festival?' said Elsa.

'Why the festival o' Lyonesse o' course.'

'What's that?' asked Elsa. Mr Penrose took a while before he answered.

'Well in old times – and I do mean old – 'twas the time that we crowned the King. The true King, Lord of the sea, the land and the air. Lord of Lyonesse.'

'Lyonesse?'

'Thass what this land was known as once my lad, and it stretched from here to the Scilly Isles.'

'What happens at this festival, what's it for?'

'Well, there is a crowning o' the King and a mock sacrifice. You'll see. Some believe the customs practised there is a way o' making sure the nets are full and the crops are bountiful.'

'Do people believe that?' I said.

'There's many do and say they don't.'

'And what about you Mr Penrose?'

'Ain't sayin' but what I do know is there's plenty o' pie and ales an' celebration and good times. Even now, when there is a war on, 'tis important we don't forget the old ways,' he said slapping his stomach and winking.

We passed a field, where a crop – wheat I think – was growing. I had no experience of farming but even I could see it was a poor looking field. Patches of it held more thistle than wheat, and where the wheat did grow it was sparse and uneven; the stems grew thin and crooked, rocking weakly in the breeze. Some of the crop had been flattened on to the ground by the wind and had started to rot. After a while Mr Penrose spoke.

'You see that, it's the same all over – not up country mind – just round 'ere. There's some that says your uncle's got some'at to do with it too seein' as this blight is particular to 'is lands.'
Elsa and I stared at him, waiting for him to say more.

'As you'll see on the day of the festival; in custom and tradition, your uncle is the King of Lyonesse and is so crowned each mid summer day. Them that are superstitious will say 'e ain't done 'is duty right. Others more practical minded might say 'e ain't attended to the affairs of 'is farms as a master of such an estate is supposed to. As I see it, people see a problem and look for someone – or something – to blame. Now giddyup!' he shouted.

Chapter 5

We descended from the moor into a maze of fields and lanes bordered by stone walls, eventually emerging onto an open road, before turning down a lane towards the sea. The lane quickly deteriorated to a pot holed, earthen track, barely wide enough for the cart, following a brook through a thickly wooded valley.

It was an enchanting valley; the brook pouring its way down steps of moss covered stones, its gurgles and ripples echoing up the walls of the steep green valley. Sunlight filtered through a canopy of branches above us, sending shafts of gold to illuminate the darker recesses of the woods, where moss crept over the stones and lichen and ivy clung to the trees. Life grew on top of life with no yard of space that did not teem with verdant brightness. Off the track, we could see a few houses, or rather glimpses of them, hidden in the thick vegetation and one other path, leading up a hill. Next to the path a rough wooden signpost bore the word 'quarry' in flaking red paint.

It almost came as a shock after a mile or more, to turn a corner and see, not trees, but the open sea, framed by a cove of granite cliffs and infinite sky. Far up on the cliff I could see where the quarry was; there were parts of the hillside missing as though some gigantic creature had taken a bite out it.

Above the sounds of the brook and horse's hooves we now heard the peaceful sound of breakers washing rocks along the shore. Beyond the shore break, the water was flat and glassy for a hundred yards or more out to sea. But towards the headland, the water chopped and rocked, being more exposed to the elements. I could see that Lamorna Cove would be protected from the prevailing winds, which explained the thick, lush life of the valley and why perhaps, boats might seek shelter here from the winter storms. It was a beautiful, hidden place. We felt we had discovered a secret.

Mr Penrose dropped us at the harbour. Before leaving he visited one of the cottages on the harbour, presumably to let the occupants know who we were and to keep an eye out for us. Then he went, leaving us to a whole new world of swimming, diving and adventure.

We climbed rocks; we explored the tracks along the cliff, and when tired and hot, refreshed ourselves by swimming in the deep, calm waters off the harbour. Later, when the tide was fuller, we found a new game of leaping and diving off the harbour wall. Each run was faster, each leap more adventurous. We had played for hours and it must have been towards the end of the afternoon when, on a particularly fast long jump, in mid air, I saw the flick of a large silvery tail in the distance. Or thought I did. I swam up for air as quickly as I could, bursting with excitement.

'Elsa, Elsa did you see?'

'What Bill?' Elsa was next to me, treading water.

'A mer… ' I paused. Had I seen it? Yes, it was clear. This time I had seen more than a mere shadow in the water. 'I don't know, a creature or some such.' Perhaps it had been a dolphin? I swam as fast as I could to the boulders at the shore, and ran back to the end of the harbour wall.

'Where Bill, what did you see?' insisted Elsa.

'There, again!' I said pointing to the shoreline, some several hundred yards towards the headland where a rocky shelf jutted into the sea. This time there could be no mistake, although it was some distance away, I saw the tail flick spray into the air, huge and powerful, covered in silver, shimmering scales – and I was sure I had seen the pale skin of her back as she rolled and dived.

'I didn't see anything,' said Elsa, 'is it the mermaid?' she asked hopefully. My skin tingled with wonder and excitement.

'You know what Elsa, I'm going to find out.'

'Wait for me,' shouted Elsa struggling to the shore as fast as she could.

We raced to don our plimsolls and put our clothes on over our wet costumes before running around the harbour, up the path, along the cliff and carefully down onto the rocks above the sea. Before long we were directly above the place where I had seen the mermaid. We stood for a moment or two, staring down into the water. The freshening wind was stirring the water's surface, obscuring the detail of what lay beneath. Other than a few rocks and seaweed, I couldn't make anything out below the surface. But I knew what I had seen, and quickly stripped off my damp cloths. Without a thought for my own safety or Elsa's, I clambered down the steep rocks as far as I could before hurling myself off the rocks and into the water some yards below.

I felt a sickening lurch in my stomach, followed by a solid 'thump' as my body hit the water. The jump had been further than I thought. I came to the surface and looked around. There was no way for me to climb back on to the rocks and I was hundreds of yards from the safety of the harbour. But I didn't think about that, I was more concerned with finding whatever I had seen. Hidden by the overhang of a great boulder, and only exposed when the sea fell, was a large gap between the rocks.

'Come on Elsa, there's a cave!' Elsa stripped down to her swimming costume, climbed down as far as she could and then stood, contemplating the jump. She was not a great swimmer and was younger and weaker than I. For a second Elsa – confident, bright, and sure of herself Elsa – looked scared. Behind her, silhouetted against the cloudy sky two crows were circling round each other, calling out their dark and croaking cries.

'Come on,' I said. She let out a short scream and then leapt into the air. When she came up from her jump her breathing was fast and shallow. I grabbed her arm.

'Look,' I shouted pointing to the cave. 'Follow me.' I swam as far as I could with my head above water, and when the overhanging rock threatened to knock my head, as I bobbed up and down in the swell, I took a deep breath and dived. Sure enough, there was a cave and with my head under water I could see it opened up beyond the entrance into a cavern. I came back to the surface and beckoned Elsa to follow me. Within a moment we popped our heads out of the water on the other side.

As our eyes adjusted to the dim light we could see we were in a sea pool at the bottom of a large, secret cavern.

'Gosh,' cried Elsa; her words echoing round the seaweed dripping walls. The water was still rising and falling, so we had to be very careful climbing out of the water and on to the rocks. We stood in silence for a while, the only sounds the wash of the water on rock and the over loud echo of our own breath. We were both shivering from the cold.

Now that I was there I wasn't at all sure I was doing the right thing. And if I had any doubts, what was I doing dragging Elsa with me? But it was too late for such thoughts, we had come this far and whatever I had seen, this was where it had gone. Besides, though I didn't say so I was also thrilled we had 'discovered' this cave. I secretly dared to hope this might be the hiding place of the smugglers' treasure Anthony had told us of.

Ahead of us I could make out a passage leading away, into the cliff. Slowly, with one hand holding Elsa's and the other feeling the way, I led us into the cave.

'Hallo,' I cried, my call echoing deep into the passageway. There was no response other than the echo of my voice and the sound of wind and water lapping rocks.

'Are you sure you saw a mermaid?' asked Elsa in a meek voice. Could I have imagined it? No, I was sure of what I had seen, and if only to prove it to myself, one way or the other; I walked on, pulling Elsa behind me.

We were some way in before Elsa noted that we were up to our ankles in water. We were nearly in pitch darkness too.

'Bill, I'm cold,' she added.

'Okay, okay, we'll go back soon,' I said, unable to hide the disappointment in my voice.

'Biiiiiiiiiiiiilllllllllll.' A long whispering voice called my name. Or was it the echo of Elsa's voice?

'Did you hear that?' I said, my own words bouncing back to me from the cold, dark hollows of the cavern.

'I didn't hear anything,' said Elsa. 'Please can we go back now? I'm cold.'

'I thought you wanted to see a mermaid,' I said, a little too harshly.

'I do Bill, but I… I… ' Her voice trailed off. I began to feel guilty that I had brought Elsa.

'Well, maybe we'll come back with Uncle Meredith and… what was that?'

'Ooooovvveeerr heeeeere Bill.' The voice came again. I stumbled away from the wall towards the source, still pulling Elsa along behind me.

'Heerrrre Biiiiiill,' it was closer now, but still hard to distinguish from the sounds of the water and wind rushing through the cave. We were up to our knees in water by then. Only later did I realise that this had been the tide pouring into the cave.

'Heere now, heere now,' whispered the voice. We carried on; my feet trembled as they sought the next foothold. Another step forward and my feet found nothing but water. I fell forwards, my hand slipped from Elsa's. I stumbled downwards, arms reaching blindly as I fell quickly over stones and pebbles, pushed by a surge of water. I lost Elsa.

I stumbled to a halt, my heart beating loudly. In my stomach, I could feel panic rising, just as surely as the cold water now began to rise over my knees, my thighs, my waist. I cursed myself for endangering us in this way. I was about to turn, to try and get back the way I had come when, directly ahead of me, in the thin light, I saw a figure.

Though I was in near darkness I could make out its silhouette. It wasn't a mermaid; it had the thickset shape of a man. There was an overwhelming sickly, fishy odour. The man, whoever he was, had a bright shell in his hands that he held to his mouth

'Cooome Biiillll,' said the voice, in whispery, soft tones. Then he pulled the shell away from his mouth and even in the dim light I could see his face. Or what was left of it.

The thin light outlined a skull, with remnants of flesh clinging to the bone. I could see the dark recesses where his eyes should have been and the glint of metal in his teeth. As the water rushed in, now up to my chest, the sound of it shook around the cave, mixing with the sound of his voice.

'Coooome Biiill,' he said in a gruff thick voice. I could see the naked grin of his teeth and jawbone, the white bone almost luminary. He laughed, and the sound of it echoed around the cavern with the sound of the rushing water.

'O God, O God, ELSA!' I turned back to the passage, my hands flailing around for something to grasp. My legs pushed against the force of the water that now flooded in, but my hands found only a wall of wet stone, and there was no response to my cry, just the cruel laughter of the ghoul and the echo of the sea rushing in. Soon the cave was near full, and my legs were no longer on the ground, but treading water.

Where was Elsa, how would I get to her? I wanted to feel strong; I wanted to know what to do. But I felt weak, confused and more afraid than I had ever done. I was floating upwards now, my head just above water. It would only be a matter of time before the water reached the top of the cave, if that is the man, or whatever it was, didn't get to me first. Then I heard my name called again.

'BIIILLLL'!

This was no wind driven echo, it was Elsa, and she was close. Her cry had come from my left, when I thought she should be directly ahead. Or had it? The echoes were disorienting. There was no time to think. I turned to my left and with a deep breath I dived and swam, as hard as I could. A few strokes and I met stone. Knowing that I could by now be above the entrance I swam down. Thank God, there was a hole. But did it lead to Elsa or to a slow and agonising death? My hand went under the stone, and I pulled myself under and along the roof of a passage. After a few strokes I reached above my head. There was no rock, so I kicked upwards, praying Elsa would be there. My head banged into something, something that wriggled and kicked. I grabbed it and heard a scream, directly above me. I had grabbed Elsa's leg. Lungs bursting, I kicked up, my head breaking through the surface.

'It's okay, it's okay, it's me!' I gasped in between breathing mouthfuls of precious air. With one hand I felt the wall of the cave and ran my hand upwards and then over our heads. We were at the very roof of the cave, trapped in an air bubble. We were alive, we could breathe, we were together. I thanked God for these mercies, but the elation was brief. It soon sank in that we had no idea how to get out, and no one knew where we were. Apart that is, from the man with no face.

For long moments we clung to each other, treading water. Elsa didn't say anything, she was obviously terrified. I did not know what to do but I was not got going to wait for the man – or ghoul – to find us, nor was I going to wait for us to drown. In any case, I was sure we did not have much time. As calmly as I could I told Elsa that I would explore by myself, coming back for air every minute until I had found the way out. Elsa's hand clung to my neck.

'Don't leave me Bill, don't leave me,' she sobbed. But I had to. I dived, feeling my way along the walls, praying for a glimpse of light, anything that would show me the way. But it was no good. I must have returned to Elsa a dozen times and each time I felt a little weaker. The faint light of hope was flickering, dying.

Gathering my strength, I dived one last time, but found nothing but rock. I thought I would return to Elsa and then wait until the tide had receded (yet knowing that we were unlikely to last that long), but instead I bumped into a body. The body of a man. I grabbed him with what little strength I had but he was both bigger and stronger than I was and after a short struggle he had me by my costume and was pulling me upwards. The next I knew my head broke the surface, I gasped for air. In my mind's eye I could see his rotting face, the naked grin of his teeth, the hollow where his eyes had once been.

A large hand reached from the water and covered Elsa's mouth, covering her scream. She was pulled under the water, I felt her hand tug uselessly at me and then she was gone.

I dived downwards. Between strokes I stretched around, my arms grasping, finding nothing. I swam down further, and further again. My hand touched something. Instinctively I grabbed. I had him by the leg. He was very strong, he must have swam for a good few yards with Elsa in his arms and me pulled by his leg. Then he kicked back and I lost him. I swam into a wall, felt along it and then must have passed the entrance to the chamber, for there was a faint glimmer of light in the gloomy depths, and I could just make out the silhouette of a large man, with Elsa held to his waist. My head began to pulsate in time with my heart, my lungs tightened. The water was clearer, lighter now; we had to be near the entrance to the cave. I could see the man and Elsa, but could not reach them for I had long used up all my strength, and now I felt movement itself drain from my arms and legs. My lungs stopped hurting, I made a couple of final feeble strokes, which seemed to be made by a body that I no longer controlled and was rapidly falling away from. My arms, the man, Elsa, the light, they were all far away now. Consciousness drained away and with it any vestige of awareness. My body turned in the still water, no longer flailing, but still, floating. The light faded to nothing, I no longer felt cold. Then blackness.

I felt a tug; I was being pulled through the water. Strong hands pulled at my limp body, a body that now only existed in the distant dream of a deep, beckoning sleep.

I was wrenched from the water. I heard a thud as my body landed on hard wood, but hardly felt it. Then, strangely, I was being kissed and air was being forced into my lungs. Light and air flooded back into my consciousness along with pain, and cold and nausea and the awareness of Elsa being pulled away by… the man, his skull! I tried to sit up, but was sick. I opened my eyes, and dizzily looked around. There was a man directly ahead of me, dripping with water. He opened his arms and moved forward, then he pulled back, then came forward again. I was sick once more before looking at him again. He was rowing. In front of him, sitting on the boat's wet floor was a woman, and in her arms a girl. It was Elsa!

'It's okay Bill,' said Elsa, tears streaming down her cheeks and into her grinning mouth. 'We've been saved.'

The man who had saved us, who I had fought so desperately, nearly killing myself in the process, was the mute servant of our Uncle Meredith. He sat in the centre of the boat, fully clothed and dripping with water. He stared at me, unblinking as he rowed, long powerful strokes. I owed him my life and wanted to thank him, but there was something in the way he sat there, still and calm, that unnerved me. He showed not a trace of emotion, and from his wet clothes came a smell, feint, but distinctly unpleasant. It was the same dreadful odour I had smelt in the cave.

The woman (who I assumed had given me the kiss of life) was in her late twenties. She wore white trousers and a thick, blue fisherman's jumper. She was beautiful, in a handsome, square jawed way. Her hair was bleached blond by the sun and cut into a short bob. She had translucent blue eyes and tanned skin and glowed with an aura of sun, sea and air.

'I'm Miss Ariel,' she said, 'you're a very lucky young man Bill,' she said, without looking at me, her eyes on the sea. 'You could have got you *and* your sister killed!' She spoke harshly, in a clipped, upper class accent. But the anger I thought was mostly feigned and could not mask the relief in her voice, nor the fact that she herself was quite shaken.

'I… I'm sorry. I didn't mean to,' I blurted out. My words sounded hollow and weak. I had never felt such a fool, nor so ashamed.

'Well never mind. You're safe now,' she said, a little more gently. 'Lucky for you I saw you jumping from the cliff. You know once we'd found the cave it took forever to find a way through. This man must have dived a dozen times and each time for several minutes,' she said, clearly impressed.

'Was there… anyone else?' I asked cautiously.

'What do you mean?'

'Did… you… see… anyone else, come from the cave I mean?'

'You mean there was someone else in there?' she said, her voice rising with panic. She looked at the man. He looked straight at me, with eyes as dark and forlorn as the woman's were clear and bright. For long moments he stared into my eyes, then he looked back to the woman and slowly shook his head.

Soon we had passed through the rough water and made for the safety of the cove. Both Elsa and I had started to shake with the shock and the cold and Miss Ariel said we were to come to her cottage for some much-needed warmth and a hot drink. Meredith's man was despatched to fetch our clothing from the cliff top.

Once inside she stood us in front of her stove, throwing extra logs into its fire for good measure. Towels and blankets appeared and we were told in a matter of fact way that this was not the time for modesty. We were to strip and rub ourselves vigorously with the towels till we felt warm, then wrap up in the blankets. In the meantime she would make us some hot chocolate, topped with a nip of brandy for the shock.

The brandied chocolate arrived and for a long time we sat in silence, watching the flames grow in the stove's open door. I felt numb, and tired but as I drank, grateful to the core of my being for every hot, life-blessing sip of the chocolate.

'Now then,' she said quietly, but firmly, from her armchair, 'perhaps you would like to tell me what on earth you were doing?'

'I… I… we thought we saw a dolphin… didn't we Elsa?' My words trailed off weakly.

'That's right,' said Elsa, more convincingly, 'and when we couldn't find it we thought it must have gone inside the cave. Miss Ariel said nothing, but she looked at me with one eyebrow slightly raised. She did not need to point out that dolphins do not live in caves.

'Will you tell our uncles?' asked Elsa with her most winning smile, and pleading eyes.

'What would I tell them? I don't know the truth. I'm afraid I'll have to tell them something. If I don't I am sure Lord Pendrogeth will.'

'Lord Pendrogeth? How… '

'He was at the harbour side when I saw you jump.'

'We didn't see him,' I said. Suddenly I felt alert, uncomfortable.

'Well he saw you. And he behaved… strangely…, very strangely indeed. When Meredith's man appeared in the harbour, I said we should go after you, to get you out of those caves. Well, first of all Lord Pendrogeth tried to dissuade me all together, saying you would be fine and if you didn't appear after ten minutes he would go after you himself. Well I know these tides and wasn't going to wait. He refused to help point blank, called me 'an interfering woman.' Then, when we had set off, I happened to look behind and do you know he was doing the oddest thing. He stood on the shoreline and appeared to be reading aloud, from a book and talking into a shell. And around his head, two or three crows were flying around, making quite a commotion. They looked quite agitated. Curious. Anyway, as I say, perhaps you would like to tell me what on earth you were doing?'

'A book?' I said. I was reminded of Uncle Meredith standing on the beach at Sennen. 'We… I saw a mermaid, and something else too, I think there was a ghost in that cave.'

'Go on,' said Miss Ariel.

I told her everything. I did not stop to think how ridiculous it all might sound, or that none of it made any sense. I told her about the hare the day we had arrived in Cornwall, about the incident on the beach and about seeing the mermaid's tail and the ghost in the cave, though I held back from describing the details of its deathly face, knowing it would scare Elsa. Miss Ariel leant forward in her chair, her hands folded on her knees. She listened intently, without interrupting. When I had finished she leant back with a sigh.

'I believe you.'

'You do?' said Elsa.

'I mean I believe that you mean what you say. But I think your uncle may have filled your head with too many of his stories – he's famous for them – and maybe your imaginations have been a bit overactive.'

'Will you tell our uncles?' asked Elsa again. Miss Ariel looked blankly into the fire for a moment or two, the way someone can when their mind is actually doing a great deal of calculating.

'If I tell your uncles what happened I am sure they will take away whatever freedom you enjoy. So I won't tell, on condition you promise, and I mean on your soul, that there'll be no more exploring of cliffs and caves. In return I'll promise to keep an eye on you myself from time to time. Do we have a deal?'

'We promise,' we said in morose voices. We meant it, but were saddened to think that we would have to restrain ourselves in any way. Elsa and I were used to our freedom.

'And no more talk of mermaids and ghosts either.'

'You don't believe in mermaids?' said Elsa.

'No, though there is a great tradition of mythology concerning them. It is said the waters were full of them when these parts were known as…'

'Lyonesse,' I said.

'Yes, though the lost land of Lyonesse is a myth too, but perhaps one based on historical truth.' We perked up, eager to learn more.

'Tell us!' we said in unison.

Miss Ariel stood up and walked over to the window. There was a table beneath the window, with a mass of sketches and maps upon it, as well as stone jars full of brushes, pots of paint and next to the table, a canvas. She turned the canvas around and showed us an unfinished painting. It was of Mount's Bay. For the most part it was a good oil painting of the sea, with the Lizard

Peninsular in the background and St Michael's Mount to the fore. But there were two notable differences to the scene we knew. In this picture St Michael's Mount was a barren rock. Further off shore, however, was another island. Most of this island was covered with a tall castle, built into the rock, with high stone walls, black turrets and battlements stretching high above the sea.

'The painting is called 'The Isle of Ictis.' Once upon a time there was another island in the bay, a long time before the castle on the mount was even built. It was called Ictis, the city of books. The Phoenicians, Egyptians, Greeks – they all came here trading for tin. The King of these parts – Lyonesse as Penwith was allegedly known – grew rich because of it. But gold and precious stones weren't the only gain he made from the trade of tin. These civilisations brought books, a rare commodity in those times. Books of maths and astronomy, astrology and alchemy, books of magic as well as science. The King's castle was on the isle of Ictis, and there he amassed a great library and a seat of learning. But you must remember that this was before the time of English books, even of the Bible, and many feared the King of Lyonesse, and were jealous of his wealth and powers… It was even said he could control the weather.

Anyway, after many hundreds of years the Christians came and the Kings of Lyonesse were cast as witches. The local people destroyed the castle, burnt the books and killed the King and all his family. That, you would think would have been an end of it. But it is very hard for a new religion to completely swallow an old one and the midsummer feast and the legend of the King of Lyonesse live on. Some believe to this day that there is a set of books, which survived the destruction of Ictis and are said to be kept hidden, to be given to the King of Lyonesse in times of turmoil, that he might use them to right the wrongs of the world.

'Who told you of Lyonesse anyhow?' said Miss Ariel.

'Mr Penrose,' said Elsa, as though he were a known authority.

'How come you know so much about it Miss Ariel?' I

asked, a little suspiciously.

'Well, research for my painting I suppose. Besides like yourselves, I'm an incomer and I find these things fascinating, though not to the point where I start believing them,' and she gave us a reproachful look, 'if you really want to find out more there's a museum being built in St Ives, partly funded by Lord Pendrogeth as it happens. It's not officially open as yet but I believe I can get us in. In fact I've been visiting there a lot. A part of the museum will be devoted to the Isle of Ictis – all sorts of artefacts have come from there, the results of an undersea excavation, also funded by Lord Pendrogeth. The rest of it's to do with the history of west Penwith; legends, pirates, mining. It's fascinating. If your uncles allow it I could take you there, at least you can't endanger yourself in a museum!'

'Yes please,' said Elsa, speaking for both of us, 'Mr Penrose could take us.'

'Oh really,' said Miss Ariel with a wry smile. She turned from the canvas, and walked to the door. From the back of it hung a thick leather coat and from underneath it she pulled a leather helmet and goggles, which she proceeded to put on. She stood facing us, her hands on her hips and a wide smile on her brown, open face. 'Are you sure you wouldn't rather fly?'

Chapter 6

Supper was a quiet affair. Anthony in particular was lost in thought, distant and sombre. We ate most of our meal in silence. Our uncles had no wish to discuss their morning's business with Pendrogeth and we were even less willing to talk about our day at Lamorna Cove, wishing to tell neither the truth nor some invention of the day's activities.

'So, you did not seek the mermaid Lamorna herself then?' said Meredith eventually. There was a hint of mischief in his voice. Elsa's eyes locked onto mine for the briefest second. How much did he know? What form of communication did he and his strange, wordless servant use?

'Meredith, your stories grow tiresome. You children swam I presume?' enquired Anthony. By then it had become a custom for us to tell them of our day's adventures over supper. I think it provided a welcome break from our uncles' worries. It might have seemed suspicious to say nothing so I told him a little about the diving and swimming and made a pretence of Miss Ariel inviting us in to her cottage for hot chocolate.

'Miss Ariel,' said Meredith, 'a true and free spirit!'

'Yes, she's going to take us flying in her aeroplane,' said Elsa enthusiastically, keen to divert their questions away from the day at Lamorna Cove. 'If we're allowed,' she added, cautiously.

'Actually it's not her aeroplane, it's ours. She rents it from us for her business ferrying supplies and rich folk to the Scilly Islands. I suppose, you can go up in it if you wish. You might as well whilst you have the chance.' Anthony did not elucidate.

'Did you see Pendrogeth at Lamorna, he was supposed to have business there was he not?' said Meredith casually, mopping up his gravy with bread and feeding it to one of his hounds, who sat obediently at his side, its great hairy head on his lap. I opened my mouth to answer, but Elsa was quicker.

'We didn't see him. Miss Ariel did though.'

'Did she say what he was up to?' said Meredith.

'Reading aloud from a book or something.'

Meredith's hand froze in mid air, gravy dripping from the bread he held. Whatever he knew, his servant had not told him this. He sat, quite still, staring at his plate for a long moment. When he spoke his voice was as calm and quiet as it was deadly serious.

'Elsa listen to me.' Meredith fixed her with his gaze. In the darkened room his eyes seemed almost black. His large, rough hands held the space between him and Elsa. 'Elsa you must tell me exactly. Was this whilst you were in the caves?' He knew! Meredith turned his fierce gaze at me. 'Bill?' Anthony looked from one to the other of us.

'Caves, what caves?' he said. Meredith now held me with his eyes. I dared not look away, nor did I dare lie.

'Yes.'

He held my gaze for a moment longer. As he watched me the fierceness melted from his face, replaced by a look I can only describe as shock. He stood up, knocking his chair over as he did so. With a trembling hand he picked up his wineglass and finished the contents in one swallow.

'What's this about caves? Will someone let me know what on earth is going on?' demanded Anthony. Meredith left, his dog in tow, leaving us to explain to Uncle Anthony what happened at Lamorna Cove. I explained as best I could, missing out any talk of mermaids or the dreadful ghoul, and being less than completely honest about just how much danger we had been in. When I had finished he sent us to straight to bed, saying he would think about how best to deal with us.

Once in my room I lay on the bed wishing for sleep. But the events of the day and Meredith's odd behaviour played repeatedly on my mind. Images swept through my consciousness like the waters in the cave, and as I had struggled against those waters, so I fought my own thoughts, desperate to control them, desperate not to have again a vision of that foul, decaying, laughing skull.

I awoke in a sweat. The room was hot and quiet, dank with compressed heat; a silent witness to my nightmares. I opened the window to let the air in and turned to go back to bed, yet as I did the wind dropped utterly, just as it had that day on the beach. I stopped in my tracks, the hairs on the back of my neck heckling, sending a cold shiver down my spine.

I turned slowly, cautiously, afraid of what I would see. Outside of the window, floating in mid-air, was the image of a hare. It wore a mask; curiously it seemed, of its own face held on a stick. On its breast was a scar, directly above its heart.

I stared at it, breathing hard. My heart was sinking, cold and leaden. My nightmares I knew were not over, yet I was no longer dreaming.

It took me a long time to speak.

'Why have you come here?'

It spoke with many voices. Voices that echoed the wind, voices that fell like water.

'You haunt my dreams,' said the voices.

'What are you?' I asked, my heart pounding. The hare said nothing; by way of answer it pulled away the mask. Behind it lay a human skull.

I opened my mouth to scream but there was only silence. I raced to the window to shut it. As I did so the hare retreated, back into the night sky.

It took a long time for me to return to the welcome oblivion of sleep.

It was to be some days before Miss Ariel could take us flying. In the meantime, Anthony told us over breakfast, he was to act as our chaperone. He assured us he wasn't angry about our adventure in the caves, but he had a responsibility, not only to us but also to our parents. Perhaps, he reflected, he had been foolish to trust us on our own.

Thereafter, Anthony, or Miss Ariel, would occasionally take us to Sennen or the beach near the lighthouse at Pendeen, but for the most part we were housebound. We were only truly alone when we walked the dogs on the nearby moors. Only there was there no risk of interruption, or worse; being spied on by Stephen. Only there did we feel truly free and would seize the chance to talk about the mermaid at Sennen, the caves at Lamorna Cove and about the strange books we had seen Pendrogeth and our uncle read.

'Meredith and Pendrogeth. They're magicians,' insisted Elsa confidently, throwing an old ball over a stone wall for the hounds to fetch. 'If you saw Meredith's books you'd realise that!' she added haughtily. Because of her midnight exploration of the house, when she had found the books Elsa believed herself more of an authority *and* an adventurer than I. And she was annoyingly smug about it. However, I was as keen as she was to get to the bottom of the mystery and knew that if we wanted to find out anything more we needed to get a closer look at Meredith's books. Elsa relished the idea. We had long recovered from our ordeal at Lamorna and our present captivity only served to make us restless for further adventure.

'Come on Bill. Let's do it. Don't be so yellow!' she taunted.

I wanted to say yes, but feared we might be discovered and *that* would ruin any chance of getting our freedom back. Worse still, we might well be sent home on the first train out of Penzance.

'I don't know Elsa.'

'Bill, we nearly died in that cave and Pendrogeth had something to do with it didn't he? And he was reading a book, *just* like uncle Meredith did that day on the beach. The book thing can't be coincidence! Besides, have you any better ideas?'

I was still reluctant to go stealing around the house in the night like a thief, and the idea weighed heavily on me. But that evening, Uncle Anthony told us something that made up my mind.

We were waiting in the dining room, whilst Meredith prepared our supper, when Anthony appeared, dressed in his linen suit. He declared he had something to tell us. He spoke with the kind, serious voice adults use when they want children to understand something important from the world of adult understanding and responsibility.

'You're to stay here till the Festival of Lyonesse, but after that you can go home… to see your mother.' We stared at him in shocked silence. We missed our mother but had no desire for our holiday to finish.

'When can we come back?' asked Elsa, a slight tremble in her voice.

'Well, that's the thing. I'm afraid you won't be able to, not here anyway.' We sat in stunned silence.

'You understand that Meredith has not really run the Estate for some time. That particular duty has been left to me. Well, the truth is that we are in debt and considerable debt at that and I have had to make the decision to sell the house and the Estate. Meredith has so far refused to even consider this option, but matters are now so bad that I'm afraid we have no choice. If he does not agree we will lose the house and the Estate to the bank in any case. Selling is our best option and frankly we are lucky to find a buyer. This will clear our debts and leave us with a small sum with which to start life anew.' He spoke in a plain and polite manner. I think he was almost relieved that the inevitable had finally arrived.

'And who will you sell the Estate to?' I asked, though I knew the answer.

'Lord Pendrogeth has made an offer. It's not as much as the Estate is worth, but there is a war on and for us to find a buyer at this time is extremely fortunate. Once the festival is over, we'll sign the papers and I will inform the Estate workers, farmers and fishermen.'

'A shame for the boy don't you think?' said a voice from the doorway.

'Meredith… I,' Anthony stammered.

'I will never sell to Pendrogeth,' said Meredith.

'Then we will lose everything,' shouted Anthony, 'and rot in prison whilst our debts go unpaid!'

'And what of him?' said Meredith pointing to me. 'We have more important dues to pay brother, dues to generations of Tregenza blood. Am I to be the last?' He left.

'What Meredith means… ' Anthony started, but faltered. He found some time to find the right words, but I had worked it out for myself.

The Estate had passed from our Grandmother to her sons. Upon their deaths the house and the lands and all the rights thereof would have passed to the next generation through the bloodline. Both Anthony and Meredith were bachelors so… I was the legal heir to Lyonesse.

We nodded and smiled as we listened, keeping our answers as short and accommodating as possible. We had no wish to add to the tangible tensions between Anthony and Meredith. Yet I too felt Meredith's fury and made promises to myself that belied the words falling from my mouth.

'Yes, we understand Uncle Anthony,' said Elsa. This house, I thought, will never fall into Pendrogeth's hands. We love you, our uncles, this house is our home, these beaches and cliffs and moors are a part of us now, and we are a part of them. Somehow we will defeat Pendrogeth and one day I will come and live here. I will grow old here. I will die here.

There and then I determined to unravel the mystery of our uncle and Pendrogeth's strange and secret powers. If the books were the keys to such powers, then they might help us to understand how we might defeat Pendrogeth. And, I vowed to myself, defeat him we surely would.

I lay awake a good few hours before rousing Elsa from her sleep. We crept downstairs and made straight for Stephens' quarters. Elsa went in alone, reappearing moments later with his keys, which she had found on his bedside table. All the time we were there we could hear his loud rhythmic snoring.

Along the corridor was our Grandmother's room. Elsa quickly found the right key. Once in I lit a match from the box I had brought, so that we could see. Sure enough, there was a table with a map or two, but no books.

'Damn,' whispered Elsa, 'they were here Bill. I swear it.' Elsa had a talent for exaggeration but I knew she wouldn't have dragged me to the room for no reason.

'They must be in the other room,' she whispered, pointing to the door at the back of the room. It was a plain wooden door. It had a circle carved into it, roughly the size of a plate.

'I don't think it's a room. Probably a cupboard,' I whispered. I knew exactly where we were in the house, and had seen this room from the garden. There was no space for a room behind this one I thought. Elsa tried the door. It was locked. Slowly, painstakingly we tried all the keys on the enormous iron key ring stolen from Stephen's room. None of them fitted. Then, instinctively, and for no reason I can explain, I lifted my right hand and placed it in the circle, pushing the door open as I did so. Elsa and I both gasped. We both knew it had been firmly locked when she had tried it.

I lit another match. Beyond the door, stone steps descended downwards, into the earth. We climbed down the steps, twenty or more, and followed a subterranean passage, hewn from sheer rock. At the end was a large and ancient wooden door.

With a push the door swung soundlessly open. We entered the darkened room, the stone floor cold against our bare feet, the only sound our breathing.

I peered into the darkness. In the gloom I could make out shelves of books and two tables, one of which had a lamp on it. I lit the lamp and cautiously adjusted it, watching carefully as the arc of yellow light filled the room. Of the two tables the nearer was covered in maps and open books, the second had a wide variety of curious instruments on it. There was also a stand for reading books upright, much the same as you might see in a church pulpit. The frame of this stand took the form of a creature that was bizarrely, both fish- and bird-like in appearance. It had a bird's face with beady, intense eyes that examined us from behind a hawk's beak of silver and gold. Wings of silver fish scales were stretched out to support a book on the creature's back, which ended in a fish tail, covered in feathers. Elsa closed the door behind us, cutting us off from the house and any danger of being overheard.

The walls were entirely covered by shelves filled by row upon row of books: thick books bound in loose leather, tall books bound in wood, thin pamphlets held by tattered and ancient ribbons, books stuffed with tracing paper and thin, flaking parchment. Most, were in foreign languages, with illustrations of wonderful and mythical creatures, some like dragons, which we knew, others which were quite beyond our knowledge or imagination. A few of the books were printed, but for the most part they were hand-written, inked and drawn meticulously by unknown authors from a bygone age, from unknown lands. We held each page in awe and could have spent hours if not days poring over the books, admiring their beauty, wondering at their hidden secrets. However, we dared not risk discovery, so with reluctance, we set to our task. We looked on each shelf in turn. There were perhaps ten books of the right size, so we placed them all on the first table, on top of the maps, which I had noted seemed to be mostly of Cornwall and of the Land's End peninsular in particular. These small books were not in English either, and with the exception of one which had careful ink illustration of herbs, had no pictures or clues as to their use or arcane knowledge. We tried to read them, but to no avail.

I had a terrible thought. Presumably Meredith had not planned to use the book that day, so it had to be a book he always carried. My heart sank. What if he had the book with him now?

Carefully we restored the books to the shelves. The room's secrets remained locked away. I was about to dim the lamp when I noticed Meredith's bag hung on the back of the door. The same bag he carried whenever we saw him.

'Wait,' I whispered to Elsa, as she went to open the door. I pointed to the bag. She took the heavy satchel from its hook and gave it to me.

With trembling hands I opened the bag. Inside were three seemingly identical books, each of them small and bound in soft leather, with no visible title or inscriptions. They were tattered, stained and very, very old. I lifted them out and placed them carefully on the table, side by side.

'Go on,' said Elsa, nudging me in the ribs. I picked up the middle one. Again, I expected print, but instead found myself looking at text that had been hand written in tiny, meticulous detail. As I flicked through I saw that the chapters had been written in different languages, scripts and styles, none of which I recognised. Clearly this was a book with more than one author.

But the book was more unusual in other ways. As I leafed through the pages it struck me that it felt wet. At first it was just a little damp and clammy, and I assumed Meredith must have somehow dropped it in a puddle or spilt a drink on it. But within a minute or so of my examining the book, drops of water began to fall from my hands.

It wasn't just the book either, since I had opened its pages the whole atmosphere of the room had changed. The stone floor was now damp, and smelt like the earth after rain. Then I heard the sound of dripping water, but it was coming from inside the cellar. Drops of water were splashing on the flagstone floor. We both looked up. Did this underground part of the house run underneath a stream? Were we about to be flooded? The longer I held the book the wetter it became, until the impossible truth became obvious. The book was welling up with water. It was as though I held a spring in my hands, the book itself being the source of the steady cascade of water now pouring over my hands. I shut the book, feeling quite shocked and more than a little worried. In an instant it was dry. Quite stunned, I held the book to the lamp. Now I examined it more closely I could see the leather cover did bear a very faint inscription. In thin blue lettering was written 'Dowr.' I had heard my mother use this word. It was the Cornish word for water.

Such had been my surprise that I had not acknowledged how I felt whilst the book was open. My head had swum with the surprise; my limbs had felt loose, fluid even. I had felt giddy, unstable. Yet when I shut the book I had come to my senses with a mighty 'thump,' like being landed on a shore by a great wave. Elsa and I gazed at each other in open-mouthed wonder.

'Did you feel that?' I said.

'Feel what?'

'I… I'm not sure. Like you were… liquid?' Elsa raised her eyebrows and shrugged her shoulders.

'Open another one,' she said. But I was reluctant. The whole room was damp, if not wet. If I opened another book what might I unleash? And it was now very, very evident that we had been in the room. Yet I was curious. I opened another. This book was heavy and as I opened it, my hands felt drier, tougher, much as they would after a day working in a garden. This time there was no discernible change in the room, but again, my own state of mind was altered. I felt a surge of power running through me, tightening my limbs. Every sinew, every muscle felt taut. Then, in an instant my senses brought everything around me sharply into focus, I could see every book, was aware of every detail. On a shelf at the far end of the room I sensed, and then saw, a spider scuttling across the tops of the book. In the silence I could hear the paper crackling ever so slightly under its tiny weight. Focussing my hearing further, I realised I could hear the wind outside the house and in the distance, the crash of waves on the cliffs. It was only when I saw the startled look in Elsa's eyes that I thought to close the book.

'What's the matter?' I said, worried.

'You! You changed. You looked really fierce. Like a wild animal!'

On the front of the book, in dark black letters, barely discernible against the brown leather was written 'Dor.' I didn't recognise this word. But I know it now. This was the Book of Earth.

With trembling fingers I picked up the last book. Though the same shape and thickness as the other books it felt very light, as though it was floating upwards and my hand was merely guiding it. I opened it. Immediately I too felt lighter, buoyant, like my body wanted to float upwards but my feet were anchoring me to the floor. From nowhere a small gust of air swept through the study, disturbing the maps and sweeping dust from the shelves. The wind grew stronger. Books flew off the shelves landing with a 'splosh' in the puddle of water on the floor. I closed the book. On its cover, in thin white lettering was written 'Ayr.'

'Blimey!' I whispered to Elsa.

'I think these might be the books he used, to call the mermaid,' said Elsa, with a smile.

'They would have been yours one day,' said a voice from the doorway. It was Meredith. 'Perhaps they still will be?'

We stared at each other for a while. Elsa went red. I felt my stomach lurch, hot and sick. But our uncle wasn't angry. He strode into the room and calmly took the book from my hands, placing it and the others in the satchel, which he slung over his shoulder.

'You must be careful. It is possible to do great harm with such books as well as good…, with or without intent.'

'Uncle Meredith. You can use your books to save Lyonesse House,' said Elsa. Meredith laughed, but without malice. His voice was gentle, deep and reassuring.

'I haven't yet found a way of making gold child, nor has any of my kind,' he fondled the back of her neck, pulling her to him. His eyes were heavy and sad. Elsa returned his affection, closing her arms around his waist.

'It can't go to Pendrogeth. It just can't,' she insisted, quietly.

'He hasn't got it yet. Besides he needs more than a set of deeds to get what he wants.'

'What do you mean?' I asked.

We had a million questions, but as we opened our mouths to speak Meredith put his finger to his mouth to request silence.

'Enough for now,' he said, and from his mouth came a 'shush' sound, a mere whisper at first, but a sound which grew, filling the room and echoing in my ears. A roar, then a crescendo; the combined song of winds and mighty waves tearing at each other on a winter sea. That was the last I remembered.

I awoke late in the morning, and rushed straight in to Elsa's room, eager to talk about our adventure the previous night.

'Elsa wake up!'

'Why didn't you wake me?' she said angrily, rubbing her eyes.

'What do you mean?'

'Last night. You were supposed to wake me… to look for the books!' I looked at her in amazement. Was this a joke?

'But the books we found. The cellar. Don't you remember?'

'What cellar?'

She had no memory of our adventure, she was adamant she had waited an hour or more for me but had fallen asleep. After a time I gave up trying to convince her otherwise.

Chapter 7

The Cornish coastline was even more breathtaking from the air. Small patchworks of irregular fields sat like pieces of an abandoned jigsaw on a table of brown and green, brushed here and there with swathes of purple and yellow gauze flower. The shadow of the tiny plane bumped across the landscape, racing speedily over the tiny cotton buds of sheep below. This hazy canvas of colours was brought into sharp contrast where land met sea; a dark rim of granite cliffs was outlined by thin lines of brilliant white shore break, beyond which, lay a blue infinity of ocean, smudging gently into the lighter blue where sea and sky met on the far horizon.

As the plane had ascended I'd noticed something very curious. We had passed over the stone circle where we had seen Meredith on the day we arrived in Cornwall. From above, the large, exposed rocks next to the stone circle looked like nothing more or less than a hare, curled up asleep. Odd, I thought, considering how Meredith had apparently revived a dead hare in that very same place.

But this was a momentary distraction from the scenery. Elsa and I grinned at each other, pointing out the wonders below, attempting shouts at each other and shrugging when we failed to hear ourselves above the chugging roar of the plane's engines. We had never even dreamt of being in a plane before.

It was over all too quickly, before we knew it we were descending with alarming haste towards the ground, bracing ourselves as the toy landscape below us became real rocks, real fields, shooting towards us. I held my breath. Just as I braced my body for impact the tiny plane tilted up ever so slightly and glided along, till we bumped into contact with the ground. The plane slowed down. The engines whirred to a halt.

The harbour at St Ives was much larger and busier than that at Sennen, judging by the clamour of shouts and seagulls and the traffic of boats and men, many of whom bore nets or crates of fish. As we passed by the quayside, men were hauling crates off the dock that were brimming with fat, silver fish. The men moved fast, laughing and shouting as they worked.

'Morning Miss Ariel,' said one, struggling under the weight of a full crate.

'Morning Bob, how's the catch?' With some effort he placed the crate on the ground, careful not to spill its precious cargo.

'Bounteous and full. Been that way for weeks. No need of nets Miss, they're prackly jumpin' in the boat. Would a brought more in too, 'cept the boat ain't that strong.' How could this be, I thought. These boats were sinking under the weight of the catch, whilst our uncles' boats came home with empty hulls.

'No doubt you'll be celebrating at the festival,' said Miss Ariel.

'Well we've got a load to celebrate ain't we? Shame for the Tregenza men I 'ear about west o' Penwith though. There's terrible. No 'arvest on land nor sea yet the weather is fine, the rivers full from the rains and the seas are brimming.' He scratched his head, contemplating the mystery, but as is the way with those whose fortunes are good, he didn't linger on this mystery for too long. 'Ah well, p'raps it'll be better after the festival? No doubt thass' what they'll be hoping,' he said with a shrug.

'Have you got your costume sorted Bob?' asked Miss Ariel.

'Oh yes Miss. This year I'm a fish! 'Ow could I be owt else?' and he lifted the crate back on to his shoulders. As he did so a fat fish slipped off the side of the overflowing crate, and lay squirming over his foot. The man lingered, toying with the idea of putting his load down so he could pick it up, but decided against it and kicked it into the air towards the dock wall before carrying on his way. Elsa made her way over to it, dodging between the fishermen. She picked the fish up, gazing at it for a few seconds before walking to the quayside and dropping it into the water as gently as she could.

The museum was situated in a side street, up the hill away from the harbour. It had a narrow entrance, which opened into a courtyard and a tall building, which might have formerly been a house, overlooking the harbour and the bay. Above the door was written 'Penwith – Its history and legacy.'

'Well, if you're interested in the history of this place, you'll find what you want here or nowhere at all,' said Miss Ariel.

The museum was far from complete. Newly installed glass display cabinets lay empty, tables were piled high with objects wrapped in newspaper, boxes lay unopened, gathering dust.

'Come to the library section,' said Miss Ariel. She led us through the museum, past rooms full of mining equipment, models of boats and cabinets full of armour and weaponry to a series of smaller rooms and alcoves towards the back of the museum, where the crates and boxes were thickest. In a darkened corner, were the books. Some had already been laid out in the display cases. Others lay in piles. There were also sea chests, some of which were opened; others had new padlocks on them.

'Really old and rare books will be on display, but there's other books for reference, books that'll tell you the history of mining and fishing, Iron Age Cornwall, ancient stones and burial grounds – all sorts of fascinating stuff. Anyway, I'll leave you to it,' she said and wandered off, with Elsa trailing behind her.

There were many books dealing with the history of Penwith. Eventually I came across a book that might tell me something useful. It had thin leaves, its inches of thickness containing hundreds of densely printed pages. The book's title was 'Customs and Folklore of West Cornwall – A Complete Study', by A N Bolitho. The book had many sections I wished to read – chapters on witchcraft, ghosts, merpeople and other mythical creatures, pre Christian religion, but my attention was caught by a chapter called, 'Festival of Lyonesse.' I turned to the relevant page. On the left hand page facing the text, was a picture of a bearded man, wearing a crown and dressed in black, flowing robes. He stood in front of a crowd of people, leaning over a stone altar to which a boy had been bound with rope. The man held a large knife aloft, threatening to plunge the blade into the boy's heart. The crowd were waving their arms, apparently cheering the man on.

I started to read:

The Feast or Festival of Lyonesse is a mid summer festival celebrated annually by the people of West Penwith It is usually held on the day directly before the June full moon, near or on the summer solstice, the longest day in the calendar year.

Though a regular feature of modern community life and adapted into the Christian calendar of festivals, the festival pre-dates Christianity in the Penwith area. Therefore, it is to Celtic religion and history that we must look for the festival's roots.

In ancient times the area of West Penwith was known as Lyonesse. This area, in legend at least, incorporated a (now lost) bridge of land from the westerly Scilly Isles to the Land's End peninsular. Its easterly border was the thin strip of land between the Hayle Estuary and the south coast. It is even possible that this border was underwater as Lyonesse has sometimes been referred to as an island.

Lyonesse was ruled by a local King or Lord, whose seat of rule was on the Isle of Ictis, an island similar to, but larger than, the isle of St Michael's in Mount's Bay which overlooked the larger kingdom. The King was purported to wield magical as well as military and economic power. He and he alone could appease or control the elements on behalf of his subjects.

The ultimate display of his power was on the full moon nearest to mid summer. A day of feast and celebration culminated in a sacrifice, (a remnant of this practice is still replicated today in the burning of straw effigies). Legend maintains that when the early show of the crops were not good, perhaps because of a drought or series of unseasonal storms, a human sacrifice would be made, usually of an adolescent child.

Modern day

  Though Ictis is long gone and the sacrificial part of the festival ceased not long after St Perrin brought Christianity to Cornwall, belief in Lyonesse lingers. Historical fact, the customs of the festival, and legend have combined to form a potent series of myths and beliefs amongst the local population. For example; some local people maintain that Lyonesse still exists as an island of ghosts, a place where those who lose their lives to the elements (for example miners killed in underground landslides or drowned fishermen) go when they die. Another common belief is that human children that had once been sacrificed are re-incarnated as wild animals. Legends abound of hares, foxes and even seals or dolphins that have been either found or caught, without a heart.

  On the day of the festival it is customary for local people to don costumes or masks and perform a version of the ancient ceremonies. They may be dressed as an 'elemental' – a spirit of earth, air, fire or water, an animal, or mythical beast. These are the 'subjects.' The most important roles however are those of the King, the jester and the Fool King. The Fool King is allowed to rule for the day, he is crowned in the morning and paraded through the streets of local towns. During the day of his reign all normal customs, hierarchies and order are thrown into disarray. Children, for example, are allowed, even encouraged, to be naughty, women may ask men to dance, kiss or even marry, local dignitaries must make mock subservience to the Fool King.

  At this time the order of time and Nature itself are believed to be disrupted and superseded by chaos. There have been reports of storms, and even snow on this day.

  After the crowning there is a procession down to the sea from whichever local town or village is hosting the festival. There, the new King (usually a local nobleman) and his 'subjects' board ships, fishing boats and gigs (large rowing boats). This procession of boats makes its way to the Bay and the site of the Isle of Ictis (given that the remaining ruins are under the sea, they usually land at Marazion).

Bonfires are built and straw effigies of animals are prepared for 'sacrifice.' When the boats arrive, the King is welcomed ashore. The jester then dethrones the Fool King and the true King assumes his crown and seat.

Thus, it is believed, that social and natural order are restored, ensuring a peaceful year, full nets and a bounteous harvest. Elemental spirits and ghosts are banished from the earth …

'…and the dead rest peacefully in their unmarked graves,' said a voice. Lord Pendrogeth was standing directly behind me, reading over my shoulder.

'You!' I said, startled, turning to face him.

'Yes… me,' he said, calmly. Up close he was more striking than I had previously thought. He had strong features, his cheekbones and eye sockets standing out, as though his skull was trying to break through his skin. He was at once more powerful, and arresting, yet seemed in himself and even in the very air around him to be the embodiment of illness and decay. His eyes stared intensely from a pale, wan face, his skin was sallow and pock marked, his eyes grey, and yellowing. He stared at me, the still and emotionless stare of a reptile. When he spoke it was from a dark, luridly purple mouth. His voice was still smooth, yet slightly cracked and rasping.

'A fascinating story don't you think? Indeed, a most interesting book. It will form part of the library here. A library I am supporting in my own humble way.' He paused for moment. 'Aren't you going to ask me how?'

'Ho… how?' I stammered.

'For some time now I have been funding an excavation of the ancient isle of Ictis, something I see you are familiar with,' he said, pointing to the book. 'Do you know what we found down there young Bill? Books… amongst other things. Books that have helped us substantially in our appreciation of the ancient customs you have been reading of.'

'Books… books from Ictis?' I said. I was over the shock now; I felt blood returning to my cheeks and with it, anger.

'Yes, most are lost in the sands, only a few have been preserved. These are being studied by myself and other… experts. Their languages are difficult to decipher, their purposes unknown… as yet.' He took a step back, the sickly smile dropped from his face. He had said more than he meant to. A look passed between us, of knowledge, of mutual understanding and with it, the veil of pretence dropped.

'You had one of these books… at Lamorna.'

'At Lamorna you say?' his look was curious, amused.

'It's you isn't it?' I said. 'You're the reason the crops are failing. You're the reason the fishermen's nets are empty. You want Lyonesse for yourself.'

'Lyonesse will be mine. With or without Tregenza's consent.'

'Never!' I said. He laughed.

'I'm not sure there is much that can stop me.'

'Yes there is,' I said, matching his arrogance with my own anger.

'Oh really?' he asked, 'and what might that be?'

'Me!'

'You?' He laughed. But his laughter was forced. I knew how ridiculous I sounded, yet felt strangely confident 'Yes. Me. I don't know how, or why, but… that's why you tried to kill me that day. I'm standing in your way aren't I?'

'Yes, that's right,' he said calmly. I felt my face flush, hot with anger and shock. I had expected outrage, a plea of polite ignorance and concern. Denial certainly. But not this, a casual, even smug admittance. He was still very close, close enough for me to notice… he wasn't breathing. My own outward breath gave out small clouds of condensation. But not him. His face seemed so still, so very calm because he was not breathing.

I stepped backward, and as I did so saw that his body was floating, several inches above the floor. I reached behind for something, anything to steady me. My eyes darted around for a book, a chair, something to protect me. I wanted to cry out, but the words caught in my throat.

'Oh, don't worry 'Heir of Lyonesse'. This is neither the time, nor the place. Besides, your uncle has protected you well... so far. Yet his powers wane, even as my own are in their ascendancy. Tomorrow, at the festival... Tomorrow boy, that is when accounts will be settled.' I stumbled, turning, running, through the alcove and straight into Elsa.

'It's him,' I cried turning and pointing to where I thought he stood. But the room was empty. Even with the darkened corners and crates and sea chests it was difficult to imagine how anyone could have escaped so quickly. 'He was here!'

'Who, was here, why did you shout?' said Miss Ariel, joining us.

'Lord Pendrogeth,' I replied. 'He was talking to me. Didn't you hear him?' A look passed between them. Miss Ariel walked into the darkened alcove and looked around.

'Well he's gone now,' she said to reassure me. 'Bill are you okay? You don't look well.'

'He was here. We talked about the festival, about Ictis. I don't know where he went but I swear he was here.'

'Well, we didn't hear him Bill and if he was here he must have crept out,' Miss Ariel looked at me a little suspiciously, but her frown soon dissolved and she smiled at me kindly, her blue eyes twinkling with brightness.

'Anyhow, you do look a little distraught. You wait here; I'll get you some water.' The moment she was gone Elsa started to question me.

'Look, just trust me Elsa. Pendrogeth did try to kill us that day at Lamorna. If he doesn't get Lyonesse he's going to try again. In truth I think he may want to kill us all even if he does get

Lyonesse House. The Estate is not enough for him.'

'Bill, we've got to warn Uncle Meredith… But he's away, he said he was 'preparing' for the festival.'

'Well perhaps he'll return tonight.'

We wanted to leave as soon as possible but on our way out I asked if we could pause as I was feeling weak and dizzy. Miss Ariel said she was a little worried about me and she would go and find someone to take us to the airfield.

'By the looks of you Bill I am not sure you are up to the walk,' she said.

As we made ready to leave we passed through a section of the museum called: 'Rogues of the Sea – Pirates, Smugglers and Wreckers.' My attention was caught by a photograph on the wall. It must have been from the earliest days of photography, as it was fading considerably, and the detail was browning on the cracked paper. The photograph was a portrait of a group of men standing on a harbour side in front of a small sail ship. The men were huddled together with their arms around each other's shoulders, or else smoking pipes or drinking from stone bottles. In the middle of the men was their captain, a proud figure with his head cocked and arms folded. What had stopped me dead in my tracks was a jolt of recognition though I struggled for a moment to remember who the man was. Then it came to me. The man in the picture was Meredith's mute servant, just as he looked a few days before when I had seen him at Lamorna. He even wore the same cap and old, black jacket. But how could this be? The photo had to be decades old. The clothes the men wore were virtually identical to those the fishermen wore now, but the style of beard, and some of the hats were all of a bygone age.

Below the photo was a plaque. On it was written:

The Seahawk, its crew and Captain, John Tanner – last of the great smugglers. In spite of the offer of a substantial reward the Seahawk and its crew were never captured. The Seahawk sank near Lamorna Cove in 18—during a ferocious storm whilst being chased by a naval frigate. All hands were lost, believed drowned – other than one sailor who made it to shore, but passed away the following day. Legend has it that moments before he died he told the villagers the location of the Seahawk's treasure. He is alleged to have said that chests of diamonds lay in a cave near the stone quarry of Lamorna.

My heart raced. Had we ourselves not been into a cave? The end of the cave had been dark as night, there could have been anything there and we wouldn't have seen it.

I looked again at the photo, with careful scrutiny. Reason battled against my wits and what my own eyes were telling me. Perhaps, my reason told me, this was the man's father or grandfather. Perhaps the photo had blurred the man's features. But no, there was no mistake. This was the man who had picked us up from the train station that first afternoon in Cornwall. This was the man who had rescued us from the caves.

When we arrived at Lyonesse House there were two pony and traps in the forecourt.

'That's Dr Gonzales' trap,' said Miss Ariel, 'I do hope everything's alright.'

I inquired of Stephen who the visitors might be. He mumbled something about 'legal business' and Anthony's study. That was curious, I thought, Miss Ariel had said that one of the traps had belonged to the local doctor.

'What's going on?' said Elsa as soon as Stephen was out of earshot.

'I don't know, but I intend to find out.'

We took a ball outside to use as an excuse should we be caught, and made our way around the house. We crawled under the study's open window. Slowly we inched ourselves into position under the window, careful not to make any noise.

'… what you are asking. It raises questions. Moral questions,' said a voice, the gravelly, serious voice of an older man.

'But is it legal?' Anthony said

'Perfectly, as long as it can be justified,' said a third voice; a younger man.

'It is the 'reasons' that concern me,' said the voice of the older man. 'You say your brother is mentally unstable. Yet the reason behind your proposed action appears to be so that you can take full legal responsibility for the Lyonesse Estate in order to sell it.' I struggled not let out a cry.

'Dr Gonzales. You know as well as I how heavily this sits with me. Yet the truth speaks for itself. This Estate has… is… suffering, it has fallen into a state of irreversible repair. A large proportion of our present troubles arise because Meredith is absent from his responsibilities, he thinks himself… that is he believes… Well, let's just say that his behaviour and actions do not arise from a rational mind.'

'Well there's the rub Mr Tregenza. Your brother's behaviour *is* widely reported as eccentric, especially over recent weeks. His beliefs are far from conventional, but that is not unusual for this part of the country even in this day and age. I cannot easily conclude that Meredith Tregenza is mad.'

'Doctor, you have attended this family for many years, you know the Estate and its workers equally well. You know how we will all suffer if we don't sell. This is the only way, and believe me I have tried or considered every possible alternative. For that reason if no other please do as I ask. It need not be for long, a matter of days even.'

'I am afraid it's more complicated than that. If I certify your brother his welfare is in the hands of the courts. He would be unable to work, to own property, to do any thing that he currently takes for granted… and, erm, it is also quite possible that his…how can I put this… delusions… arose because of the stress and strain of the Estate's affairs. If you then lose the Estate all together… who knows how it might affect him.'

There was a moment of silence before Anthony responded, sounding a little desperate.

'Surely, you must see the reasoning?'

'I understand the reasons but they provide no comfort.'

'So you'll do it?'

'Wait until tomorrow, after the Festival of Lyonesse. If you haven't managed to persuade him by then I'll do it.'

'Will there be time?' asked Anthony of the third man.

'Lord Pendrogeth *is* putting pressure on us. He did say we had until tomorrow. So, arguably, yes. Then it will be a matter of a few days to transfer all legal and financial responsibilities to yourself. Once that has happened, we can proceed with the sale.'

I had heard enough and so had Elsa judging by the tears streaming down her face. As soon as we were out of sight of the window Elsa stood up and began to run. I called after her but she ignored me.

I followed her down the garden, through the gate, catching up with her on the cliff path.

'They can't Bill, they just can't.' But I knew they could, and they would. Our uncle Anthony was not a bad man, not in his heart. But this was wrong – badly, fundamentally wrong. Whatever he stood to gain, was it worth this betrayal?

We determined to tell Meredith as soon as we could. But Meredith didn't appear that afternoon, nor at supper, nor did Anthony know of his whereabouts.

That night I awoke from a restless sleep to the sound of the window creaking and banging in a gentle breeze. Strange, I thought, I had left it shut as was then my habit on all but the most stifling of nights.

The room came into focus, its shapes and shadows bathed in a flood of blue moonlight. I went to shut the window, but as my hand reached out I froze. The first I saw was a mere speck against the moonlight, a small indistinct shape making its way towards the house. It must be a bird I thought, but there was no tell tale bobbing up and down in the air. This shape was floating, silently, relentlessly towards me. There was another behind it, and yet another. The near full moon allowed a full view over the tree tops and towards the moors. These shapes, whatever they might be, were coming from all directions, straight towards the house. Some it seemed, were rising from the moors, into the night sky, to join the procession.

'William,' whispered a voice. I looked down. There was a boy on the lawn, directly below. The boy took a step forwards, then another, but he was not only moving forwards, he was floating, rising up towards me. I shut the window. The other dreams had felt so real, yet they were nightmares. This could be no more real I reasoned with myself. Yet the days had brought even stranger truths. The dead could not walk I told myself, mermaids did not exist, books could not magic water from thin air. I returned to my bed and sat there with my eyes shut. For the first time since arriving in Cornwall I did not wish to know the heart of this or any other mystery, I wanted to be home, away from this godforsaken, haunted land.

'It's a dream,' I said, 'a dream,' as the voices began to whisper and then cry.

'Wiiillliaaaaaaam.'

'Only you can rescue the heart of Lyonesse.'

'Only you, only you,' the voices whispered, cried, shouted, desperate and damned.

'How?' I shouted, opening my eyes, daring to confront the horror. Outside of the window was the boy, floating in mid air. His glazed eyes were as dead as the moon, but just as bright. He wore hessian trousers and was stripped to the waist. Behind him were other children, shapes floating, still in the night air. I could not tear my eyes from the boy, nor he from me. With a weak and sick smile his hands reached towards his chest, to a scar above his heart. He stuck into his fingers into his chest.

I opened my mouth, but before I could give voice to my fear I heard the sound of another's scream. Elsa! The door was flung open and she ran straight to me, leaping onto my bed, embedding herself in my bedclothes and under my arm.

I looked to the window, but there was nothing there.

'Oh Bill, Bill, I've had the most terrible nightmares.' She clung to me, her face pushed hard against my chest. 'There are these children,' she pushed each word out between her sobs, 'and they've got no hearts!'

I stroked her hair, hushing and comforting her, the way I hadn't done since she was a little girl. The whole time I kept my eye on the window.

Eventually she went to sleep in my arms and in the morning she was to have no recollection of her dream, nor why she had woken in my bed. For my part, I did not go back to sleep. Whatever thin fabric had separated my nightmares from the waking world was now utterly broken.

I watched the ink blue of the night fade, leaving for a short time a grey, dull complexion on the sky and distant moors. Then the detail of the moors vanished into shadow and the sky was filled with the blinding tide of the sun's rays.

The night was over. It was the dawn of the longest day. The day of the Festival of Lyonesse.

PART 2

THE STORM

Chapter 8

The scene, to begin with, was nothing more or less than a provincial market town on a day of festival; a town that had put on its finest clothes, swept the streets and set out is finest wares on its stalls. By the time we arrived in St Pirans in the later hours of the morning, the streets were already heaving with people, busily parading up and down the cobbled street. The better off posed leisurely in their Sunday best; the men all top hats and waxed moustaches, the women in fancy, flowery hats and dresses that stretched from their trussed up necks to the ground. The rest of the crowd were dressed as smartly as they could afford, the men (the young, the old and those exempt from soldiery) tipping their straw boaters to the women, who wore long white smocks and straw hats decked with fresh flowers.

Above us, the sky was bright with that white, breezy light so peculiar to seaside towns, and I could hear the ever present cry of seagulls (attracted no doubt by the commotion and smell of food). There were spit roasts of pigs and lambs, coconut shies, stalls selling lemonade and figgy pudding, ginger bread, sticks of peppermint, slabs of toffee and numerous other confections. A band pumped out jolly tunes on trombone, bugle trumpet, and accordion.

Crowds gathered around the cider and ale stalls and I was surprised to see several of the men – gangs of miners and sailors – drunk at such an early hour. They called after the groups of young women, that moved in gaggles up and down the street, dressed in their finery of bonnets and tight, bodice hugging dresses. There were a few injured soldiers present too, returned from the war. They were regaled wherever they went, none of them would be short of friends or drinks that day. Children darted between the crowds and numerous stalls, searching for toffee apples and mischief, chased by their parents.

We kept close to Uncle Anthony, as we made our way down the street, stopping to chat with people, especially soldiers who had worked for our uncles before the war. Anthony was buying a round of drinks for some of these men when he was interrupted by an elderly, bearded gentleman. He was very distinguished; being tall, with a long white beard and bushy eyebrows and dressed in tweed jacket and breeches with a matching deerstalker hat.

'Ahh Anthony. You seem to have acquired some children.'

'Bill, Elsa, this is Dr Gonzales.' Behind the beard the man's face was warm and bright, his eyes sparkled with a curious intelligence.

'Very pleased to make your acquaintance,' he said. In spite of what I knew he and Anthony were planning for our uncle Meredith, I couldn't help but like him a little. I shook his hand limply.

'Where's Uncle Meredith?' asked Elsa sharply. She might just as well have said; 'What have you done with him?'

'Why I've no idea child. Is he not with you?' Dr Gonzales looked around. He wasn't acting. We didn't know why Meredith was not present but were sure they hadn't got to him. Not yet. We moved on, steadily making our way up the street through the crowds of people. The air was bright with sunshine and full of the shrieks of delighted children, the songs of sailors and laughter and chatter of the women. It was a joy to behold, marred only by my fears for Meredith.

As we made our way towards the top of the town, I could hear a strange tune rising above the din of chat and laughter and band music. It was faint at first but as we got nearer, the clear tones of an accordion playing a folk tune slowly drowned out the other songs and noise of the crowd. Here people had ceased talking and laughing, their attention instead being focussed on the source of the music. One or two drunken voices began to accompany the accordion, slurring indistinct words in time with the music, and as we got nearer, the song was picked up by first one voice in the crowd, and then another. In a matter of moments more voices had taken up the song, and the accordion was joined by an unseen drummer and a fiddle. The song was rhythmic, repetitive. I found myself humming along and noticed as I walked that some of those around me had linked arms with each other and were swaying, gently, from side to side in time with the music. I looked behind me, all eyes were facing up the street and everyone I could see, was now linking arms, swaying and singing or humming, rocking as one body.

I felt intoxicated, the very air being filled with the steady thud of the drum and the steady swagger of the song. And everyone; man, woman and child, our Uncle Anthony included, was joining in with this song and linking arms. It was clear they had expected this and by the looks on their faces, they were enjoying it immensely. There were verses to the song, belted out by an unseen singer and in between the verses a chorus which the whole crowd seemed to know. The song was irresistible, hypnotic even. The crowd sang with hearty voice:

keep the blessed harvest growing
may our cup be o'er flowing
catch be full and harvest plenty
nets and barns be never empty

We were still making our way up the hill, pushed by a groundswell of people behind us, who all seemed intent on reaching the top of the hill and finding whatever it was that drew the crowd to it like a magnet. The song was almost deafening now. The crowd was so tightly jammed together it would have been impossible to leave even if we had wanted to.

Then, without warning, the crowd surged, and I fell forward, into an open space. The crowd had formed a large circle, fenced by rows of swaying people, all singing the song. In the middle of the space and right in front of me was a jester. He wore bright, multi coloured trousers and tunic, and on his head wore an enormous tri-cornered hat festooned with bells and ribbons. In one hand he held a stick, covered in feathers and bells, in the other a wooden crown. His face, garish and hideous with clown's make up, leered into mine. By the look in his eyes and the smell of his breath it was easy to tell that he was drunk. In mock deference he bowed before me, then to the delight of the crowd, placed the crown on my head and danced around me, singing and shaking his stick.

'A Fool for a King, a Fool for a King,' he sang in his high pitched, drunken voice.

'King for a day boy hmmm?' he said to me, then implored the crowd with open arms.

'No, not him,' said one voice.

'Not the boy Mr Trinkle,' cried another.

'No? ooooh!' he said, and made a momentary pretence of looking heartbroken, wiping imaginary tears from his eyes – before snatching the crown off my head and prancing off to try the crown on someone else. Hands pulled me back into the crowd, linking arms with me. I was in a wall of people, surrounding the large open space, which as well as the jester, held an accordion player, a drummer and a fiddle player. Next to them were two large chairs, held on rails, which I guessed were for raising on men's shoulders.

The first throne was made of dark, age stained wood with a high back topped by three carved points. It had long thick arms and was sturdy and old, though finely crafted. For the comfort of the 'King' a large, plump, red cushion filled the seat. The other throne was made of wicker and though it looked as old as the other chair, it had not weathered the years so well. The wicker was worn and thin. In places it had rotted and holes had been repaired with wire and string. The wicker work had been decorated with rabbit feet and fox tails, bells, ribbons and small statues. It was a rickety, shoddy caricature of the throne beside it.

Just as suddenly as it had started the music stopped, yet the drummer drummed on, slowing the beat down, banging the drum with ever heavier beats. The crowd stopped singing, but continued to sway in time to the steadier, slower drum beat. Above us I could hear the gentle wind and piercing squawk of seagulls and, tellingly, the throaty, rough call of crows circling high above, just as they had at Lamorna. Another, unseen, drum joined the first, and then another. As more people joined the circle, so it grew, ever wider and larger. The atmosphere was expectant, heavy with the heat of the crowd.

The crowd parted. Into the circle walked Meredith followed by two drummers. He was dressed in a long, black, robe and from its folds he produced a metal crown, which he held aloft to a great cheer from the crowd before placing it carefully on the cushion and making his way back to the edge of the crowd. The tune started up again. Like a mechanical puppet controlled by its rhythm the jester sprang into action and once again began leaping around; lunging into the crowd, pulling each unfortunate victim into the centre where he would hold the mock crown over his victim's head and look to the crowd to cheer their enthusiasm or boo and hiss their disapproval. He was a superb mimic and would cruelly and accurately imitate each chosen person, picking one attribute; their size, their walk, their stance and exaggerating it for the amusement of the crowd. Though the others laughed I felt uneasy with the nature of this strange custom. For some of those the jester chose were drunk, or very old. One man looked, by the utter bewilderment on his face to be perhaps mentally retarded. Another man, a tramp by the state of his clothes, looked a little mad.

'Nooo!' the crowd cried as the crown was held over his head. I tried to make my way around the circle towards Meredith. It would be impossible to talk to him, but I hoped that as soon as this part of the day's ceremonies were over I could at least warn him of Anthony's plan and tell him about my encounter with Pendrogeth the previous day. I waved, but he did not see me. His attention had been caught by someone in the crowd. My heart missed a beat. Amongst the sea of grinning, singing faces was the face of a gigantic bird. Of course it was a mask, but it had given me a shock, not least of all because it was so life like. The 'mask' covered the wearer's head entirely and was made with real feathers and glass eyes. The bird's beak had been fashioned from metal. To my left I then noticed a fox. He, also wore a head-dress apparently of real fur and a cloak, so he looked as if he had the body of a man and the head of a fox. Then another, a hare this time, and a badger, then a fish's head, ornately made from metal and shiny, pebbles. But these masks were of no concern to Meredith. He was staring at Pendrogeth.

The Lord Pendrogeth was set far back in the crowd, talking to Stephen, our uncles' butler. He noticed me staring at him almost immediately, his face blank and impassive. Then Stephen saw me too. The butler smiled a low, secretive smile and lifted a bottle of wine to his lips, taking a slow, long gulp. It crossed my mind that he was drinking from one of my uncles' wine bottles and mocking me as he did so. He made his way through the crowd until he was at the front, directly in front of the ridiculous jester. Mr Trinkle stepped back, feigning surprise that someone should apparently, be offering himself in this way. He quickly placed the crown on Stephen's head and looked to the crowd for judgement. There were a few 'ayes' and few 'nays' but for the most part they were indifferent to this particular candidate. As Mr Trinkle moved to pull the crown off Stephen's head, the butler leaned forward and said something into the jester's ear. Mr Trinkle's face lit up with a lunatic grin. Grabbing the crown and pushing Stephen back into the crowd he launched into a high stepping dance in time with the music, leaping and jumping around the circle in increasingly frenzied movements. With a sudden violent lunge he jumped into the crowd, causing people to gasp and scream, he literally fought his way through the crowd and in a moment had disappeared. In the commotion the jester moved amongst us, low and unseen, worming his way quickly around the circle.

Meredith was caught by surprise, pushed into the circle

with some force. Quick as a flash the jester had circled around him and was holding the Fool's crown on his head. He looked to the crowd, his face mad with ecstatic joy. There was an audible gasp from the crowd. The music came to an abrupt halt. The sense of shock and confusion was almost tangible. No one, it was clear, expected Meredith to be picked for the Fool King. Yet none shouted out against it either.

''E's bin a King awready, and we know 'e is a fool,' said one voice.

'Why not?' said another 'dun' 'e deserve it?'

'Frank!' Exclaimed a woman, 'to say such a thing of the master.'

'Not my master. Not no more.' There was a murmur of agreement.

'No!' shouted Elsa.

Uncle Meredith took the jester firmly by the arm and with his other hand slowly lowered the crown off his head and threw it on the floor. This was a mistake. To disrespect the jester was one thing, to openly scorn the crown, quite another. Releasing the jester's arm he walked backwards into the crowd, only to be met by the arms of several men, who forced him back into the circle. Stephen stepped forward, picked up the crown and after another long swig from his bottle offered it to Meredith.

'You've dropped your crown Sire,' he said, with a snigger.

The men surrounded Meredith, then forcefully picked him off the ground and carried him to the Fool's throne. Stephen and the jester followed, and when the men had unceremoniously dumped Meredith in the chair, placed the crown on his head. There was a cheer from the crowd. The awful, giddy music started up once more.

'Nooo!' cried Elsa, struggling to free herself. But both she and I were held back by strong arms.

In such moments time slows down, details normally unnoticed or soon forgotten become burnt in the memory. I remember the crowd was a blur, swaying, moving, an indistinct flow of faces and bodies. But I saw the masks, clear, still and silent amongst the chaos. Observing. Waiting. And I saw Anthony, I saw Dr Gonzales, I saw the local vicar and the Head of the Hunt I had seen on our first day in Cornwall. They too were watching. The vicar and the doctor looked at Anthony expectantly. Would he protest at this outrage? But all they saw in his face was shock. Worse still, fear. And in that mask of fear, acceptance. Anthony did not permit what happened to Meredith, but he did not try to stop it either. Then the moment was gone, and with it any chance of reprieve; any hope of redemption.

They held Meredith to the chair and took belts and rope to fasten him tightly so he could not escape, then they hoisted it on to their shoulders with Meredith above, looking helplessly down on the cheering, jeering crowd. Elsa and I were held back by chains of arms, our voices were drowned in the tumult of jeers and cruel laughter. Meredith was paraded through the crowd, which parted like a sea, bowing and scraping in mock deference to the new 'King.'

''Ave a drink my Lord?' said one man, throwing a full tanker of cider into the air. The drink splashed over Meredith's face and shoulders. Others threw scraps of food and clumps of mud at him.

'Fool!' they shouted, 'Fool for a King!' As he was taken away from us, the crowd began to move and Elsa and I were able to break away from the arms and bodies that held us back. We followed, crying and shouting, fighting to get to him, to do something – anything – to help him, to stop the cruel parade.

I still feel the shame of that dreadful day. I can still feel the sickening disbelief that churned my stomach over and over, the burning sense of injustice, the tears of futile rage. Then came the final insult. A horn was blown, or perhaps a conch shell, it's deep clear tone, cutting through the crowd's cheers and laughter. I looked behind. The other throne had also been raised, and was being carried by six men. On the throne, dressed in a long black robe sat Pendrogeth with the crown on his lap. Two crows swooped down, one of which flew over the crowd, round and round, but always returning to Pendrogeth. The other settled on Pendrogeth's arm, shaking its wings and cocking its head so it could survey the scene with one and then the other of its cruel, black eyes. The crowd held up their faces to Pendrogeth as though facing a sun after many years in darkness.

A rotten cabbage flew through the air, hitting Meredith, much to the delight of the crowd. A large stone followed it, landing on his head. Blood poured down his face, mixing with what I thought were tears. Whatever voices there were to object were silent now, smothered and beaten by the will and voice of the crowd. Meredith stared straight ahead, seemingly oblivious to what was happening. But then I noticed he was struggling against the ropes, twisting and turning, reaching within his robes. I caught a glimpse of leather.

But he was seen. Stephen jumped up and reached inside the robes. With a violent tug, he yanked the satchel off Meredith, breaking the leather strap on which it hung. Stephen fell backwards. The satchel flew though the air.

Pendrogeth sat bolt upright in his throne, threatening to jump. But he decided against it and instead pointed to the books. Stephen and Trinkle tried to fight their way back through the crowd, to where the satchel had been thrown. I threw myself to the floor and crawled between the legs of the people blocking my way. There were shouts of indignation and more than one person fell over me. I was kicked, stifled, unable to breathe, but I made my way through the crowd and, breaking free, jumped and dived onto the satchel as though my life depended on it.

'Run Bill run!' shouted Meredith. I didn't hesitate. I went as fast as my legs could carry me, down one alleyway then another, over a fence, through a garden, back onto the road, not stopping until I was sure I had lost Trinkle and Stephen and the music and shouts were a long way off, eventually stopping to rest in a shop doorway. From where I stood I could see the procession making its way down the hill to the small harbour where a flotilla of boats awaited. I looked inside the satchel. The three books were inside. But what now?

I slowly started making my way back to the crowd, I had to help Meredith. But I knew I would have to stay hidden from Pendrogeth and his cronies. They would be looking for me, or more specifically the books.

Chapter 9

I followed the tail of the crowd down the steep lane to the sea. When I had almost caught up I ran straight into an angel accompanied by a giant hare.

'Bill,' said the angel, 'what on earth are you doing?'

The 'angel' was Miss Ariel, though it was hard to recognise her. On her back she wore large wire and silk wings, and for her dress a robe of a light, silky material that seemed not to have a colour at all, but instead reflected the colour and movement of whatever was around her. It was quite disorienting to look at it. Her face was painted silver and white.

'What do you think? I'm an Air Spirit. Fitting, no?' she said. 'You'd better get down there or you'll miss the launch of the boats. I'm not coming on board though; I'm going to do a fly over! In fact I've got to hurry or I'll never get to the airfield in time and…something wrong Bill?' she asked in her bright, perky voice.

'Didn't you see? What they did to Meredith?' The incomprehension and concern in her eyes told me she hadn't. 'Look there's no time to explain. Can I borrow your costume?' I said to the 'hare.' 'Miss Ariel, it's vital. I've got to help Meredith!'

'Very well but why on earth do you need a costume?'

'Please!' I insisted. I could feel my eyes welling up with tears. Miss Ariel gently held my arm and looked into my eyes. She turned her attention to the boy. He wore a cloak and a complete head dress, in the likeness of a hare. As with the other head dresses I had seen that day, it was covered in fur and had been so cleverly made that it looked for all the world like a real hare's head, albeit of a size large enough to cover the boy's head.

'Listen Bob, young Bill here needs your costume. I can't

tell you why, but I know it's very important.' The hare didn't move or reply. 'Look, if you do this I promise I'll persuade your mother to let me take you for *another* flight and for longer too!' The boy needed no further encouragement. In a minute he had stripped and I had donned the head dress. I mended the satchel's leather strap and slung it over my shoulder. Then I put on the boy's cape, being careful to cover the satchel.

'Thank you,' I said, giving Miss Ariel a clumsy hug. With a wave I ran down the hill towards the sea.

By the time I arrived most of the crowd had boarded the vessels waiting to take them around the peninsula to Marazion. There were sailing boats, fishermen's boats, gigs and other large row boats, every type of craft that could enter the small natural harbour, formed by the rocky peninsular of Cape Piran.

I ran to join a queue of people boarding a gig, but noticed another boat with half its hull on the pebbles, and the other half rocking gently in the water. An old man leant on the side of the boat, filling his pipe with tobacco.

'Where'll it be Master Hare?' said the man without looking up.

'To the boat that carries the King?' I said

'O'er thar,' he said pointing with his pipe. Some fifty yards off shore a small sailing ship was anchored. I had the peculiar feeling that I had seen it before. As many people as it could carry were crammed on board and I could see Elsa leaning over the deck, no doubt looking for me.

'And unc… the Fool King?'

'What of him?'

'Is he aboard that ship?'

'He is.'

On the top deck of the ship I could see Pendrogeth, still on his throne. He was holding the crown on his lap. There was no sign of Meredith.

'Please take me there?' I said, pointing to the ship.

The crowd were too busy singing and dancing to notice me

climbing aboard. Stephen and Trinkle were on deck, handing out cups of wine tapped from an enormous oak barrel. I made my way up the ship.

'Maybe he's gone home,' I heard Anthony say to Dr Gonzales.

'No, not Bill. He wouldn't leave us, not now,' said Elsa.

'What's happened to Meredith?' I said.

'Bill!!'

'Don't give me away Elsa. Where is he?'

'We saw them carry him aboard. We think they must be holding him below deck.' To the back of the ship was a small doorway, which led to the hold.

'Now listen my boy,' said Anthony in shaky voice. 'Don't cause any trouble. Once things have calmed down a bit I'll make sure they let Meredith go. They've had their fun.'

'Fun!' I spat the word out. 'Elsa stay here. I'm going to try and help Meredith.' I moved away from them, to ensure I wouldn't attract Pendrogeth's attention.

Finding a place right at the front of the ship, I sat and waited for us to set sail. There was a gentle tilting of the boat as it was pushed softly but firmly by the breath of the wind, and we were soon on our way, sailing down the coast and around Land's End. I watched the coastline bob up and down as the boat surged through the ocean swells, listening to the creak of the wooden ship, the booming rush of water against the hull and the sound of wind picking up the canvas sails. Wind and spray poured into the mouth of the mask, cooling my face. I closed my eyes, listening to the crashing whispers of wind and sea. I longed to take the mask off but didn't dare to. Pendrogeth and his men would be upon me in a moment.

The celebrations were in full swing now and I noted that no one was guarding the door to the lower deck. Making sure I wasn't being watched I began making my way back up the ship. But then I heard something that stopped me dead in my tracks. An echo of a song, smooth and gentle was running like an undercurrent beneath the ocean's own music. But where was it coming from? It seemed to be both near and far, as much from sea as in the air around me. At first I struggled to make it out above the sounds of wind and water but as I listened it became clear to me. The sound of the whispering song, was the sound of the wind and water, as though whoever spoke these words, spoke in a voice of elements. Yet it was distinct and undeniable. The hair on the back of my neck stood up on end, my hand instinctively clutched at the satchel. I looked to Pendrogeth, he was reading from a small, leather bound book which he held in one hand, his other hand was held to the air with his palm open.

As though taking a cue, the crew started to sing a sea shanty. The song was slow and rhythmic, rising and falling with the boat in the waves.

Blow the wind down now boys,
Blow the wind down

As we sailed round a final headland the great bay of St Michael's Mount came into view. I could see the distant shore and on it an enormous bonfire, waiting to be lit. Around it were statues of animals, made of straw and wicker.

A small gust of wind blew from the shore, buckling the sails, quickly followed by another; only stronger and faster. The wind that had so speedily carried us from Land's End dropped off, robbed of its strength, by this new force. Beneath our feet the timbers of the boat creaked and rocked as though the ship itself was confused by this sudden change. There were gasps and confused cries from the passengers. But in all this commotion the sailors sang on, and the loudest of them was their captain, a man wearing a dark navy suit, a fisherman's roll neck jumper and an old worn cap. Though he sang with a full and hearty voice, his eyes were cold and still as the deepest heart of an arctic sea. He was just as I remembered him from Lamorna, from the day of our arrival, from the picture in the museum at St Ives.

There was a low rumble of thunder. We all looked to the

sky, but it was as blue and clear as it had been all day. I turned to a sailor standing near me, holding to the deck rail to steady myself.

'What ship is this?' I asked. He stared straight ahead, bellowing out his song. He seemed not to have heard me. I leant over the side of the ship. The name of the vessel was painted on the side of the bow. Though I was reading upside down I could easily make the words out. The ship's name was the *Seahawk*.

I fell backwards. In the sky seagulls were squawking and crying. The same birds I had so often watched rising and falling on the airs gentle currents now tumbled and turned, fighting against a violent, chaotic wind; useless and panicking in the very sky they usually owned with ease.

The sails billowed and waved, the mast timbers creaked. There was crack of lightning, a rumble of thunder. Then the very fabric of the world was ripped apart.

Chapter 10

The air was disturbed by a loud rumble of thunder. The ship's passengers looked skywards, confused as to where the sound might be coming from on such a bright and sunny day.

'Look,' shouted a boy, pointing to the shore. At first I thought he was pointing at Miss Ariel's plane, for the small white aircraft was over the sea, heading towards us and bobbing and weaving erratically in the air. It whirred and buzzed like an angry insect. But this isn't what had caught the boy's attention. Behind the plane, seemingly chasing it – and moving swiftly in our direction – was an enormous shadow in the sky.

A blanket of rolling cloud was steadily rising over the horizon of hills and moor, sucking up the sunlight in its path and turning the light blue sky into thick, dark cloud. In seconds the cloud had cast its shadow over the land. A shadow that was moving steadily across the sea towards us.

Long moments passed as we waited for the curtain of darkness to draw over us.

'Whassat?' said one man.

'Where's the Cap'n? Wass goin' on?' asked another. But their shouted questions could barely be heard above the first claps of lightning and growls of angry thunder.

Miss Ariel's plane passed overhead, and in its wake came the darkness, blocking out the sunlight, turning the fresh, bright waters to wine-dark ink.

The wind began to blow in ever-stronger gusts, billowing the sails, causing the boat to rear up like a startled horse. It howled as though filled with fury and vicious intent, tearing at the sea that lay in its path until what had been calm azure only moments before now rose and fell in bruised, darkened peaks of ever greater size and force. As the ship ploughed on, urged forward by the wind, thick waves of spray shot over the bow, drenching us with cold water. A mighty crack of lightning filled the sky, followed in an instant by deafening thunder and before long the rolling clouds unleashed curtains of rain in cold, hard sheets.

The rain awoke the crowd from their torpor.

'Get us ashore,' cried one man.

'Head for Lamorna!' shouted another.

But it was futile request. So dark had the sky become, and so thick the rain, that the shore could no longer be seen at all. Nor could any of the other boats. People screamed at the captain, but neither he nor any of the sailors responded to their pleas, they just carried on with their singing.

In the confusion I was able to sneak up to the doorway that led to the hold. Inside was a set of steep stairs. Grabbing the rope which acted as a rail, I descended the steps, steadying myself against the roll and rock of the ship. Meredith was in the bowels of the vessel, still tied to that dreadful wicker throne (now divested of its carrying rails). He was slumped in the chair and looked, for all the world, as though he were asleep. With sickening horror, it dawned on me that they must have beaten him unconscious or that the rock that hit him had concussed him. I tore off my hare's head dress and threw it aside.

'Uncle Meredith!' I grabbed him by the chin and lifted his head. His skin was warm, but when I raised his head his eyes lolled around their sockets.

'Uncle Meredith. It's me Bill.' When my efforts to revive him failed I set about untying the belts and ropes that bound him. He was a thickset, heavy man, but I still imagined I could bring him to his feet and somehow walk him out.

'A rescue!' said a voice. Pendrogeth stood between us and the steps. He wore a ceremonial cape and in his arm held a staff – which I could not remember having seen before. I paused, struggling to hold Uncle Meredith upright. But I didn't need to. At the sound of Pendrogeth's voice, Meredith sprang back to life. The body that had hung in my arms with such heavy, dead weight was now alert with movement and power.

'It's okay Bill. I'm back now,' he muttered to me in that soft deep voice of his, a voice that could reassure and comfort even in the most dire of circumstances. 'Your quarrel is with me Pendrogeth. Let the boy go.'

'So speaks the Fool Tregenza. The boy has something I need, I can take it now or later.' Pendrogeth raised his staff, as though to strike, though there was no way he could hit either of us with it from where he stood. He took a step forward. Meredith held up his hand, punching the open palm of his hand forward. As he did this the boat rocked backwards. Pendrogeth fell backwards, dropping his staff. In spite of the ship rising and falling like a rollercoaster, he recovered himself remarkably quickly and was about to raise his staff once more when we he was disturbed by a woman falling down the stairs. She was drenched to the skin.

'God have mercy upon us,' she said, grabbing Pendrogeth's cloak. Behind her, first one passenger then another hurtled down the stairs. They had seen quite enough of the storm and were now seeking shelter below deck. A look of contempt and disgust passed over Pendrogeth's face as he shoved the woman to one side.

'Run Bill! Do as I say!' Meredith's large and firm hand propelled me towards the steps. A girl of about my own age was climbing steadily down the steps, urged on by those impatient to escape the storm. I grabbed the side of the steps, using them like a ladder so I could climb past her. At the top I took a look back. As Pendrogeth raised his staff Meredith was running towards him.

'Go!' he ordered. 'Help your sister.'

Pendrogeth turned his piercing eyes on me. I still wore the cape, but I am sure he saw the satchel. In that fleeting second his face was no more or less than a mask of naked hunger. He lunged towards the stairs, knocking the drenched passengers aside. But Meredith caught him. Pendrogeth turned as Meredith's fist lashed out. The magi began to fight; the two masters of ancient ceremony and natures' secret paths fell to the floor and began to wrestle like dogs.

I found Elsa huddled on the deck, wrapped in Anthony's jacket. He and Dr Gonzales had their arms over her, as much to prevent her from being thrown into the sea as to protect her from the rain, such was the force with which the boat was thrown up and down the terrifying waves. I crouched down with them. There were no words to say now, we just held each other, bracing ourselves against the sheets of water that swept over the deck. Before long we were saturated.

As the minutes went by I lost all hope of us making it to shore. Occasionally I would sit up and scan the horizon for any sign of boats or land, but only darkness and rain met my gaze, and from this darkness, monsters of waves reared up from the ocean, sucking the ship into valleys of shadow one moment, throwing us high over their peaks the next.

Then I saw the spirits. The first appeared as a flash of blue light, racing overhead, diving and swooping in between the sails and rigs. It was not easy to follow its movements, as the boat was heaving so violently and it – the figure – moved so quickly and erratically. But when I trained my eye on it I could make out a body, coated in robes of silver that blended almost completely with the sky and rain, as though it were itself made of air and water. Then I saw another, and then another. Soon, the sky was full of them. Some of them dived into the sea, racing in and out of the waves.

One flew from the water, over the bow and swept by me. It was followed by its companions and before long they were swarming in, diving through the sails, weaving in between the passengers.

People screamed and wailed. A man grabbed the captain by his arm.

'For God's sake man. Where are you taking us?' he shouted. As he tugged at his arm the captain continued to sing and I noticed that as he did so, water fell from his mouth. I stood up, grabbing the rail of the portside to steady me, but the wood crumbled in my hand. Dozens of woodlice, climbed from the rotten wood and over my arm.

The man pushed the captain aside and tried to take the wheel himself. One of the spirit creatures swept in, weaving in and out of the rigging at incredible speed. The man held an arm up to protect himself as it rushed at him but the spirit went right through him and shot upwards into the sails. The man fell backwards, taking a part of the wheel with him. He stared in amazement as the wood in his hands crumbled into sodden dust. Looking up I could see the sail was now tattered and full of holes. A woman screamed. She had fallen into a hole in the deck. Then another hole appeared and the terrible truth dawned on me. The whole ship was disintegrating before our very eyes, decaying and rotting until it became its true form; the rotten, sea lice infested skeleton of a ship that had sunk many years before.

There was another scream. A woman was cowering on the deck. Next to her a sailor had collapsed and was lying face down on the deck. A man turned him over, as though to help him, but immediately recoiled in horror. The sailor was dead, long dead. Where his eyes should have been there were empty, black pits. Bone and teeth shone through what was left of his face. A crab crawled from his mouth.

A glance across the deck revealed more of the same. All of the crews' bodies now lay on the deck, or slumped against the hull. I saw one fall overboard. The captain himself was now no more than a skeleton, dressed in rotting clothes.

Panic set in. Many screamed, raging uselessly against the evil storm, others threw themselves overboard, prepared to brave the waters rather than stay another second aboard the haunted ship. The boat dropped suddenly as we were sucked into the pit of a gigantic wave, time slowed as a monstrous wall of water reached slowly into the sky. It paused for a frozen, dreadful moment before crashing over us, washing men and women from the ship. I was thrown by its force, rolling down the deck of the ship. Looking up I saw something racing towards me. I dived and rolled. The mast crashed onto the deck, smashing into pieces, followed instantly by a sodden mess of sail and rope.

Then, above the sound of raging wind and waves, I heard a low, ill cry of straining timber. For a brief moment the ship felt sturdier and was suddenly stable in the tumultuous waters. But this could only mean one thing. Water was flooding into the hull, claiming the ship. Before long the *Seahawk* would be sucked into the abyss.

I started to make my way up the ship, towards Elsa. But she was gone. As the boat surged upwards on a wave I took a deep breath of air, stepped onto the side of the ship, and leapt into the sea.

A shock of cold went through me. I had barely a moment before a wave broke on me, but in that moment I saw the last of the *Seahawk*, swallowed by the waves.

A series of mighty 'cracks' echoed through the air, as though the sky itself were breaking apart. For long moments the world was illuminated in the pale blue of the lightning. It was a scene of pure havoc. The ocean heaved and fell like a roller coaster and on its peaks and in its troughs, were the heads and waving arms of the *Seahawk's* passengers. Above them, the spirit creatures raced and swooped in circles, no doubt ensuring their ghastly work had been completed.

Clearly they were creatures of the storm but whether they were its masters or its slaves I could not tell.

'Elsa, Elsa!' I shouted her name again and again.

Away from the shouts and screams of the other passengers I stopped swimming and trod water, clumsily freeing myself of my boots and of the robes I had taken from the boy, yet even in the midst of the chaos I was careful to keep a hold of the leather satchel holding the books.

A sheet of lightning shattered the sky with a deafening crack. The sea was lit for a fleeting moment and in that moment I saw a head, and an arm that could have been Elsa, held up to the sky no more than fifty yards away. I shouted again but my voice was drowned by wind and thunder. I swam with all the strength and speed I could muster, but each stroke seemed heavier and slower than the last.

My heart leapt. No more than twenty yards ahead a body surfaced. Even in the storm I could see it was a girl.

'Biiiilll!' It was Elsa. She had seen me.

'Biiilll,' her voice was faint even at close quarters. I was nearly upon her now. Her head dipped below the surface for long seconds, then reappeared, her face held upwards. But Elsa was not looking at me. She did not look afraid, nor was she struggling. Her face was empty of emotion. She sank beneath the waves.

Taking a lung full of air I plunged downwards. The world below the surface was dark and silent, but a crack of lightning lit the undersea world for an instant, followed immediately by another. I saw her face, a beacon of pale light in the fathomless dark. The light flickered, and then it was dark once again. Long, tortuous moments passed. Though my lungs were beginning to ache with pain, I swam ever downwards.

Another sheet of blue-white light. Elsa was far below me now. She opened her mouth as though to speak, letting out a stream of bubbles. Then the light vanished. I waited in those desperate seconds, but there was no more lightning, no fleeting illumination. My searching hands found only water. Again and again I dived, but as the minutes passed strength and hope began to seep slowly away.

It is not easy to describe the way I felt then. I was engulfed, drowning, not in water but in a sea of emotion; struggling to grasp the sheer horror of losing Elsa, fighting my fear of dying, feeling tears of frustrated rage blurring my vision. Confusion and bewilderment swept over me as surely as the strong, dark waters.

I could no longer see nor hear any of my fellow passengers. I expected the end would not be long in coming. Yet I did not succumb, I trod water for a while, then started to swim, with no aim or purpose other than to stay afloat. I don't know how long I swam for but after some hours the light, what little there was, began to give way and I knew that night was falling. And though I had found reserves of strength within me that I had not known existed, my strength wouldn't hold much longer. I decided to rid myself of the satchel. Then a memory flickered across my mind, a memory of Meredith's study. Grabbing the satchel, I reached inside. My hand fumbled about till I found a book. It was sodden as you would expect. I felt another. It was dry and light. My hand started to tingle. A shot of what I can only describe as 'dryness' leapt up my arm and then over my body like a fresh breeze. I found the third book. This too felt dry, but solid and heavy. I clutched the two books together. Miraculously, now I felt almost completely dry. Somehow the books were protecting me from the wild sea. The waters around me began to bubble and swirl. My foot touched something solid. Instinctively I reached out in the water. A large block of wood had floated to the surface. It was a piece of wreckage; several thick planks nailed together. I closed the satchel, and making sure that the leather strap was securely around my shoulder, reached my arms over the wood and lifted my body on to it.

The sudden ability to rest came almost as a shock. Exhaustion flooded through my muscles and I was sick, regurgitating all the water I had unwittingly swallowed. I started to shiver with the cold as the rain lashed my limp, exhausted body. I was cold, dizzy and barely conscious, but I was alive. Careful not to lose my buoy of wood I turned on to my back, so I could lie facing upwards, my hands gripping the sides of the planks. Gradually, night descended.

Time after time in the night I struggled not to lose consciousness for if I had fallen asleep, even for an instant, I might easily have lost the precious wood.

I don't know how long I remained like this, certainly it was several hours, and in that time I saw no more of the spirit creatures, nor did I see or hear any of the other passengers.

Eventually, the storm began to abate. The huge mountains of water became hills, the fury of the raging wind subsided and the rain merely fell where before it had cut and beat in iron, grey sheets. After several hours in near total darkness, holding on for life itself, there came a point when I could relax my grip on the wood without fear of losing it. The thick black cloud began to dissolve and in between the dense clouds small patches of the night sky appeared. Stars peaked through these gaps. Above the sounds of the slowing wind I heard the call of seagulls and above that a familiar, welcome sound. Waves crashing on a shore.

Whatever fury had possessed the seas and sky was gone. Ahead of me, set against a rapidly clearing sky of blue night, was a great shadow, and at its base, thin lines of white. The shadow had to be land and the white lines, the waves I could hear breaking on the shore. Slowly, carefully, I reached my hands over the side of the wood and started paddling.

Once into the breakers, the waves carried me forward. They were large and quite ferocious; a legacy of the storm, but I was grateful for each pounding surge of white water pushing me towards the shore. An enormous wave crashed over me, and in my weak state I lost the wood. I was carried forward in a foaming mass of white water, tumbling over and over. When the force of the wave finally waned my feet found sand and rock beneath me. Water poured from my nose and mouth as I gasped for air. I struggled through the last few yards of water towards the beach. When I was sure I was a safe distance inland I collapsed into the sand.

Slowly, the grey twilight of dawn seeped into the sky. I was on a small crescent beach, of the palest yellow sand, backing onto a bed of rock. Beyond the beach was a cliff face steeped in the shadow caused by the rising sun. I wondered how I would ever scale it, but then noticed on the left side of the beach were rocks that looked as though they might be climbed, and at their top a stream poured out of a gulley; a cleft in the rock, out of which I could just see the tops of bushes and long grasses.

Gasping and shivering, I crawled over to where the stream tumbled off the rocks into the sea. Putting my face into a pool of water I drank deeply. Slowly my senses returned to me, washed clean by the waters. After a time I found I could stand without feeling too dizzy or weak. I walked over the base of the cliff and began to climb the rocks.

Upon reaching the top I saw in the distance – of all things – a hare. It was some way off the cliff path, half way up a steep verge. The hare had not seen me, and lolled slowly up the verge to an outcrop of exposed rock. I decided to follow it, thinking that if I could climb the rock I would get a view of the peninsular and find my bearings.

By the time I reached the rock the hare had disappeared and I found that beyond the rock lay a path leading steeply up a hill at the top of which was a tor, an exposed peak of bare rock washed and blown by the Atlantic weather. It took a while to reach it but I knew that when I did I would be able to get my bearings.

Sure enough, from the top of the rock I had a view of almost the entire peninsular, though its furthest reaches were covered in sea mist, being slowly burnt off by the morning sun. Directly below me, no more than half a mile off I could see a cottage, with smoke billowing from its chimney. I could see Penzance, or a part of it directly in front of me, and out to sea a dark grey shadow, which I guessed, was St Michael's Mount. If I followed the path to the cottage I reckoned, I could get help and find my way to the coast road. Then it would be no more than a few miles to Lyonesse house.

I was climbing down from the tor, when I was struck by a distinct and sharp feeling of unease. I climbed up onto the tor again. There was Penzance, right in front of me, and in the bay St Michael's Mount, and to my left the familiar outline of the distant moors. But the moors had a distinct, unmistakeable crown of snow. Had the storm been so severe? I thought. Slowly, the mist began to evaporate. I could see that the island wasn't St Michaels'

Mount at all. There was no castle. But further out to sea the mist was revealing another island and for a fleeting moment I thought I saw a tall black turret, pointing skyward from the white clouds in which it was shrouded.

Then I realised; some of the patches of white and blue in the distance were not mist at all. Where the Lizard peninsular should have stretched southwards there was nothing, nothing but an expanse of blue sea. I turned around, looking vainly for land. Beyond the distant shore, the curtains of mist were rising, fully revealing the truth. In the bay, ahead of the town, stood an imposing, mighty castle, its black walls and ramparts rising out of an azure sea. It was exactly the same as Miss Ariel's picture.

Before my legs could give way I sat down on the rock, my head spinning with confusion and disbelief. I was lost, marooned on an island no earthly navigator could ever find.

'Tell me boy, are you washed up by the storm?' A voice boomed. It was like a whisper, yet was almost unbearably loud. I reeled, this voice seeming to have come both from inside my head and from far away. It sounded un-unnervingly like the voices of my dreams. I turned. There sat the hare. Its large, deep eyes returned my stare.

'How came you, to the island of Lyonesse?' it asked, cocking its head. I think I must have fainted, for I don't remember what happened next.

PART 3

LYONESSE

Chapter 11

My senses dragged me from a deep slumber. I could hear voices nearby, the whistle of the wind and a steady patter of raindrops.

But the wind and rain were muffled, heard through thick stonewalls, and above the voices I could hear the gentle crackle of a fire. The air smelt of firewood and cooking. I was dry and warm, tucked up in a bunk of wood, lying on a straw mattress and covered by a thick blanket.

As my senses awoke to my surroundings, memories swept through my mind. I remembered the festival, the ship, the storm… and a hare. A hare that had talked.

'It's the boy I tell you. The same I have seen in my dreams,' said a voice. It confused me, seeming to be spoken in my ear, yet at the same time, having the echoing quality of a voice speaking from afar.

My eyes quickly scanned the room. There was a table, two chairs and a fire with a pot hanging over it. Sat in front of the fire was a man, dressed in hessian trousers and a leather jerkin worn over a coarse shirt. He had straggly, dark hair that brushed his shoulders and was smoking a long, thin pipe. Next to him, apparently talking in fluent English, was the hare.

'There's others too,' said the man, 'they come ashore all round the island.'

'What others?' I said, sitting up in the bunk. I groaned as I spoke. Every muscle ached, every bone creaked.

The man came straight over to me, followed by the hare. His eyes bulged out of his long, unshaven face. He was very curious, but seemed wary of me.

'What others?' I repeated 'Where am I?' I said, pulling the blanket up to my chest. This was a dream, I told myself, it had to be. I'd had vivid enough nightmares whilst staying at Lyonesse House. This was just one more.

'Never mind that boy! 'Ow did you get 'ere and in what manner?' the man grizzled, pointing at me with the stem of his pipe. He obviously thought he should be the one asking the questions.

'From the mainland of course. I… we were in a ship. A storm hit us, just south of Lamorna. The ship sunk and I came ashore here.' The man and the hare exchanged a look.

'So you drowned then?' said the hare, as though this were some kind of reasonable conclusion. Did I need to point out that if I had drowned I could not very well be sitting in the bunk, talking to them? I noticed that above his heart, the hare had a thick scar.

'I didn't drown,' I said, staring at the scar.

'I'm afraid you did,' said the hare in a matter of fact way, 'you see…otherwise you wouldn't be here. We have many of the drowned. Did the merpeople bring you ashore?'

'Merpeople? No, I clung to a piece of wreckage. I'm alive. Can't you see that?'

'Many think that… at first. Show us your chest then,' demanded the man, 'you'll soon see.'

'I beg your pardon?'

'Your chest,' he insisted.

Reluctantly I undid the buttons of my shirt. The man reached out and placed his cold, bony hand over my heart. His hand lingered for a second before he recoiled, as though he had received a shock.

'Saints above us,' he said in a shaky voice, 'this boy is alive!'

'Of course I'm, alive! How else could…,' I looked again at the scar above the hare's heart and again at the man. What exactly were they trying to tell me?

'Why… wouldn't I be… alive?' I stuttered, dreading what

the answer might be.

'Only the dead come here,' said the hare in a kindly voice.

Nightmares were now the stuff of waking life, and the world I had once thought of as real was a distant dream. I had a hundred questions, but for now I wanted only to know one thing.

'These others. Where are they? Was there a girl, shoulder length sandy hair?'

'I dunno,' said the man, 'but I 'eard there was men.'

'Could you take me to them?'

'I might, if I knew where they were. You been out a good few hours young man. They could be anywhere on the island. Be night time soon. P'raps we should wait till morning till we decide what t'do with you. Meantime, we'll 'ave supper. You can tell us 'ow you came to be 'ere… ' he paused, looking searchingly into my eyes, then he reached under the bed and produced the satchel. 'And how exactly do you come to be in possession of the Master's books?'

The 'dead' it seemed, needed to eat just as much as the living. A fish stew was produced from the pot hanging over the fire and ladled out into rough wooden bowls. It was made of fish and tomatoes and potatoes, flavoured with herbs and wine. But such a simple description does no justice to how rich and warming the stew was. It seemed to nourish parts of me that had withered and hungered my whole life. I ate so eagerly that the liquid burnt my mouth and throat. But I didn't care. Each mouthful seemed to pour a little more strength into me till I felt quite recovered. No one spoke till I had finished my third bowlful.

Afterwards, they told me of the island and of Meredith's other life, as Lord of the domain of Lyonesse. In return I told them everything of my experiences in Cornwall, of Pendrogeth and my uncle Meredith.

The man and the hare seemed to believe my story, though the man had seemed very surprised that the *Seahawk* had delivered us to the island, and even more surprised that its crew may be – as he put it – 'in the pay of' Pendrogeth.

'If this Pendrogeth has triumphed… well, many will go to him, and if 'is power is strong enough many will 'ave no choice,' said the man, whose name was Bob Trelawney. The hare cocked his head to one side.

'This may be why he called the storm. Here his powers are at their fullest. This magus wants more than land young Master. He will stop at nothing until you are dead. You are not dangerous to him. Not yet. But you have the blood of the magi in your veins. If you were to learn the ways… then you would be his worthy enemy.'

'Why didn't Meredith do anything? Why didn't he prevent the storm?' I said.

'Perhaps he could not. I warn you, for this Lord Pendrogeth to have brought you here does not bode well. We must hope your uncle has vanquished this magus somehow, for the magic used in the world of the living is but a thread, drawn from this place. It is but a thin whisper of that which may be spoken here.'

'If Pendrogeth lives it is only a matter of time before he finds you,' added the man. He picked up the satchel and dropped it on my lap. 'It may be too late for the master boy. But not for you. If you 'ave authority to use these books, you'd better start learning.'

Loer Skovarnek and I, (for that was the hare's name), made ready to leave before dawn of the next day. Bob Trelawney had given me some of his clothes to wear. I was quite tall for my age and he was short for a man, so the clothes were only slightly outsized; a leather sleeveless jerkin, hessian trousers (which had to be cut short and re-sown to fit me), a linen shirt, boots (with straw stuffed in the ends) and a hooded cloak. When I was dressed he thrust a staff into my hand.

'Keep those books hidden,' he warned, tucking the satchel under the cloak, 'if you come across anyone, or anything, don't trust 'em unless you are sure they are loyal to the master. If you're sure of 'em tell 'em you are a friend of Bob Trelawney. In the meantime I will make contact with them we *know* are loyal to your uncle Meredith and let them know the state o' matters… and I'll warn 'em of Pendrogeth.'

The door shut behind us and we walked out of the cosy hut, and into the cold and rain. I looked back. I shivered as rainwater trickled off my hair and ran down my back and longed to be back inside where I had been safe and warm. But the hare was away already, bouncing along at great speed in first one direction, then another, pausing only to stand and sniff the air. I pulled the hood over my head and using the staff, started to climb the hill.

We were headed for Ictis, the castle on the island I had seen from the moors. Bob and the hare believed that within its walls was the library of the master. If I was to learn the ways of the magi, this library was my best, if not only hope.

'We must cut across the land now and follow the cliff path,' said Loer 'it is better that you are not seen. Come'. He bounded over a stone wall, off the track and into a field. I could see that he meant to take us to the east shore of the island, that part of Penwith that in the real Cornwall, adjoined the peninsular to the mainland. I climbed the wall and plodded after him. The rain stopped eventually, and the sky began to clear, allowing columns of light and patches of blue through the dark rolling, clouds.

'You see' said Loer, nodding and pointing with this head 'the forces of nature are in a flux! Mark my words, young Master, it will be high summer within the hour and mid winter before the day is up.'

We walked for several hours. The path followed the top of a cliff, which was for the most part sheer and dizzily high above the sea. But in some places the cliff had collapsed and I could see it would be possible to make one's way up or down the scree and rubble to the sea.

We had travelled the path for a good few hours when Loer suddenly froze in his tracks, his ears erect, his nose twitching.

'What is it?' I cried.

'Look!' said Loer, his unearthly voice echoing in my head

(it was only when I was close to him that I noted that as he spoke his mouth did not appear to move). On the beach below were the bodies of several people lying in the sand, close to the shore. Around them were strips of wood, coils of rope and other debris from the wreck of the *Seahawk*.

'I think we should go down, some of those people might need our help,' I said.

'This is no business of ours young Master. The books are our concern. We must hasten for Ictis.'

If Pendrogeth was on the island, no doubt he would be seeking entry to Ictis himself. But I could not in all conscience ignore what I had seen. Besides, I thought, what if Elsa, Anthony or Meredith were amongst those bodies?

Carefully, and quickly as we dared, we climbed down the rocks towards the sea. There were quite a few bodies littered along the shore; men, women and children. I recognised some of them from the day of the festival. Followed by the hare I ran to the nearest body. It belonged to a young woman. She was lying face down in the sand, her hair and clothes were sodden, and she was draped in seaweed. With a great deal of effort I turned her limp, heavy body over. Her eyes rolled listlessly in their sockets and her mouth opened as though to speak. But only water poured out. I put my ear to her chest. There was a weak but regular heartbeat.

'Bill!' Loer cried with alarm. He was near the base of the cliff, hiding behind a large rock. I looked around, searching for what might have alarmed him. A man was swimming through the breakers to the shore. He stood up, waist deep in the water, and began wading towards us. I froze in horror, for the man was one of the sailors from the ship, just as he had been as the boat went down. His teeth shone through a gaping hole where the flesh of his mouth should have been; one eye was a black, bone rimmed hole and the other had his solitary eyeball, swivelling loosely in its socket. His clothes were in tatters and, so was his flesh; the skeleton fingers of his hands pushed through the flesh as though the skin and sinew were worn out gloves for his bones.

I cowered in revulsion and fear, wanting to run, yet was unable to tear my eyes away, and somehow, to turn my back on this 'thing' seemed unwise. Besides, he was moving at a pace now, he would easily catch me if he had the will. The man, or what had once been a man, strode steadily onto the beach and then made a bee line towards the cliff. He did not seem to even notice me, or if he did, I held no interest for him.

As he came nearer so my fear grew and I was about to run when I noticed that his fingers, did not in fact seem to be bone and torn flesh, but now looked quite normal. His face too, suddenly seemed to have features where before there had been bone and tatters of flesh. The truth was; as he passed me he was undergoing a sudden and dramatic transformation; the flesh grew back on to his face and his clothes, which seconds before had been rags, re-formed into trousers, a smock, a jacket. It was a precise reversal of what I had seen on the boat. It happened so fast, that I doubted what I had seen, as though his previous, deathly appearance had been a trick of the light or the projection of my own fearful imagination. When he reached the cliff he began climbing the route of rocks and scree that we had used in our descent. Loer reappeared, taking nervous glances at the cliff and then out to sea as he hopped over to join me.

'Well?' he said, glancing at the bodies on the beach.

'They're alive. But they won't – or can't – wake up,' I said, hearing the wonder in my own voice.

'And your sister?'

'She isn't among them.'

'The ones that are here. You say they do not wake?' He was looking past me down the long beach. Some distance away, one of the 'bodies' was walking about. I set off immediately, with the hare following close behind. As we got nearer I fancied that the figure was a man, and as we got closer still it became clear that he was wearing a large hat. It was Mr Trinkle, the jester that had so cruelly and horribly ridiculed my uncle Meredith at the festival of Lyonesse. Of all those who might have survived he was the last person I wished to see! We stuck closely to the base of the cliff, running between rocks, advancing on him but being careful not to be seen. Eventually we came to a place where there were caves and many fallen rocks at the foot of the cliff. We hid amongst them.

There were a few more bodies on this part of the beach. Trinkle was moving between them, searching their pockets and checking their hands, necks and ears. The rogue! He was not concerned with whether they were dead or alive, he was searching them for jewellery and money.

Then I had an idea. When I had first seen the books, the night Elsa and I had sneaked into Meredith's secret study, one of them had empowered my senses. I recalled sharper vision, and acute hearing. I also recalled an overwhelming sense of power and strength in my body. I fumbled in the satchel. The first book felt damp. This had to be the Book of Water. My fingers found another book. This one felt heavier and dry. I picked it out and opened it. The page I chanced upon had dense text, in a language unknown to me. Of course I could not understand it. But, as with the first time I had held it, the mere act of holding the book, had an immediate and profound effect on my senses. My hands felt dry and heavy. A warm feeling slowly crept up my arms and through my entire body. My breath and heartbeat were suddenly uncomfortably loud in my ears and the colours and texture of everything around me was brought sharply into focus. Every bubble of foam on a breaking wave was visible, every shade of turquoise and glimmer of light could be seen clearly, as though the wave were mere inches from my eyes. I found I could focus my hearing too, moving in on the crash of a particular wave as it broke or picking out the squawk and cry of a seagull high above, almost *feeling* its crystal clean echoes in my head. I listened to Trinkle.

'Quickly, quickly,' he said to himself, still yanking on the poor woman's finger, 'before another one comes.' He was so involved in this activity that he failed to notice that further up the beach was a man, or something in the rough shape of a man, crawling along the shoreline on all fours. As I concentrated my new sense of sight, it became clear that this was not a man at all, but some kind of creature. He (I assumed it was a he) was roughly the shape of a man, but by the look of his hide, and the way he moved seemed at least half animal, though a half of what kind of animal it would be difficult to say. He was covered in a thin coat of hair, beneath which I could see a thick leathery hide of what I can only describe as scales. There was undoubtedly something ape-like about him, yet he moved across the sand like a giant lizard, his hands and feet supporting his movement equally. In fact, he was at once as much a giant lizard as he was a primate as he was a giant fish. His face when I saw it was ugly beyond reckoning; large black eyes bulged out of his face, his nose was wide and snubbed, his mouth was large and full lipped, like that of a fish and when it opened, it revealed three rows of sharp teeth and a long pointed tongue. In spite of this unfortunate appearance he moved with a great deal of poise and grace. He would crawl along at great speed and then, for no apparent reason, pause, his body frozen in action, much like a lizard when hunting an insect. He would then lower his face to the sand and sniff before plunging his arm into the sand, up to his elbow. In itself this meant he had to have enormous strength and power. When the hand was retracted it contained a large shell, which he placed carefully into a sack he carried over his shoulder. He would then repeat the process and as he did so, was moving closer towards us. Neither he nor Trinkle seemed to have noticed each other.

Trinkle still held the woman's hand, but he was staring out to sea. His expression of frustration had been replaced by a look of abject terror.

'Oh, no, not again,' he said to himself. He dropped the poor woman's hand and started running.

At the shoreline, two more deathly, rotten bodies of sailors were hauling themselves ashore. The creature, who had been so busy looking for his shells, also saw the men, and in alarmingly quick time also ran full pelt towards us, first on all fours and then, upright, like a man. When he was no more than a few yards from us, he ducked behind a rock.

Trinkle turned and ran, at first back the way he had come and then, towards the caves and rocks, also towards us. I tensed, dropping the book. My normal senses rushed back to me and indeed, we were so close to them that we could hear and see what was going on without need of the book. I picked it up and carefully placed it back in the satchel.

Trinkle ran around one rock, then another, till he found one to hide behind. Neither he nor the creature could see each other; both of them were clearly petrified of the sailors. But they had no need to worry; the sailors, now fully restored to their full bodied selves, were some way off, climbing up the cliffs. Then I heard singing and as the singer grew nearer so the words of the song became clear:

> Barmaid, I've waited way too long
> For you to pour another one
> That is why I sing this song

'It just gets worse,' said Trinkle. 'Now they're singing, just like they did on the boat!'

'What speaks?' replied another voice. This voice, the voice of the creature, was low and rasping. It was the voice of an animal with a human tongue. Fortunately for Trinkle, he could not see who it was that addressed him.

'Oh Lord… I think I hear them coming… ' said the jester.

The singer had taken no small amount of time to reach our part of the beach, but when I saw him it was obvious why. A tall, thin man dressed in an old frock coat was rolling a barrel along the sand. From each pocket of his coat a bottle stuck out. He stopped when he got close. He leant against a rock, which he needed to do on account of being rip-roaring drunk.

'What has the master sent to torment me now?' said the creature, sounding genuinely scared. 'I'll do what he wills, I'll bring the shells home, I'll dig potatoes. I'll fetch wood and cook his supper and curse him no more,' pleaded the creature.

'If you have voice where is your mouth? I'll give you sustenance?' Stephen took one of the bottles from his coat and made towards the rock hiding the creature.

'I know that voice, but, but... he is drowned surely. Are you a... (gulp)... ghost?' said Trinkle's voice.

'Almost definitely,' said Stephen, with a burp, turning toward the rock hiding Trinkle, 'but a rich one!' He laughed, fishing out of his pocket a fistful of rings and necklaces, no doubt torn from the bodies on the beach (low minds think alike, I thought).

'Have you a face?' asked Trinkle weakly, perhaps thinking Stephen too was like the ghostly sailors. Stephen, who seemed to have taken everything in his stride up to this point, seemed rather taken aback by this question. As carefully as he could, considering his drunken state, he felt the contours of his face, being careful to steady himself against the barrel with his other hand.

'Two ears, eyes, nose, mouth, yes, all there.' For a second Stephen looked awfully sober. I think he was pondering if he might indeed have been cursed like the crew of the *Seahawk*. He shuddered, shaking off the ghastly thought.

'St... St... Stephen. If you are him truly and still himself and... and not like... them sailors, well, don't you know me? It's me... Trinkle.' The jester crept out from behind the rock and Stephen fell backwards. They looked a very sorry pair, especially Trinkle. His jester's costume was covered in sand and seaweed and the three corners of his hat hung limply round his face. The two of them stood up.

'Trinkle!' shouted Stephen with drunken joy, opening his arms.

'Stephen,' sobbed Trinkle. They fell into each other's arms like long lost lovers.

'You are not sprites sent by the master to taunt me, then you might be men,' rasped the creature, appearing from behind his rock. Trinkle didn't seem to hear what the creature said. He stared though and the more he stared the tighter he clung to Stephen. It took several seconds for him to emit the scream that welled up from the very core of his being; a cry of desperation, disbelief and – above all – terror.

'Shut up, shut up for god's sake man. There's nothing can harm you on this island,' said Stephen. He took the empty bottle and from the tap at the base of the barrel, filled it with wine before handing it to the creature. 'Speak Monster, who are you? And who is your master?' The creature drank long and hard before replying.

'My name is Cabal-En. I am dortriger. Earth dweller in your tongue. I know this isle like no other; the fertile ground from that which shows a weedy crop, the fresh brook of sweet water from the brackish stream. I'll fetch the master the best berries, the eggs from the cliff nests, the fish from the river, the whelks from the rock. None know these things like dortriger, and none are quicker or sharper than Cabal-En. And my master is the magus Meredith, master of this Isle when he comes from the land of the living. I think you are new here to ask such questions!'

'Well, he must love you for being so…helpful. How does he… erm… reward you?'

'Reward! Reward? When I do his bid my reward is slavery, when I disobey he plagues me with the prickles of hedgehogs, sets the flies on me, orders his sprites to place ice and fire under my skin. He says it is the only language I understand. But it is a language he taught me and in time I will curse him with this same language!' The dortriger spoke with great bitterness and broke his speaking with swigs of the wine bottle. The dortriger looked towards the cliff and shouted to the air; 'Come then Master. Will you not punish such words!' The shouts echoed along the cliff, and in the dark recesses of the nearby cave. 'Can it be true? He does not hear me, his powers wane?'

'Don't be afraid Monster. He will not punish you. He is gone. There is a new master now,' said Stephen.

'A new master! This juice of yours drowns my fear and *your* reason or else we would not speak so… though it is said his power is absent of late.'

'And what is the source of this 'power'?' asked Stephen, sarcastically.

'Why his books of course. Without them he is as nothing. But your magic is stronger, it must be so to free me from his wrath and the wrack he would put me in?'

'That's right Monster. A strong magic indeed. We serve a different master and if you serve him too you will be rewarded. Never fear Monster, you will have all the reward you wish for and so shall we dear Trinkle,' he said, taking the bottle from the dortriger and offering it to the jester.

'When you said we should follow Lord Pendrogeth you never said anything about monsters, or storms, or islands or… ghosts. You said the on the feast of Lyonesse accounts would be settled, Tregenza would be made a Fool and Pendrogeth would be in charge, but you never said nothing 'bout… '

'And he is in charge dear Trinkle and Tregenza is no more. When we last saw your master Monster, he was wearing a crown of eggs and cabbage. The King of Fools, tied to a throne and now I do believe, master of the ocean deep, with crabs and sea lice for his subjects. Now, why don't we see if we can't find the new master, the Lord Pendrogeth?' Stephen placed a bottle in Trinkle's trembling hand and helped him bring the bottle to his lips.

So this was it then. Meredith was drowned and Pendrogeth was the master of Lyonesse.

'Now Monster. We have a rendezvous to keep. To Ictis, you know the way I trust and shall lead us there,' said Stephen. The dortriger lifted the barrel onto his shoulders with ease.

'Come then. This tunnel shall take us there,' he rasped, and he bounded towards a cave mouth, but stopped dead in his tracks at the entrance

'Truly, the liquid does dull my senses more. The way through the cave is thin in places. Good for us, but the barrel shall not pass. Will we leave it here?'

'Is there another way?' asked Trinkle hopefully. From the

sound of his voice I think he did not relish a crawl through a dark, dank cave.

'Oh, yes. It is longer, but we shall make that path easily with the barrel,' replied the dortriger.

'Then we shall take it, and not leave our 'friend' behind.' They all laughed.

We waited till their drunken voices were no more than an echo on the breeze before coming out of our hiding place. They were a long way down the beach. Stephen had started singing again.

'Meredith… ' His name fell from of my mouth.

'We must go!' said Loer. There was compassion in his voice, but urgency too. 'Drunken fools these may be but dangerous too. The dortriger are base indeed, but powerful. If more of their kind join this Lord Pendrogeth's camp, then the isle will soon be his. And if this man's words are true our quest is ever more urgent young Master Bill. We must hasten to Ictis.' And with that he bounded off towards the mouth of the cave.

Chapter 12

Inside the cave were the remnants of a fire and a crudely made bed of straw and dried seaweed. No doubt this was the resting place of the dortriger. We walked further in, till the sand floor gave way to rock. We soon reached the point where the long fingers of daylight could reach no further.

'Be still young Master. Our eyes will adjust to the light. Then we will find the way.'

Our eyes did indeed adjust and in the weak light I could see the way forward split into several passages, any one of which could be the route we sought. Beyond the entrance of each passage we could see nothing but ink-black, darker than the night. The hare of course, was used to the dark of night and burrows, but I wasn't convinced that even his keen senses could guide us through. Besides, to feel our way would take a lot of time. Time that we did not have.

I reached inside the satchel and felt for the Book of Air. With the other hand I thrust my staff forward, using the stick to feel the way. There was an instant rush of power up my arm and into my whole body, but it was a light and delicate energy, quite unlike that of the Book of Earth. It was several seconds before I could breathe steadily and focus my mind on how the book might be useful. This was difficult. The energy released into me, merely by holding the book was almost enough to override my mind, as though my senses were supercharged with a will all of their own. I concentrated, reminding myself of our task, focussing on the darkness ahead.

'Show me the way to Ictis,' I whispered.

I tried each route in turn, feeling my way in some distance before deciding – or sensing – that this or that particular route was a dead end. The last to be tried was a small fissure in the rock above. For this the books and staff were no good, I had to push them ahead of me and wriggle through like a snake. A few feet in the gap widened. What had the dortriger said about not being able to take the barrel through the passage to Ictis, had he not said that parts of it were too narrow?

I could feel a vein of cold, salty air, brushing my face. We travelled as quickly as I dared, given that we were after all, in pitch blackness, but the deeper into the cave we went the more confident I became. The books imbued my body with strength and agility that was more than natural, so we could travel through spaces barely big enough to crawl through, or climb steep rocks, with comparative ease, and all the time accompanied by a cold, gentle breath of wind. In fact, as we explored the cave further and after travelling an hour or two, I had the odd feeling that the breeze was guiding me, whistling past my face when we went in the right direction and disappearing altogether when we took a wrong turn. It was a mad thought, yet it persisted and the longer it persisted the more I came to believe that the breezy air was some kind of presence. Eventually, the feeling of being helped became so strong that I became truly sure there was a presence with us in the dark. I stopped still, wondering how 'it' would react. Surely enough, after a few moments I felt a cold rush of air behind me, as though it were pushing me forward.

'Who are you?' I whispered.

'Fear not, I can not harm you. I am Ayr.' The voice spoke in a soft, feminine whisper. It was the sound of wind rustling through leaves, the sound of the sea in a shell held against your ear, the sound of a breeze on the night air.

'Where are you?' I felt my heckles raise. My muscles tensed against the breeze.

'I am the very air around you. You called me to this task.'

'I did? Must you do what I tell you?'

'Aye Sire. Your will is that I should lead you from this cave?'

'It is.'

'I take breath from the air which draws across the stones of Ictis,' the voice whistled. 'Come!' There was a rush of air past may face.

'A spirit of air. As dortriger are to the earth, so this spirit is to the sky and the wind,' explained Loer, 'the power you draw from the books will call such spirits after a time.'

Before long we were in a wide tall passage and the thin whisper of air became a breeze of salty wind. Ahead of us we could hear the distant, haunting call of seagulls A few more steps and we saw a gradual dawning of light in the darkness ahead and in the light I could see a vague ball of light, which grew more distinct as we approached the entrance to the cave. In the centre of the light was the outline of a human figure. As we watched the ball of light began to form features; the face and body of a young woman was revealed, apparently floating in the air. She was entirely made of light and seemed to have no colour at all, her form only being visible in the twilight of the cave entrance. If I blinked she vanished, but if I looked long enough the form of the woman would again reappear in the air. She wore robes and had silvery hair that floated around her, as though she was immersed in water. I realised I had seen her before, and more of her kind. I had seen this creature in the storm, ripping through the sails of the *Seahawk*.

'You… you were there… in the storm.'

'I was its agent. There never was a storm seen on this or any sea until that day, and I was afraid for what I had done. The waves and winds were fury, and the fabric of the sky was torn by such magic.'

'So, you were commanded to bring the storm?'

'I was. I long for my freedom. For in my bondage I have done such deeds and carry a burden of shame for my part.'

'But now you are *my* servant?'

'My will is not my own. Whilst your magic holds Master, I am your humble servant.'

'Then you must do as I say?'

'I must do as the reader of the books decrees.'

'Then tell me. I command you. What has happened to my uncles?'

'One is subject to a powerful magus. The other lies on the ocean bed. His blood is now salt water. His bones are of coral formed. His flesh is the sand, which the storm has scattered all round these shores. He suffers a change… '

'And my sister Elsa. I saw her when the ship went down. She was taken by the storm. Is she… dead? '

'The word has no meaning here.'

'Do not meddle with me spirit. Does she… is she alive?'

'She also has suffered a sea change. She too is not as she was. She is of a different race.' A different race? What could it mean?

'Can you take me to her?'

'I cannot.'

'What happened to her?'

'I will show you… Master.' Her voice faded into the darkness. I took a step forward to follow her, but my feet could not find a foothold. The light ahead disappeared, instantly.

'Loer,' I whispered. There was no reply. I was aware of three things. That the gentle breeze that threaded through the stale air could no longer be heard or felt, that my feet had no hold on the cave floor and that my calling of Loer's name had no echo, no resonance.

Indeed in that moment I was not only aware, but sure in the knowledge, that I was no longer in the cave at all, but in a void infinitely darker and emptier.

A pale light, shimmered above me. Slowly the light increased, revealing a murky, silent world of shifting shadows, swirls and clouds of sand, jagged black rocks and towering bushes of seaweed that twisted and waved in violent currents. Impossible as it seemed, I was in the sea, or at least that is how it looked, for I had no physical sense of it, or indeed, of anything. I also had no trouble breathing. It dawned on me quickly that I was not there at all, but in my mind's eye I was being shown whatever the spirit wished me to see. And on the seabed, her eyes, open but unseeing, her hair, swirling in rhythm with the seaweed, was Elsa. As in a nightmare I tried to move towards her yet had no body with which to move and knew, immediately not only that I was not in that place but was witnessing events that might be past as easily as present.

In the distance were shapes; strong, dark shadows were snaking in powerful and fluid movements towards Elsa. They were merpeople, two mermaids and one merman. They went straight to Elsa, enveloping her with their bodies, their thick tails working with the water's currents to steady them. Their arms were around her quickly, picking her from her watery grave. In so doing they kicked up a storm of sand, making a fog through which I could not see.

When the sand had sunk or washed away I could see one mermaid had Elsa in her arms, supporting her from behind. The other mermaid and the merman were crouched over her, apparently biting Elsa's neck. The image was shocking and profoundly strange. Blood oozed into the water, making smoke like vapours in the water.

Elsa shuddered. Her eyes moved, then saw. I was relieved of course, but there was something in her eyes…then the shocking truth hit me. When Meredith had told us of the merpeople he had spoken of the common legend of sailors becoming merpeople, joining their chosen sweetheart in the underwater world. I had wondered when he told us, how a human could be converted, could be changed, into a merman or maid; suddenly able to breathe, to live underwater. And here was the answer. This was how. Like vampires they knelt over her, taking god knows what from her, but also giving something of themselves. As I have said, it was strange, being moving and disturbing in equal measure. Elsa was saved, but in how many ways was she changed?

She did not fight them; her eyes – her new eyes – were fixed on the distant surface. When they drew away I saw she had bite marks at the base of her neck, almost imperceptible, but there nonetheless. Then they swam off. Elsa swam with them, not as fast as they could, but still with short thrusts that sent her quickly and more easily than her young body was capable of (she was – had been – a weak swimmer). And as they swam I got a closer look at their features. The man's hair was dark, the women's both light. He was handsome, the women beautiful, yet it was a cold beauty; ageless and pure. There seemed to be nothing warm, nothing human about their features, their eyes were too light, their skin too pale. They had the marble-cold beauty of statues, a beauty to captivate, to beguile; a beauty that could break your heart – as attractive and compelling as the sea they made their home. And just as dangerous.

Before I could look upon this scene of wonder any longer it disappeared. The light withdrew, the rocks, the sand and shafts of grey light retreated into an infinite night.

I opened my mouth to speak, but the light returned, stronger this time; a light that blew away the dark like a fierce wind, revealing a world I could now hear and see; a sky of blue, the cry of gulls, a rocky shoreline, a reef of rocks dressed with muscles, limpets, sagging seaweed and pools left by the retreating tide. Smooth, regular waves licked at the foot of the shore. This was the shore of the island after the storm; a calm and shallow turquoise, a world away from the scene I had just witnessed.

The waters were disturbed by a commotion. A mermaid's head burst through the surface, her hair, wet and silky, framed her perfect face. She was followed by the other merpeople, and Elsa. My sister hugged each of them close, in turn, but she did not hold them out of simple gratitude, she held them – and they her – as though parting with a loved one. As though she were indeed, one of them.

They swam to the shore and I noticed that Elsa now swam as they did, with her feet bound together, waving and rolling through the water. This way of swimming, if that is the right word, was of the element of water, quite different to the awkward mechanical strokes of a… (I gasped as I thought it)… human. Elsa crawled onto the reef, hoisting herself up with her arms and practically dragging her legs onto the shore. Those limbs that had been so lithe and swift in the water, now looked like a deadweight, something quite heavy and useless out of the water. She gasped and coughed, sucking in huge lung-fulls of air, but never seeming to have enough. I feared for her, but eventually her breathing regulated and she was able to steadily haul herself to her feet. She staggered like a newborn foal, before finding her balance and stumbling over the rocks to a small beach.

Elsa hugged herself, rubbing her arms with her shoulders hunched against the cold. She was shivering. She looked back toward the sea, perhaps hoping for guidance from the mermaids, perhaps hoping they would beckon her to join them once more. But they were gone.

Poor Elsa looked very much like a drowned rat; cold and miserable and afraid, and it hurt me to the core, knowing I was powerless to help or even warn her, for she, like me, would have believed that she was 'home'. But there was no Loer or Bob Trelawney to give her a warm bed and fish stew. Who knew what welcome she would receive. She cried tears of frustration and misery, but Elsa, being a tough spirit, stamped her feet in frustration before the tears could take hold and spoke sternly to herself.

'I've been rescued by mermaids. And… and I'll bet Bill and Uncle Meredith and Uncle Anthony have too, and as soon as I get some help I'll find them and we'll all… we'll all be okay.' She was shivering violently now and using her hands, not only to keep the cold at bay but to control her shuddering shoulders. I think she must have been in shock. So much so, that she did not notice the dark shapes crawling out of the shadows. From between the rocks and from a sea cave and from behind a tree, dortriger were emerging. They crept silently and softly towards her.

'Elsa. Elsa… Ayr,' I cried, 'take me to her, take me to her!' Panic rose in my voice as they inched towards her. The mermaids had saved Elsa but they had also delivered her into the claws of the dortriger, though whether by chance or design I could not tell.

'Hark! I am called!' said Ayr. Elsa, the dortriger and the beach all dissolved. I was back in the cave, with the sound of gulls and waves in the distance and the steady breath of salt wind upon my skin. I could see Ayr in the vague half light. She began to float away, towards the entrance, and vanished as she met the light.

'And what of my sister?' I spoke the words quietly, almost to myself, knowing it was too late for the spirit to provide a response. Loer and I followed the path of the Air spirit. We were nearly at the entrance when we heard voices. Holding ourselves tightly against the wet wall of the cave we inched forwards. The voices echoed down the cave, mixed with the sound of wind and rain. It was hard to hear all of what the voice's owners were saying but I picked up fragments.

'All is done as I commanded of you and your kind?' it was a man's voice that spoke.

'All tasks are done Master.' This was Ayr's voice, the sound of a thousand sighs, filled with sadness and regret.

'And the cargo?'

'Strewn to the wind and the waves.'

'And now… they are here?'

'It is done. I and other agents of the storm have brought them hither.'

'And the boy?' My heart stopped. I could only just hear the voice above the sound of the wind and the cries of the gulls, but I strongly suspected the man's voice belonged to Pendrogeth.

'He and all the passengers are ashore, washed up like driftwood, and scattered all round the shores of the Isle.' I breathed a sigh of relief. She had told the truth, but not wholly.

'Good. Your obedience may be rewarded. Now be gone!' ordered the man's voice. The figure of light and air reappeared as it backed into the cave. Her head turned, until she was looking straight at me, yet even as she saw me, and as our eyes met, so she began to fade from view and in seconds had disappeared altogether.

The cave was above a shelf of rock leading to the sea a few yards off. We could see the entire bay, with the Isle of St Michael directly ahead and beyond that, the castle of Ictis. Its walls were sheer and dark and it towered above the sea, ruling the land and sea before it with the still, all seeing power of a great mountain. Directly beneath us, at the shoreline was a row boat tied to the shore by means of a short rope and anchor. Next to the boat, sat on a rock, was a thin old man, dressed in rags, playing a flute. And walking up to the man, with his back to us, was Lord Pendrogeth. He was dressed as I had last seen him, in dark black robes that reached to his feet, and dragged behind him in a trail. In his hand he held a staff of wood and on his shoulder a crow perched.

'Are you the ferryman?' he asked of the old man.

'I am stranger,' said the man in a high-pitched, croaky voice.

'Then you will take me to Ictis.' It was not a question.

'Only the master may enter there stranger… or those he might call friend.'

'Oh, I see,' said Pendrogeth, seemingly amused by the old man's words, 'well then you should grant my request because, you see…' the humour fell from his words like a veil '… I am the master of Lyonesse.' The old man pondered his words before replying.

'Why then you've no need of my boat. You can 'magic' your way across,' he said with a laugh. The old man stood up, flapping his arms around in wild arcs to indicate flying, or swimming or perhaps the conjuring of a spell. He had a thin body, a long, wispy beard and wild, unkempt hair. The effect of him bobbing up and down as he acted out his suggestion was quite comical. Pendrogeth stared hard at the man. He held a quizzical expression on his face for a second, then he burst out laughing and clapped his hands together. I breathed a sigh of relief, thinking the old man had had a lucky escape.

'My dear man, you are quite right, but this is not the time for tricks. Besides, my fellows will need passage also.' He pointed along the shore. Beyond the rocks was a long beach stretching for a mile or more. At its end lay Penzance, or whatever version of it existed on this island of ghosts. And from the town, walking down the beach towards us was a small group of men.

'You must go,' whispered Loer. I thought quickly. Could I swim to Ictis? What would I do when I reached it? I hesitated.

'You must prevent him from taking the seat of power,' urged the hare. 'The master's secrets, the ways of learning, they are within the walls of Ictis. Now go. Do not worry about me, I will find you when you need me.'

I crawled out of the cave and into the daylight, keeping behind rocks so that neither Pendrogeth nor the old man would see me. When I reached the water's edge I pulled from the satchel the Book of Water. Within seconds of holding the book it felt wet to the touch and a moment later water was pouring from it. As with the Books of Air and Earth there was a distinct feeling of energy, reaching from the book, through my hands, up my arm and into my body. But this was not a surge of raw power, like the Book of Earth had given me. Instead, whatever properties the book held, poured down my arm and into my whole being. I did not merely feel, I became fluid, and –strange as it seemed – had an overwhelming desire to merge with the sea. With some relief I sank into the water, feeling it seep through my skin as easily as if it were muslin cloth. There was another effect too, something that had not happened before. As I slipped into the shallow water, words and sounds poured forth from my lips. Words that would defy any attempt to write them, for they were not of any human language. I spoke, but the sound was like a waterfall, like the rain, like an ocean; gurgling, splashing, bubbling, roaring, yet whispering also. All the songs of that element. I did not pull the words from any knowledge; they welled up inside me and streamed outwards; an unstoppable, liquid language where words were as inseparable from the whole speech as a drop in an ocean of water.

And as I spoke this new language, I knew somehow, that I did not need to hold the book to use it, merely to keep it close and separate from the others, for it was the properties of this book and this alone that I needed. Still speaking the words as my head sunk beneath the water I placed the book between the belt of my trousers and my stomach. There was a rolling, disturbing, yet not unpleasant feeling as the book seemed to open up my stomach and pour its powers into me. Reaching my staff ahead of me and grabbing it with both hands I was propelled forwards. I felt every nuance of the current, every slight change in temperature as my body flowed and fluctuated in the water, riding its secret streams and currents.

I surfaced. I had covered a great distance in a matter of seconds. Steadily, keeping my head above the water, I moved towards the isle of Ictis. As I passed the rock of St Michael, Ictis hove into view. Now that I was close I could see that the 'castle' was really a citadel; beyond the outer wall I could see the roofs and chimneys of several buildings and beyond that the inner keep of the castle, towering upwards in a complex of towers, ramparts and walls peaking in a single round tower fronted by a level open-air court. At the bottom of the castle walls, leading straight into the water were steps, and at their top a portcullis gate flanked by statues of lions hewn from the black stone of the island.

Pendrogeth and his companions were climbing aboard the boat, if I was to find a way in to the castle it had to be quick. I soon reached the steps and pulled myself out of the water. Behind me, I could hear the men talking, as the boat neared the island. A few more seconds and they would pass through the harbour gates.

Taking a deep breath I took a step towards the gate and willed the portcullis to open. But the portcullis remained stubbornly shut and there was no time to try and figure out how to open it. I picked up my staff and leapt back into the water.

Chapter 13

I swam down as far and fast as I could to ensure I would not be seen from the surface. Below me I could see where the steps ended and the rock dropped vertically, like a cliff, to the sea bed. Above me, the underside of a large row boat sluggishly pulled into the harbour, its oars breaking the surface in rhythmic patterns. The boat docked at the steps. When I was sure they had disembarked and my lungs could hold no longer, I floated upwards.

I surfaced as near to the boat as possible, to ensure the men would not see me. I could not see them either, but I could hear them all right and as they talked so I recognised their voices.

'We demand some answers Lord Pendrogeth,' said the voice of an elderly man.

'Answers, Dr Gonzales?'

Pendrogeth was instantly recognisable by the smooth, mock politeness of his voice.

'Do not try and make fools of us man. It has been quite clear to me ever since the storm broke that powerful and unnatural forces are at work. If I had not witnessed these events with my own eyes I should never have believed them. Yet, nothing that has happened seems to have been a surprise to you!' Pendrogeth let out a wry laugh.

'For pity's sake man!' It was another voice. I had to suppress a cry of surprise. The voice belonged to Uncle Anthony. 'My nephew, niece and brother are missing, possibly drowned. If there is anything you know about this place, or why we might be here then you must tell us.'

'Must?' Pendrogeth interrupted, 'all will be revealed

Tregenza… in time.'

'I have wronged my brother. I doubted him, and trusted you,' said Anthony quietly.

'It is a little late for that wouldn't you say? Your faith is given, and if you have any sense you will not change that now. You can only return to where we came through me and when you do you will have no memory of this place – should I wish it – and will sign your Estate to me as you have planned. Did you not plead with your brother many times to sell your Estate, entrusting the legacy of generations of Tregenzas into my hands?'

'How would you know of what passes between Meredith and I… Stephen!' Anthony said with disgust.

'Yes, Stephen. A spy in your own house, but a faithful servant to me. As you will be.'

'Never!' I heard a crow. It let out a long, croaking cry, which sounded unnervingly like a laugh.

'As I say, it is too late for such questions. Your will, Tregenza, is mine. Now, please, your quarters are ready.'

There was a low murmur of words, almost a whisper, mixed with the sound of wind and a rough noise that sounded like a chain grating against rock. The sounds and the words were as one.

Daring to look, I saw that Pendrogeth had turned to the gate, with his arms outstretched. The lion statues sprang to life at his command, letting out deafening roars. With a clunking, grinding of chains the portcullis began to rise, pulled by unseen forces. When it was fully open Pendrogeth commanded the men to enter. One by one they filed through the gates, cowering as they passed the lions, which paced up and down the steps, herding the prisoners (for that is undoubtedly what they were) into the citadel of Ictis. As well as my uncle and Dr Gonzales I recognised the local vicar, the head huntsman we had seen on the moors the day we had arrived, and a couple of the local fishermen. When they were all inside the gate, the lions, having done their master's bidding, returned to their stations and in a moment had turned back into statues. I watched Pendrogeth's back recede into the darkness as the portcullis drew slowly down.

I had to grab my chance. Pulling myself quickly out of the water I made a dash for the gate. The portcullis was low now, but there was still enough space for me to roll under and I was about to dive onto my side, ready to roll under the gate, when I froze. Was it instinct that stopped me? The gate was rolling down a little too slowly, Pendrogeth was walking away, but not quite fast enough, and as I dived had he turned his head? Something was wrong. I sensed – a trap. Pendrogeth turned, thrusting his staff towards the gate. The portcullis smashed down.

'Damn you boy!' he cried. He uttered another incantation, thrusting his arms upwards. The portcullis rose in a second.

I started backwards, falling over myself as I tried to stand. As he strode back into the daylight I got a good look at his face. Thin, pock marked skin stretched across his skull. It was a mask of death yet his yellow eyes were alive with hate and lust. I was mesmerised for a heart stopping, near fatal moment as he stormed out of the gates, raised the staff over his head and unleashed from it a wave of raw power.

Whatever came forth from his staff was invisible, yet the very air in front of it collapsed in a wave of distortion as it raced towards me. I dived backwards, tumbling into the boat and falling clumsily into the water. He strode forward, raising his staff again. Then there was a loud 'clunk' inside my head, and I was engulfed in blackness. When I came to, my head was throbbing with dull pain and a warm trickle of blood was pouring down my face. The boat lay in pieces all around me. I was weak and dazed, yet alert enough to know that another blow would surely kill me.

Pendrogeth was at the waterfront, towering over me. As I lay on the steps in the water, fighting to keep myself conscious, my eyes met his. He smiled, lingering over the moment as he raised his staff once more.

'Bill!' cried my uncle. 'Run!' Anthony ran out of the castle and lunged at Pendrogeth grabbing the staff and knocking him over. Pendrogeth was caught off guard for a moment, but with a mutter of some spell under his breath, composed his powers and hurled my uncle back up the steps with inhuman strength. Anthony landed with a loud groan. Then the dark magus turned his attention to me once again. I didn't wait for him to finish his incantation; I immediately plunged into the water and swam into the depths.

From my mouth the language of water poured forth, welling up from the book, surging from it, up through my body and out of my mouth. It was unstoppable, a spring of blinding, intoxicating power. The more of this language I spoke the faster I swam, quickly passing the end of the steps and hurtling down the undersea rock face as though it were a cliff.

Pendrogeth's power exploded in the water like a bomb. The water shimmered and trembled with the might of its force. I was pushed downwards, feeling its power squeeze my flesh. But when the blow's power subsided I was unhurt.

Pendrogeth unleashed several more of his blows into the water. Sand on the sea bed swirled into clouds, shaken by the sudden violence; fish that had been idly cruising the reef, jolted into spasms when the bolts hit, then collapsed in the tremor and floated serenely to the surface. I waited for while, till I was sure that Pendrogeth would think I was either dead or had escaped, then moved, swimming quickly along the seabed and out towards the mainland, away from Ictis. I heard, and felt more tremors in the water, but they were far behind me.

I broke the surface when I felt I was a safe distance away, gasping for air. He was still there, standing on the steps. He was looking out to sea – towards me – and reading from a book. Then Pendrogeth walked off the steps and onto the water and across the surface. When he had walked a few yards he stopped walking and simply floated above the water, his staff held aloft.

In an instant, the weather changed.

A cold, harsh wind started to blow, billowing Pendrogeth's black robes around his body. The sky, which had been grey and dark a moment before, lightened and thickened as a blanket of white-grey snow descended on Ictis; a great web of icy chill, with Pendrogeth at its core, spread its way steadily across the bay. I felt it in the water, a sudden shock of icy current penetrating my clothing and freezing my flesh.

Taking a deep breath I dived and fled, but had gone no more than a few yards when a shadow overtook me. Above me a sheet of ice was forming, spreading quickly across the water. Thrusting my staff forward I lunged through the now freezing water making for the shore as fast as I could. But Pendrogeth's magic was fast and strong. A web of numbing ice, now stretched all the way to the mainland. I was trapped.

I heard a crunching sound above as he landed on the ice, almost directly above me. Muffled laughter echoed through the ice.

'Do you hear me boy? Don't you want to come out to play? You can't stay down there forever can you?'

I made to swim towards the harbour at Penzance, at least to get away from him. I stretched my arms out, waiting for the surging power to take me forward, but my arms were shaking and my fingers, wrapped around the staff, had precious little feeling left in them. My brain was slowing, steadily turning to ice as surely the water around me.

I heard his voice again coming from directly above.

'There's no fight in you boy.' Fight? Did he think that in mocking me I would come to him and let him have the pleasure of killing me in cold blood. 'Come on boy. What can I do to you? You who hold such powers. Don't you know how to use that which you possess?' he taunted. I tried to focus my mind, but everything within me, even my thoughts, were slowly freezing. I sank to the bottom of the seabed and moved, foot by foot, towards the harbour.

Once inside the harbour I could see the hulls of boats in the ice white ceiling above me. Three of these hulls were very large. They rocked gently in the wind, grating against the ice sheets that threatened to still them in its icy grasp. I lunged upwards, breaking the surface by a large anchor chain. My frozen hands grabbed the chain links as though they were life itself, straining with every fibre of my being I managed to pull myself up. Once I was clear of the water I climbed faster and in a moment was aboard the ship.

I took a quick look around. There were two other ships; warships by the look of the cannons jutting out of the upper decks, and a small flotilla of fishing and lobster boats.

On the furthest point of the harbour, a ramparted jetty jutted out into the sea and upon its walls stood a group of perhaps twenty men, looking out to sea; shouting and pointing. They were a motley bunch; some wore navy uniforms; others were dressed in simple smocks and trousers, others had long coats, tri-corn hats and large thick belts with pistols and swords shoved into them. Some were clearly English, others were natives of more exotic shores; mulattos and corsairs amongst them. Like the boats, the men had come to this place from across the seas, and the centuries.

''Tis the master returned!' shouted one man.

''Tain't 'im,' insisted another. 'The time 'as come for a changing. That is a new master bringing this power. Look, see 'ow 'e makes 'is way across the spreading ice.'

'Wass 'e doing? Seems like e's 'unting someat!'

'He is. He's hunting me!' I shouted. They all turned.

'I am your true master's nephew and his rightful heir.' For a moment the men said nothing. Several of them wore expressions of disbelief, even amusement.

'You're of the magi are you?' asked one man.

I didn't get a chance to answer. The men were now pointing and shouting at something on the other side of the harbour wall. They stood back. Pendrogeth's head, then body glided into view as he floated above the harbour wall surrounded by his crows who heralded his arrival with 'crawk's and 'squark's.

Ducking behind a wool sack I immediately began groping with numb fingers in the sodden satchel until my fingers connected with the Book of Earth. With trembling fingers I switched it with the Book of Water still tucked into my belt. I felt no less wet or cold, yet in an instant, in place of numbness and fear I felt in the core of my soul an animal, untamed anger. My chattering, frozen teeth let out a growl.

'Quick Master!' I turned, my keen eyes focussing through a fog of falling snow and finding Loer on the jetty.

'Don't let him tempt you. Run!'

'Here I am boy,' he came down to land, floating gently on to the harbour wall, to the amazement of the assembled crowd of sailors, soldiers and brigands.

'You might use it now might you not boy?' He scoured the harbour. His staff was raised, poised to strike.

'Run Bill, run.'

Walking towards the harbour were Stephen and Trinkle. Their friend the dortriger followed, lugging the wine barrel on his shoulders.

'You're not allowed 'ere monster,' shouted one man.

'Nor you hare,' said another. For a split second I was torn between running and fighting but with enormous self control I quelled the images of violence running through my mind and focussed the power of the book into my body. I took a last glance at Pendrogeth.

'The time for running is almost over,' I whispered to myself. I bounded along the deck and leapt into the air, catching a rope and swinging onto the great beam at the base of the sail rigging. I ran down the entire length of the beam and leapt a great height and distance from the ship to the harbour wall. In seconds I had reached the hare.

'After him!' shouted Pendrogeth. With Loer at my side I ran full pelt into the narrow, winding streets.

Since Elsa and I had arrived in Cornwall we had visited Penzance more than once and I had begun to know it a little. But this Penzance, the Penzance of the ghost island, was as strange as it was familiar. In form and character it was the same place, but I didn't recognise a single one of the buildings. Rough cottages, made of huge granite bricks nestled in between tall timber framed buildings with wooden roofs. All of the buildings were very old in style, yet in paradox, looked newly built. The overall effect was of the harbour's whole history been crammed together in a single moment. The streets were busy, the inhabitants of these buildings having been drawn outside by the sudden arrival of the snow. We ran down one street, then another, taking turns whenever we could.

After a few minutes we stopped and looked behind us, daring to hope we had lost Pendrogeth. But above us was a crow, circling and crying, clearly giving our position away to our pursuers. Besides, we had left a trail of noise and commotion a child could follow and sure enough, Pendrogeth appeared behind us, with Stephen, Trinkle and some other men. I cursed under my breath. As we ran down another alley he was shouting:

'Gold for the boy. Twenty pieces to the man that catches him.' Our only hope was to make our way through the town, up the hill and into the country. We ducked and dived, turning into an alleyway here, leaping a fence there.

More than once we met small groups of men who had been stirred by the commotion, or had heard Pendrogeth's offers. Followed closely by one such group, we scarpered down an alley and found ourselves in a terraced row of houses on a steep hill. There was a commotion from around the corners of both ends of the street – ahead as well as behind and one stubborn crow remained above us, annoyingly calling to its master. From the top of the hill came the sound of numerous boots, their hobnails clammering on the cobbles. It was the only sound in the snow filled air. With a curse I noted that the street behind us was nothing but a sheet of speckled white, patterned by my boots and the hare's tell tale prints.

Quickly as I could I grabbed the Book of Air. My arm felt hollow, my body light. As though summoned by the book, a gust of wind arrived from nowhere, speeding through the narrow street. From my mouth came a high, breathy whistle. It seemed not have come from me at all – but to be an echo of a wind rushing through some distant cave. Without meaning to I found I had raised my staff over my head and brought it down in one swift arc. The wind, gathered from all around, hammered at the thick wooden door of the nearest house. It rattled for a moment and then collapsed inwards, ripped cleanly off its hinges. I stood still for a moment, quite stunned. Then, gathering my wits I pointed the staff skywards. I aimed at the crow, which had been joined by a friend, equally keen to tell of our whereabouts.

'Crawk, crawk,' they cried, sounding jubilant, as though they were shouting: 'Here they are, here they are,' over and over again. The wind raced through my staff and in one powerful jet of air, blew the crows fifty yards or more into the air. They tumbled over and over, trying to get control of themselves.

'After them… ' came a cry. Without looking to see who might be calling after us Loer and I ran through the doorway, through a small, cosy living room, through the kitchen and straight out the back of the house. We found ourselves in a tiny yard, which led to another narrow street. At one end lay the road, at the other a wall. The road echoed with cries and footsteps. I decided we should take our chances over the wall, or would have but for the hulk of a man who had appeared from nowhere, and now blocked our way. He wore black, buckled, knee high boots, a thick belt, a long buttoned coat, leather jerkin and tricorn hat over his immense frame. Every piece of his clothing was as black as his long wavy hair and round, glaring eyes. His beard though, was red and tweaked into two forked points. He had a sword, a dagger and pistols tucked into the front of his belt. He grinned, flashing a mouth of gold and rotten, yellow teeth.

'Well now, what 'ave we 'ere?' He looked, and sounded, every inch how I imagined a pirate would look, right down to the mad, gleeful look in his eyes, his many ringed hands and the two flintlock pistols he was pointing at me.

'I… I'm a friend of Bob Trelawney's,' I forced the words out.

'Are ye now?' he said as he cocked one of the guns and

raised it. There was a loud 'bang' and a 'whizz' sound as the shot raced past my ear. I spun round. Two men, deck hands by the look of their striped shirts and baggy trousers stood a few yards off, eyeing me like hungry, wild dogs.

'Thass juss a warnin,' said the pirate. 'One step and the next'll find your head.' There was the sound of a scuffle on the other side of the wall, then two things happened at once. Some more men came round the corner and joined the two in front of us, no doubt drawn by the gunfire. One of them had a musket which I noticed – it seemed in slow motion – he was aiming at us. At the same time, from behind the pirate, over the wall appeared first one face then another. The pirate fired his other pistol, and in a flash had dropped both his weapons and from the inside of his long coat drawn two more.

'Damn. Missed,' he said. Up the street the man with the musket lay on the floor clutching his bleeding arm. The injured man's companions shuffled nervously, not knowing whether to attack or retreat. The men from over the wall jumped down and took a position alongside the pirate. Then another jumped down, and another and soon there was a whole gang of them. The pirate reached out, grabbed me by the shoulder and in one movement pulled me behind him where a man was waiting with cupped hands for me to use as a toe hold. I climbed up, grabbing the arm that was reaching down to help me.

Then I saw the face of the man whose arm I held. It was a face I knew. Only the last time I had seen that face it had been nothing more than a skull, covered by a mask of decomposing flesh. I tried to recoil, but it was too late for he held my arm firmly and was pulling me towards him.

'Do not fear young Master Bill. I am John Tanner, Captain of the *Seahawk*,' he said. On the other side of the wall were the mariners of the *Seahawk*, queuing to get over the wall and join the fight that had broken out between them, the pirate and my pursuers.

'At 'em lads,' shouted one of the crew, and was greeted by

a hearty cheer.

Loer jumped over the wall, helped by unseen hands.

Captain John winced and grimaced at the sounds of crunching, thumping and shouting. He tried to pull me down the alley, away from the trouble, but I stayed grounded to the spot. This man had saved Elsa and I at Lamorna, it was true. But then it was his ship that brought us here, and apparently under Pendrogeth's orders. Now it seemed he and his men had saved me from my pursuers. None of it made any sense. Reading the confusion in my eyes, he grabbed my shoulders and placed his face inches from mine. He stared straight into my eyes.

'I know what you must be thinking lad, but I have always been your Uncle Meredith's true servant both in this place and when called to aid him in the land of the living. He made me promise to keep you safe and keep you safe I shall. Remember Lamorna Cove.' His gaze was steady. To trust this man was a risk. Nevertheless, one I took. Any enemy of Pendrogeth's, I reasoned, had to be an ally of mine and if he and the *Seahawk* had been under Pendrogeth's control at sea, they certainly weren't now.

'But Pendrogeth… ' I said.

'Ne'er mind 'im. The lads'll cause a distraction and then slip into the shadows like they was never there. Meantime we'd best get you away young Bill. We'd best get you to the Admiral!'

John Tanner, Loer and I ran through the maze of snow filled streets, stopping occasionally to make sure we were no longer followed. Before long the ghost town of Penzance lay behind us and we were trudging through thick snow onto the moors.

Chapter 14

The snowstorm had robbed the day of most of its light and after a few hours of walking, what little remained began to fade as night descended. We walked for many miles, sometimes on the road, but frequently climbing over stone walls and heading across the moors; the wind and snow covering our tracks almost as soon as we made them. After a time we saw a faint orange light ahead of us; a light coming from the window of a low, stone building.

The Admiral was a run down, ancient inn; its walls of thick granite supported a crooked roof of large irregular slates, at the top of which a chimney billowed smoke into the night air. From the grubby windows came the glow of firelight and a chorus of voices. Taking a last look round to ensure we hadn't been followed, John ushered us through the door.

The inn was as ramshackle inside as out. Several thick wooden pillars supported low beams, preventing the smoke stained roof from falling in. Arranged in between and around the pillars were benches and tables covered with pipes, tankards and plates. Every seat was occupied, but so dark was the room that I couldn't see most of the Admiral's customers, just their beards and hats lit by the few lamps and candles that stood on the tables or hung from the beams.

Table by table the men ceased their talking and drinking, till the only sound was the gentle crackle of the fire. John pushed me gently forward and, without warning, pulled my hood back to reveal my face.

'Well ain't 'e the spit of the master?' said a voice, breaking the silence. The whole pub gave up a rousing cheer. Several of the men left their benches and came up to greet us, tousling my hair and patting me on the back. The clients of the Admiral were dirty, scruffy and mean looking, but they were smiling and seemed genuinely pleased to see me.

'You found 'im then,' spoke a voice from the shadows. Bob Trelawney stepped into the light cast by the fire.

'That I did, but not without some trouble,' said John Tanner. 'Is everyone 'ere?'

'Every man I could find that's still loyal to the master, or least to 'is kin,' replied Bob.

'Better the loyal few then. Now listen up you all!' John shouted. The men sank back into the shadows, taking a seat or standing against pillars so that John had a clear space in which to stand and talk.

'You'll be wanting to know why Bob 'as called you to the Admiral. These dark times, the cause of 'em ain't the master. I should know, I 'ave been in 'is service these past weeks in the land of the living. No, 'tis due to a certain Lord Pendrogeth. Like the master and many Tregenzas afore 'im , this Pendrogeth is of the magi. How he came by the powers is anyone's guess, not in the normal way of things to be sure. Don't matter, we are where we are. This Pendrogeth is well versed in the craft. Difference is, e' ain't no good not by a long measure of rope. 'Tis 'im that's brought this discord in Lyonesse and on the mainland of the living too. Fishnets are catching nought but seaweed and flotsam, crops is blighted and not growing. All by his hand… and more besides. I do believe 'twas 'im that brought the storm and for my part me and the boys were powerless to resist his magic!'

There were cries of dismay, even disbelief.

'But 'ow can it be? Ow can 'e do these things without the books?' asked a voiced from the crowd.

'He has his own books,' I said.

'That's not possible! The books is handed from generation to generation.'

'I'm afraid it is possible,' I replied, thinking back to mine and Elsa's visit to the museum. Miss Ariel had told us of Pendrogeth's excavations at sea, of how he had found sealed chests of books. The site of the excavation was where the Isle of Ictis had once stood. 'He has his own books and he's learning more of their uses as each hour passes.' John Tanner nodded.

'What's more, Pendrogeth seeks the seat of Lyonesse and is already on this island. Even now 'e gather 'is forces and makes his allies. That is why Bob has gathered you 'ere,' he said.

'And the master?' asked a voice from the shadows. John gave me a worried look.

'I'm afraid I 'aven't got good news on 'im either. As some of you know the master called me back into the world of the living. 'Is will was that I should find the *Hawk's* treasure trove, believed by many to be at Lamorna Cove. That we didn't do, though we might 'ave got close.' John glanced at me. 'Anyhow, at the Festival of Lyonesse the master was taken by Pendrogeth's crew, tied to the Fool's throne and pelted with rotten vegetables. After that what should happen but the *Hawk* appeared, and some of its crew. But called by who? I thought it 'ad to be the will of the master. But I fear it weren't. Then a mighty storm come, as though from nowhere and we was bid by a force o' strong magic to come back to Lyonesse, bringing our cargo of the living with us.'

There was a cry of horror. Clearly for the living to come to Lyonesse transgressed some ancient and important law.

'Anyhow, master was aboard the *Seahawk* when it went down. As is normal twixt this place and that, me and the boys went through the changing. As that 'appened I could not tell where he was to. What I do know is that amongst the number was Pendrogeth and his cronies. He used the *Seahawk* to get to Lyonesse. 'Twas strong magic, there was no way we could disobey.'

'Wait a minute,' I said, 'you were helpless against Pendrogeth?'

'We cannot refuse the power of the books lad.' said John. 'If 'e is as powerful as the Cap'n says then once 'e gets to us we're 'is and so is all of Lyonesse,' cried a panicky voice from the shadows.

''Twill be 'arder for 'im than for those that gives up willingly, and sure we can fight it. But each of us knows we cannot ignore the call of the books,' said one man gravely.

''Tis just a matter 'o time!' said another. There was a moment of silence as the men pondered their fate.

'But p'raps all is not lost?' said John. He tapped me on the shoulder. 'For on that same ship was this lad, the master's nephew. As is evident, me and some of the men got to 'im afore Pendrogeth did. But that's not all. Go on Bill. Show them.' I gave him a quizzical look. He raised his eyebrows and nodded his head downwards, pointing to my cloak. Of course! I thought. From under my cloak I produced the leather satchel. The crowd gathered round, necks were craned, fingers were pointed.

'Are they in there?' said one man, his voice wobbling with hope, but also awe.

'The master may not be 'ere. 'E may be gone,' said Bob. 'But 'is books and 'is blood are present, and that's enough for me. Pendrogeth ain't the master of Lyonesse. Nor will he be.'

'I'll drink to that,' said one man. The men shouted 'aye' in return.

'Whaddya say lad?' said John, picking up a tankard of ale and offering it to me.

'Well?' said Bob.

I took the tankard. 'I say 'aye'. Nor will he be!' and with that I took a long slug of the ale. The men cheered. From the shadows came the strain of an accordion inhaling. As the music started, a drum picked up the beat and the men burst into song.

I ran away to sea
For a girl that's fair and sweet
Yes, I ran away to sea
To sail the ocean deep
Her body's firm and fair

Her cheeks are lovely pale
And you've never seen a prettier sight
'Less you've seen her in sail

Oh the Seahawk, *the* Seahawk
I'll follow to th'end of days
Till she rests on coral beds
I shall be her slave
She'll be my mighty mistress
I'll be her loyal knave
And she can take the heart of me
To a watery grave…

'Lucky you found 'im,' said Bob to John Tanner, shouting above the singing.

'Weren't hard as young Bill left a trail of trouble, and as Forkbeard can find trouble without even trying, sure enough they ran into each other! Didn't 'elp 'imself by carrying 'is Familiar,' said John pointing to Loer.

'Am I to be your Familiar? This would explain the nature of my dreams. It would be an honour,' said Loer, his words echoing in my head.

'What's a Familiar?' 'I said, 'and who is this Forkbeard? Is he the man who rescued me from Pendrogeth?' I said, recalling the giant of a man with a long beard, dyed red and tweaked into two tails.

'Come lad. There's a lot of explaining to do and plans to be made. You and yer Familiar sit down in a quiet corner. I'll fetch rum and vittles,' said Bob.

'Erm, rum might be little strong for the lad?' said John.

'Oh. Yes. I'll fetch ale too… with water added!' said Bob, looking quite embarrassed.

John led me away into a dark corner of the inn, and sat me down on rickety old bench before going off to help Bob find food and drink. Loer sat at my feet. We shared the table with a short, thin man who promptly introduced himself, holding out a hand so thin and bony it resembled nothing so much as a claw. He wore many rings, some were gold, but others had precious stones inlaid, which twinkled in the dark. I guessed that none of the rings were being worn by their original owner. He had masses of wiry black hair, a beard, a huge pointed nose and two enormous eyes. He puffed steadily on a pipe.

'Jethro's the name.'

'I'm Bill and this is Loer.'

'Oh we knows 'im already and more of 'is kind. Them that has kept close company wiv the master knows 'is kind and knows not to be afraid of such creatures, though they are strong in magic.'

'Why would you be afraid? He's just a hare.' As soon as I said these words I realised how false they sounded. Loer was a great deal more than that which he appeared to be. His very being sung of the powerful, magical forces that ruled the island.

'Sho! you're alive are ye?' said Jethro. He sounded like a crow might, if it could talk, and in spite of his Cornish name, spoke with an accent heard in London's docks more often than the ports and inns of Cornwall. 'Dya mind if I…?' and he pointed to my chest. At first I wondered what he wanted. Then I remembered Bob's shocked face when he had realised I was alive. I nodded. Jethro leant forward and placed his claw like hand on my chest. When he was satisfied I had a heart that was still beating he sat back with a look of total awe in his face. A shiver ran down my spine. So lively and likeable were these characters that it was easy to forget that under their shirts and coats not a single heart was still beating. I was in the company of the ghosts.

'And you're… um…?' I couldn't bring myself to say the word.

'Dead? Oh, yesh, as a dodo,' he nodded and grinned, or rather grimaced, as most of his teeth were missing (this made his speech slightly slurred, he pronounced some of his s's with a 'sh' sound as though he was drunk, which for all I knew he was). Those few teeth he still had, glinted with gold and silver.

'How did you di… come to be here?' I asked, 'are you a pirate?' I asked. Jethro was taken aback.

'I've never been sho insulted in me life,' he squawked. 'That Forkbeard what you have met, 'e is a pirate lad. When he sailed he'd set on any ship wiv 'is men like a pack of hungry dogs; English, Spanish, freetrader, warship or cargo – it din't matter to Forkbeard and 'is men. If you'd see 'im fly the skull you give'sh up what you've got and then pray 'e won't take yer life as well. That is a man wivart loyalty to no flag and no cause but 'is own greed, 'cepting the master of course 'oo 'as been kinder and more forgiving than many might to his sort. No, I am glad to say I ain't a pirate. I'm of the *Seahawk* lad. One of Cap'n John's men, a few of my comrades I believe you 'ave already met. We are freetraders. What is commonly called smugglers.' Jethro looked at me intently to see if I was following. 'We take'sh goods from folk that want to sell 'em and make sure they gets to folksh that want to buy 'em. We make sure this enterprise can 'appen wivart either party 'aving to pay extortionate taxes wot is unfair and contradictory to the interests of good business. That was me life and a good one at that. I come to be 'ere 'cuz I went down with the *Seahawk* I did.'

'You've been here all those years. How long ago was it?' I asked. His eyes bulged and rolled. He stroked his beard and then held up his finger.

'I've got no idea,' Jethro laughed.

'I couldn't tell you if it was one year or a thousand. Time in Lyonesse is not like the mainland of the living. Time is different 'ere lad, not for us to understand. What I do know is that I 'ave been 'ere all that time and unlike some of me crewmates never gone back to the mainland of the living. I dunno why I weren't called, probly 'cuz I ain't much of a sailor, though I am 'andy in lots of other ways,' he tapped his large, pointed nose and winked. 'You know, it ain't so bad being 'ere. The worst of it is that we died wivart ever spending our ill gotten gains,' he sighed.

'The treasure of the *Seahawk*! It's rumoured to be at Lamorna!'

'Din't John say 'e was called to the mainland of the living to 'elp find it? Well I'm surprised there's anyfink to find! The only man 'oo knew where it was, was Davey Jenkins. 'E went down wiv the *Hawk* same as us. But as 'e 'aint 'ere wiv the rest of us we've always assoomed he'd got ashore and taken the treasure and lived his life a rich man… as he was entitled to seeing as none of us could enjoy the fruit of our labour.' I thought back to mine and Elsa's visit to the museum of St. Ives.

'But one man did survive – it must be the same man – he died not long after he came ashore. Before he died he tried to tell those that had rescued him where the treasure lay – there was a poem… '

''Tisn't a poem lad, it's a riddle. We crew knows the riddle. When put together wiv Davey's map – which was full of symbols and dates – anyone could find the diamonds.' He noticed the look of confusion on my face. 'Oh yesh lad, forget ideas of gold and silver sat in a mighty chest. 'Tis all in diamonds. None of us could carry or easily hide gold and silver. Many a smuggler and pirate knows, put 'yer money into stones! Easy to carry, easy to hide!'

'How is it Captain John doesn't know where his own treasure is?' I asked.

'Oh lad, ye've got a lot to learn. For a start the treasure don't belong to one man, the booty is shared between the Cap'n and his crew. Now the Cap'n trusted Davey, as did we all, and Davey was given the task of hiding the booty. 'E created the riddle and drew the map, which was put in the possession of the Cap'n, 'oo could find the treasure if 'e needed to. You see, if ever 'ed been caught they might 'ave tortured it out of 'im. None of the rest of us knew the location either, for the same reason and besides, though we trusted each other, who knows who might tell a sweetheart or even the law – under duress you understand. But, if the Captain ever wanted to find the booty he could do so 'imself, or even pass any of us the map if 'e was captured, and we could find it as long as we had the map and knew the riddle. For neither made any sense wivart the other. Clever ain't it?' Foolproof!

'So where's the map?'

'Alright, not quite foolproof. The Cap'n 'ad the map when the ship went down but it 'erm, got lost,' said Jethro.

John Tanner had been called back to the land of the living to help Meredith locate the treasure. That was why he had been at Lamorna!

'And the only man who knew for sure didn't die like the rest of you. He made it ashore and would have had a Christian burial.'

'Well 'e ain't 'ere is 'e? One fing I do know, 'e didn't go down wiv the ship. Every man, woman or child on this island 'as got one fing in common,' he leaned closer, his massive eyes were like dark pools, 'not one of us died of illness. Not one 'ere died of sickness, or gun-shot or at the end of a cutlass. Every one of us was taken by what you might call natural forces, rather than causes. Some is men lost in the mines by way of flooding or rocks. One man was caught in a bog and sucked into it. But for the most part we drowned – them that's fallen off of a boat, them that's gone down wiv a ship. It's like the sea was claiming us for its own… and 'ere we must stay in the twilight 'twix life and death, till the master that controls them forces wot claimed us 'as decided our time is up.'

'Jethro, I think the treasure is still there. Pendrogeth nearly killed me in a cave near Lamorna. There was a ghost there. Perhaps he was guarding treasure… '

'It's possible Bill,' said John, as he placed a plate of meats, cheese and bread in front of me. Bob Trelawney joined us, carrying tankards of frothing ale. 'That's where your uncle thought the diamonds were. We were going to wait till after the Festival of Lyonesse to really explore those caves. As you found out, the tides are fierce, yet on a particular moon, and at a particular date there'll be parts of those caves that could be reached that'll be flooded most of the year. The riddle would lead us to think that after the mid summer moon, we could get in there.'

'But why didn't you just explore them anyway. I mean, you couldn't… you know… '

'Die by drowning? No, but if I swam in those caves a hundred years I'd never find the treasure, not in the dark.'

'John, the man who came ashore at Lamorna, he said the treasure was near the quarry?'

'Thass right lad and that's what makes me think the treasure is at Lamorna. The riddle don't mention Lamorna directly, but it does mention the quarry of stone, and Lamorna's the only place in Penwith where there *is* a stone quarry:

> *Racing, jumping, running fast*
> *In shadow it shall be found*
> *In mid-summer moon, deeply cast*
> *Yet sleeping gently in the ground*
> *Who was the first but now is last*
> *Will lead the way by quarry of stone*
> *The face of the future shall become the past*
> *And then the treasure trove's your own*

It made no sense! How could something be racing and jumping, yet sleeping in the ground? But perhaps the riddle did indicate that the treasure could only be found at specific times, as it made reference to the moon. The tides are controlled by the moon and can be stronger or weaker at different times of the year. Could it be that on the midsummer moon the tides would be so low that all of the cave could be entered for a brief period and not just the parts Elsa and I had explored? A part that was full of water for the rest of the year. And if that was true, was the treasure buried there? If I ever returned to Cornwall – the real Cornwall – I would found out.

Bob held up his hand to silence our talk of treasure and indicated to Jethro that he and John needed to be alone with me. Jethro went off to join his crewmates and the other men, who were still singing and drinking.

'Talk of treasure's all very well young Bill. But it ain't treasure that's needed right now is it? This Pendrogeth, his power is growing. Even now he will be forcing his will upon those in Penzance. Them that was loyal to your uncle are here, but once he reaches them even they will be forced to bend to his will. Sure they may struggle, but without no force to counter his magic it's a fight with only one possible end. Our only hope is in those books and how you might use them. You have learnt something of their ways. But how much?'

'I am beginning to know them Bob, but I never made it to Ictis and I don't understand the languages in the books. There is no doubt, Pendrogeth knows more of their secrets than I do.'

I put the satchel on the table, and pulled the small leather books out one by one. Bob and John sat back, trying not to show their fear. I didn't touch the books, I just looked at them, hoping I suppose, for inspiration. If there was an answer, it lay within their pages.

'You are an apprentice on this isle Master, but you are not the first,' Loer spoke these words with great care. 'I am Sakrifis, one who has been human and animal, one who is of both the land of the living and this place, I have known this isle through many a master.' He was right, there must have been many 'masters,' each of which, in turn had to learn the ways of the magi. But how? From the previous master of Lyonesse, from the books of Ictis? Or was there another way?

'There is creature Master, like me, a creature of magic. He is as old as the books and once travelled with them from far off lands. He knows their ways. I am a creature of earth. He is of the sky and of the water. He is to be found within Ictis but not at all times. Pendrogeth may not yet know him. Nor do the menfolk know him, he converses only with the magi. If you can find him, or call hi... '

As Loer had spoken neither Bob nor John had looked at him. It dawned on me that neither of them actually heard what the hare had said. His words were in my head. What manner of creature? I thought, testing whether Loer might also hear my thoughts.

'To the eye he is half bird, half fish,' came the reply. I tried to picture what such a creature might look like, and in an instant realised I knew exactly what the creature looked like, and where to find the secret library of the magi.

I was about to say something to the others when the door to the Admiral burst open. Forkbeard strode into the inn, followed by some of the *Seahawk's* crew. He was panting heavily and was covered with snow.

'Now listen all… ' his voice boomed, '… and listen good ye varmints and scoundrels. I 'ope ye've got yerselves a plan for we ain't got much time. Pendrogeth now rules over Ictis and most of Lyonesse. 'E says the storm and the snow and all chaos is the anger of the gods, anger wrought because Master Meredith 'as forsaken us.'

'Well we know different,' said John.

'Thass as maybe, but who will believe it? Besides he has cunning this Pendrogeth. He has promised to right what's wrong. To bring order where there is chaos. He says he will do this in the old way. For 'tis nearly mid summer.' Time then, really was different in Lyonesse, the events at St Pirans had happened on the summer solstice in what the folk of Lyonesse called 'the land of the living.'

'The old way?' said Bob, his voice full of dread.

'Thass right. Sacrifice! Tomorrow he will prepare his magic. The day after tomorrow, in the open court of Ictis, the deed will be done where all can see it.' A murmur went round the assembly of men.

'That is old and dark magic,' said Bob, 'it requires the death of a human child.'

The huge pirate took his tricorn hat off. He looked directly at me.

'O, 'e's got one alright. A young girl, washed up by the storm.'

All eyes were upon me now. I stood up but found I could not speak. After a long moment, during which I tried – and failed

– to gather my thoughts, I ran past Forkbeard and into the night. As I ran out I saw John move towards me, but Bob held him back.

'Give the boy a moment will you?' he said.

When I was a long way from the inn, I collapsed in the snow. I felt like I was going to be sick. With shaking fingers I searched within the satchel and found the Book of Air.

'Ayr!' I cried into the night 'Ayr!' The wind and snow whirled and howled around me. In the night I could neither see nor sense her, yet with my firm grip on the book I pulled at its powers with a desperate need. I knew she would come. She had to.

'Master, you have called… '

'Show me spirit. Where is my sister?'

The snow and wind were sucked into the night, leaving a dark void, which lifted slowly, like the curtain of night revealing the dawn. Once more the tableau shown me was underwater only this time I was being shown something at the surface, something shaped like a box, or perhaps a crate floating amongst chunks of broken ice. But as the floating, indistinct shapes became solid, real, almost tangible – I saw that the 'box' was in fact a cage, seemingly suspended in the water. I was taken by Ayr to the very edge of the cage. Inside it, huddled into a corner was Elsa. The top of the cage was above the water line, clearly so that – if she stood – Elsa might breathe. But she had no need. He mouth was open, and I could see at her neck the faint ripple of the incisions the merpeople had made. She was breathing underwater, staring around with those green eyes of hers, (eyes that now had a light, almost transparent quality to them) and holding herself, though I believed out of comfort, she did not shiver against the cold.

As though on an invisible chain the cage suddenly jerked upwards, shaking Elsa out of her trance. She grabbed the rails of the cage as she was hoisted into the air. Then I saw indistinct shapes and sounds floating around me, gradually forming into people, buildings, the voices of a crowd.

I found myself in Penzance, among a crowd, standing at the quayside – the very place I had come ashore, when Pendrogeth had chased me from Ictis. And the dark magus was there, floating over the crowd, which included (though under guard) Anthony, Dr Gonzales and others. In one hand he held one of the books, in the other his staff. He was dressed in his black robe, with only his hands and face visible. The skin on his bony hands and skull was like a thin veil beneath which the purple and yellow workings of his flesh could be seen; sinew and muscle like meat in a butcher's window, purple vessels of blood and the grey of his bones and skull. Only his piercing eyes seemed alive; though yellow and ill they swept over the crowd with greedy intent. I could almost feel him absorbing the crowds' will, sapping its spirit and strength into himself. He seemed now a perverse parody of a vicar giving sermon to his congregation; a congregation that cowered in his presence, looking upon him with wonder and fear. And in the air next to him, held in the cage like an animal at a fair, was Elsa. Again, it took a while for Elsa to be adjust to 'air' breathing, but as soon as she did she found her voice.

'Your master has forsaken you,' Pendrogeth preached, 'but with the sacrifice of this young girl I may… '

'Don't believe him!' she shouted, 'it's a trap …' His head turned, like a puppet's head on a stick, so his body was towards the crowd but he was facing her. His eyes grew large, both with mocking and barely contained anger,

'I do not like to be interrupted,' he said turning his staff as though it held a cord around her neck. He had her in his grip, but her eyes glared back defiantly.

'My people will not allow you Pendrogeth… ' she croaked before he could silence her. And for a split second he looked confused.

'Your 'people' are dead or captive,' he said, then turned to his audience. 'This child will be the sacrifice, tomorrow we will make the preparations, then, on the next dawn, in the way of the old magic, her blood shall anoint the altar of a new day… ' His voice faded and the night descended once more.

'Lad! Bill lad!' the voice of John Tanner strained through

the howling wind. The glow of a lamp was swinging its way towards me.

'Ayr?' I said, but she was gone.

'Ye alright?' John's concerned face loomed out of the darkness.

'He's going to kill Elsa.'

'Tomorrow we'll… '

'No. Tomorrow I will travel alone. But in the night, when I am ready… we'll face Pendrogeth, together. Tomorrow night, in the early hours before dawn, you must gather the men at Lamorna Cove.' He smiled and nodded, offered me a hand, and pulled me out of the snow.

Chapter 15

Loer and I left at dawn the next morning. As we trudged through the snow the day crept slowly into existence, the night fading gradually to reveal a white quilt of snow upon the land overhung by a granite, featureless sky. It was a still and silent world that we faced; a world that had been covered in the cold, dark magic of Pendrogeth.

Loer and I made our way to the top of the nearest hill. A thin mist was forming, rising in clouds from the snow-covered ground, but we could just see Penzance, its spires and roofs coated with thick wedges of the night's snowfall. Having made our bearings we headed north. Progress was slow. The snow had drifted in places and nowhere was it thin or firm enough for us to move freely. As we climbed steadily the cold and effort of wading through the snow began to take its toll.

'This is no good,' I said between gasps for air, 'we'll never make it.' Loer hopped about in a circle, his long and wide paws effortlessly bearing him over the snow.

'A magus has many ways to travel does he not?'

He stood on his haunches and stared at me with his head cocked. He was right. Had I not seen Pendrogeth fly, or rather float through the air, as lightly and easily as a feather on a gentle breeze? I wondered if I could do the same. I reached under my cloak and took from the satchel the Book of Air. I immediately felt bouyant and sensed the force of air, a force coming from the book, which was all together lighter and fresher than the air around me. I tried to concentrate my mind, focussing the lightness I felt, mentally pushing myself away from the ground. I took a step forward, half expecting – or at least hoping – to rise into the air. But I was still glued to the snow. I tried this for a few minutes, imagining myself flying, willing my body to free itself of its weight. After a while the effort of focussing began to give me a headache. I cursed, throwing my staff into the snow.

'Too much effort Master,' said Loer.

'Maybe Loer, maybe.' I decided to rest for a few moments. I sat in the snow, looking back at the distance we had covered. It wasn't far for the time we had spent. Through the clouds of mist I could still see the Admiral and between it and ourselves a steady track of prints. I closed my eyes for a moment and breathed deeply, gathering myself for the next effort. If it didn't work I thought to myself, we would just have to persevere through the snow, though it would take a long, long time to reach our destination and no small amount of effort. I opened my eyes, ready to pick up my staff. But my staff had vanished. All I could see was mist. I gasped in shock and felt a lead weight in my stomach pulling me downwards. I landed deeply in the snow with mighty thud. Whilst I had rested I had still had the book in my hand. Without trying, or even thinking about it I had floated a good ten yards above the ground. But the moment I registered what had happened, I had fallen like a stone.I laughed out loud, a release from the shock of falling. And flying.

'I can do it Loer! I think the trick is that I must empty my mind. The thing is not to try.' It was like flying in a dream, it would come effortlessly, or not at all. If I thought about it, if I tried too hard, it wouldn't work. I picked up Loer, tucking him into me with one arm and the staff in my hand, holding the book in my other hand. I closed my eyes and waited. But of course it didn't work. How could I not try to fly, how could I not think about it when it was the very thing I was trying to achieve? My legs stubbornly clung to the snow.

'We must hurry Master!' said Loer, hopping out of my arms.

'Do you think I don't know that? Why do you think I'm trying to...?' My words of frustration faded to nothing. Loer ran several yards off and stood on his hind legs. His ears were pricked and I noticed the heckles on his neck were raised.

The mist was thick now, more of a fog, and we could no longer see the Admiral.

'What is it?' I whispered. I was answered by the distant 'craw' of a bird, probably a crow. Then another 'craw', and another, and then a whole crescendo. Though some way off I could tell there were many of these birds, if that is what they were.

I used the Book of Earth. One moment they sounded far away, the next quite close. Somewhere in the back of my mind I knew I was floating now, some distance above the ground. The hairs on the nape of my own neck now tingled with expectation. In between the 'craw' sounds, I could hear the air itself being beaten by the sound of many, many wings. The white mist was suddenly grey with great flapping shapes. An enormous flock of birds broke through the mists and descended upon me. I had no more than a second to cover my eyes as the first of them lunged their claws and beaks at my face. The birds pecked viciously at me from every quarter. Those that weren't attacking me directly had their claws around my staff and the book, tugging frantically to rob me of my only protection. The sound of their evil cries was almost deafening. And what is more their cries were more than the crescendo of craws and squawks. They were forming into a pattern. A rhythm. Words.

'Give us the books! Give us the books! Give us the books or die!' they screamed and all the time their beaks were stabbing at me relentlessly. The cloak and the clothes I wore were thick, but they would not offer protection for long. I had to act.

I drew the power of the Book of Air up through me like drawing a breath of pure air. When my very being felt fit to burst I threw my head back and opened my arms, with the staff in one hand and the book in the other. The birds fell back against each other, thrown by an explosion of energy that emanated from my very core. Now I could see the sky was full of them, not hundreds, but thousands of large crows. More than a few fell like rocks, stunned or possibly killed, but for every one that fell a dozen or more flew in to join the attack. I had the urge to run, but I couldn't, I was floating in thin air. Instead, with an effort of will, I shot upwards, faster than I could have hoped. I raced through the wall of black, flapping wings with my staff above me, knocking and bumping against those too slow to get out of my way. Within seconds I was above the dark cloud of crows. Looking down from far above them the crows became mere spots of black, like particles of dust forming into a thick cloud, a cloud which now swirled around in a shapeless, confused mass for a moment, before forming into a point, like a spearhead and racing towards me. I sent another blow downwards, only this time, almost unconsciously, I thrust my arm downwards as I released the energy of the Book of Air. This seemed to concentrate the force of the blow, which shot through my body, down my arm and out of the staff. The force blew the cloud of birds apart. I had no intention of letting them re-group. Without knowing how or why I could do it, I flew down into the centre of the birds and begun to swing my staff around in an arc. I spoke the words of the elemental language of Air, feeling the flow of its energy rise up from a storm that was within me and which I felt would tear me apart if I did not release it. The sounds that rushed out of my mouth were deafening and violent, as the fiercest of gales raging in a winter storm.

The air was moving swiftly around me in a circle, picking up the crows and the mist in a whirl of wind, till they blurred together in a grey rush of air and speed. The crows were helpless; as the vortex grew they were sucked into it, their wings flapping uselessly as they tried to escape. I rose upwards, all the time swinging my staff around, weaving a helter-skelter of air and birds.

When I was sure all the birds were trapped in the air stream I had created I rose above them and with one mighty blow from my staff smashed the cloud apart. The bird's bodies were thrown in every direction, spinning and somersaulting into the air till the wind could no longer carry them and they dropped like stones. Some lay in the snow, clearly dead, but most of them were just stunned, and with an unsteady gait walked a few steps off before taking flight, or simply stumbling off into the fog, pulling their broken wings along the ground. The mighty wind dissolved into the still fog. The air was silent once more.

I landed gently in the snow and with trembling hands placed the Book of Air back in the satchel. Though pleased to have survived I was horrified at what the book could do, and at how easily I had used it to turn my fear and anger into a force of destruction. When I looked at the twisted black forms of dead crows lying in the snow, I felt no victory, only sadness. Loer, who had been hiding behind a stone wall, bounded over.

'You must use the book, Master. They followed our tracks here and will do so again. They will return soon,' he said.

I knew, he was right. The crows were really only scouts, perhaps part of an entire web of dark forces that Pendrogeth was using to scour the land. For all I knew they might have followed Forkbeard's tracks to the Admiral. There had been a good few men in his company and I had no idea how long it had snowed after they had arrived the night before. They would find us again if we left tracks so I picked up Loer and tucked him under my arm. I didn't want to touch the book and some how knew I didn't need to. With my thoughts firmly on our destination we rose into the air.

Though hampered by the fog, we found our way. It was easy enough to get to the top of the moor and then we followed the stone walls, flying in a north-westerly direction down to the sea. When we came to the cliff top we followed its contour until we came to a headland I recognised.

'This is it Loer,' I said, and veered away from the sea until we found the woods that was the site of Lyonesse House in the land of the living. Of course the house was not there, all the buildings in Lyonesse were ghosts of buildings that had once existed in Penwith and the house was still very much in existence. But the cellar of the house, the place where we had first encountered the books, I reasoned had belonged to much older dwelling and if I guessed correctly was as much a part of the lost island as the so called 'real' world.

I recognised the small hill near to the site of the house and came down to land at the edge of the woods, roughly in the spot where the house stood.

We had reached our destination but now we had arrived I was reluctant to enter the woods, I had been expecting a building of some sort but there was nothing under the trees but rocks and summer plants. There was no building that I could see, just the eerily quiet interior of the wood. It made a very strange sight; the branches – in full leaf – hung heavily with a burden of snow, affording what protection they could to the summer blooms of plants on the woodland floor, which wilted and shrivelled in the cold.

My hand crept towards the satchel but by now I had no need to touch the books. In place of my hand, my mind reached within, delving into and finding the Book of Earth.

Loer sniffed the air.

'Listen Master.'

My eyes sharpened, my ears pricked up.

The sound we both heard was a 'crunching' sound, some way off, but closing rapidly. I found I could attune my hearing, focussing it like a searchlight to locate the strange noise. The sound we heard was feet stepping in the frost crusted snow and there were a good many of them. The rhythm of their feet was regular, akin to the beat of horse hooves. Who, or what, ever they were they were not at all hampered by the deep snow.

'Dortriger!' said Loer.

Loer bounded towards the woods. He hopped around until he found large hole between my hiding place (an oak tree) and a boulder. The hole looked like the sett of a fox or badger, but Loer had to take the risk. I rose into the air and dashed for the cover of the trees. I hid behind the thickest tree, floating effortlessly some ten yards in the air.

The dortriger appeared – a dozen or more galloping over the snow on all fours. They found Loer's prints. One of them lowered his face to the ground, sniffing.

In a dark rasp of a voice he said: 'His Familiar – it is a hare is it not?'

He followed Loer's prints to the set's entrance. The hole was big, large enough for him to crawl into. But he hesitated.

'What do you wait for? If it is not the hare we seek then it will make a meal anyway, quick but tasty,' said one dortriger. Several of the others grunted approvingly. I couldn't see his face directly but he was behaving cautiously, almost scared. I don't know what he was afraid of, and I'm not sure he did either. The creature put a tentative arm into the hollow, peered into it and when he felt confident enough, stuck the top half of his body into the hole. Yet he was hardly in before he let out a blood-curdling scream and bolted from the hole, falling over himself as he ran backwards. Across his face were three red lines of blood. Something had made three deep gashes across his face.

The other dortriger burst out laughing.

'A fox has had the hare and now will have you,' said one. The others laughed.

'No hare will go to a fox hole willingly,' said their leader, sounding suspicious.

'Unless it heard us coming,' said another, 'come,' he picked up his injured companion by the scruff of his neck, 'we'll find herbs and roots for poultice, you'll heal soon enough. Now let us hunt his boy!' And on they went.

The woodland regained its unearthly silence. I strained my ears, focussing on the set entrance, pushing my animal like hearing, reaching down the hole, into the darkness. I heard only silence, but sensed… I did not know what.

'A presence!' said a voice, finishing my thought. I almost fell to earth with the shock. The voice was not Loer's. It was high-pitched, croaking and very old. I floated down and stood at the entrance with my staff raised.

'Loer,' I spoke silently, using my thoughts.

'I am safe Master,' came the reply. The mysterious voice broke into cackling laughter.

'It is true, he is safe. But are you, young Master magus?' I poised my thoughts, my staff, my very being. 'No, no, no. You have nothing to fear from me. But the dortriger, they may return.'

Whatever it was it had seen off the dortriger and meant no harm to Loer. I crouched down on all fours and climbed head first into the hole.

The hole I had climbed into opened up into a chamber. I was able to stand freely and sensed that the chamber was quite large. Using my thoughts like fingers I opened and accessed the Book of Earth. I felt my pupils widen and my skin grow alert to the dry, cool air of the cave.

Without quite 'seeing,' I sensed Loer ahead of me and next to him, something shining and glimmering in the dark – something that absorbed, and wore, the light streaming through the hole I had climbed through. The 'shape' moved and like a dance hall mirror-ball, a hundred shafts of light illuminated the darkness. The owner of the voice was a bird of sorts, standing some three feet high and in shape, very much like an eagle. Yet in place of feathers it had scales and I noted, the tips of its wings and tail were more akin to those of a fish. Each scale was like a small coin of some rare and bright metal, shimmering white and blue, like sunlight on water.

'Braaarrrkkk,' it croaked, and moved its head from side to side in stiff jerking movements, eyeing me fully first with one of its perfectly round and glassy eyes, and then the other.

'An apprentice!' it said. 'Come to learn the way of the magi?'

'Who are you?'

'My name is not for you to know. I have met you before, though you did not know it. You came stealing secrets in the middle of the night, braarrrkkk.' He stretched his wings. I was almost blinded by the light reflecting off him. 'You have come again, and again, also to learn. No?' The bird-fish stepped sideways. Behind him was a door and on it a carved circle. I stepped up to the door and placed my hand on the sign. The door did not move, but began to shimmer as though I had disturbed a reflection on the surface of a pond. My hand met no resistance. I waved my hand around, searching for the solid door that I thought was in front of me. My touch obviously had an effect for the door continued to shimmer violently. Then it simply evaporated. I took a step forward into the darkness.

I reached out with my staff and found something hard ahead of me, something wooden by the dull 'clunk' sound it made. That had to be the table. I reached my left hand out. My fingers brushed over the soft leather spines of the books in Meredith's study.

I groped forward till I found the table with my fingers. I located the matches and lit the oil lamp. I had the most curious feeling. I had endured the storm, witnessed the sea changes and deep magic that were necessary to rent a hole in the world I knew and create a corridor to the island of Lyonesse. Yet here was a doorway that took a second to walk through. It made perfect sense of course. Meredith would have needed to travel back and forth between the two places frequently, and this was his gateway.

As the bird-fish creature moved into the lamp light its scale-feathers filled with the dull orange of the oil fed flame, as though the bird-fish were a lamp itself, or had no substance other than a self of mirror and crystal that absorbed, reflected and amplified the light around it. Though very bright, it was now bearable to look upon.

'Where do I begin?' I said.

'The magus must master three stages of the books, three ways to use the elements and all their qualities. The first is to use these elements to master oneself, to bend the powers to your will, to control your own body. Braarrk. Have you not already mastered this? Using the Book of Air to fly, to escape those that would pursue you? Sensing your way into this cave through the power of the Book of Earth? In your travels has this book not provided for you? The ears of the hare, the eyes of the hawk. He, he, he haaaah.' He let out a dry and croaking laugh.

'You saw me? But where... how?'

'What would be the point of studying for as long as I unless you can master a few tricks haaaa, he, he, braaark, braark.' I was a little annoyed at how amusing he found the whole situation. 'The second way is to control not yourself, but that which you have allowed to flow through your body... ' As he talked I was mindful of when I had swum through the water to Lyonesse, run through the streets of Penzance and flown through the air. I was indeed controlling myself at those times, but when I had fought the birds I had manipulated the very air around me.

'And the third way?' I asked.

'This is the hardest. Everything is of the elements young Master. Everything. You and I according to the will of our true selves are but a mix of these elements. For without will the elements are themselves only. For each of the elements would be unto itself and only itself were it not for the will, the force that separates or binds – that is what the magus must master.'

'I don't underst... '

'Will, Spirit, Essence. That which determines what each thing is, for as I say without it, the elements will gather unto themselves only.' I felt my brow furrow as I struggled to understand.

'So the magus must use his own will to control, to change, the will of Nature?'

'In a sense, but control is a false word, an illusion. It is not what is true. The magus knows that the will of Nature itself, neither the gods nor man, is the true master and he is its humblest servant. For he may master the elements, but he cannot alter the ultimate will of Nature, the will that truly binds or divides us,' I sensed some truth in what the bird-fish said, but still did not understand.

'Do not worry young Master. What I am telling you are the

rules of the game, mastering the game may take a lifetime…
sometimes several.' He laughed.

'You said the elements will gather unto themselves?'

'Braarrk, each will gather itself unto itself, only the will of
being can prevent this. Now see!' He cried, making me jump. He
spread one of his wings, (and it was astonishing how far his wing
span spread) and tilted the feathery fish fin tip towards me. The air
shimmered, then thickened into something not solid, yet
undeniably real.

What appeared was nothing more or less than a pool of
muddy water, albeit a pool of muddy water floating some three feet
in the air. Slowly the 'puddle' began to glow, throbbing with an
inner orange light.

'Observe. This is an illusion and an illusion only. There is
no spirit, no will, no essence, only the elements mixed,' said the
bird- fish. Like a goldfish bowl full of sediment, the puddle started
to clear as the 'muddy' elements sank to the bottom of the pool.

'See how the earth sinks, gathering itself unto itself, the
lowest, the basest of the elements. Brarrrk. Upon it everything else
must rest.' At the base of the apparition a thick layer of muddy
earth now rested. Above it, the last few specks of earth floated in
the eddy and flow of what could only be water. The water too now
'gathered' dripping, flowing, pouring out of what was left of the
primordial ball until the fuzzy, now very light ball had two lower
tiers. One of earth, and above it, another of water. On top of this
a fuzzy ball of light remained, hovering in the air.

'Over water and over earth, air. And lastly, the element
the magus knows to be the purest. The element of truth, of birth,
of destruction. See how it gathers itself, for all fire must by
necessity return to its source, the sun, this is why flames rise, and…
are you listening?' I was aghast, wide eyed and open mouthed at the
small sun now forming above the layers of earth, water and air.

'Four!' I barely whispered.

'Yes, though I doubt you have had reason to call upon the
Book of Fire, as yet. Now if we may contin… '

'I… I don't have it,' I could feel the blood draining from my cheeks, turning into lead and filling my stomach.

'But you have the books,' reasoned the bird-fish as though for me *not* to have the Book of Fire were an impossibility.

'No. When I received the books there were only three.' Nor, had there been a fourth book that night when Elsa and I had first come to Meredith's study. Perhaps it was here, in his study all along, I thought. The bird-fish must have seen my eyes searching the shelves.

'No, no. If it is not in your possession it would not be here. Too dangerous.' I gulped, audibly. There were more than one copy of the books.   What if Pendrogeth had it, or another copy? The bird-fish sensed my thoughts.

'Young Master. If Pendrogeth had the Book of Fire you would not be alive. This book is rare indeed.

Hmmm, if not in your possession, it is deep within Ictis, in a place where the master of Lyonesse keeps it safe. It is the most powerful of the books. If Pendrogeth has it your battle is lost.'

'Wait a minute!' I said, thinking out loud. Pendrogeth had taunted me, whilst chasing me from Ictis to Penzance. What was it he had said? Something about using what I possessed? Of course! He thought I had the book but had not yet garnered enough experience to use it wisely! That was why he had been so keen to hunt me down so quickly. He wanted to get to me before I could learn the proper uses of the books and the Book of Fire in particular. That was why he had covered the water in ice, to tempt me to use the Book of Fire!

Yet it was in his grasp and he did not know it.

'Be warned. It is the most powerful of elements, the most pure, and as I have demonstrated, the highest. There is no creation without fire, and no destruction either. To use the Book of Fire is to call on spirits, forces that cannot easily be tamed, it is a power that will go far beyond your intent if you do not take care. It may consume he who would be its master.'

'I'll cross that bridge when I come to it,' I said.

'So… ' said the bird-fish jumping nimbly onto the table. 'You can unleash what lies hidden within the books. You use their forces, changing your body, becoming a vessel for their qualities and when needs be, unleashing them. Now you must go further. You must use your influence upon an object, a being which has a will or spirit not of your making. Make your will stronger than others; you must call others to your will as surely as the sun calls the flame of a fire or the sea beckons the water of the river. Pendrogeth knows this. Each being is merely a vessel of elements, held together by will. It is the will that determines a things true identity, not its substance.

Now, use the Book of Earth. Call the animals whose composite is most base. But be warned, you must focus your call, if you draw on its power too long or too widely you will call dortriger. For this you may touch the book. To be near them is enough, but you are a novice.'

I took the satchel and placed it on the table. Reaching inside, my hand *knew* where to find the book. Before I had even taken it out I felt the creeping dryness that was its signature, a power that spread like roots into my arm, along my skin and into my body.

Just like the first time I had opened the book the atmosphere within the library changed, becoming thick and dry. I noted every spine of each book as my eyes flitted quickly across the shelves. I smelt the thick mustiness of the chamber, a cloying but not unpleasant mix of earth and ancient books, and heard the tiny clicks and scratches of insects in the earth around me. The more I listened the louder they became until the smell and sights of the place were forgotten entirely and my head was filled with a building crescendo of noise. My reasoning mind grew smaller, drowned out by the new strength of the force. This was so much more than I had felt previously. Before this power the 'I' that had opened the book threatened to shrink and vanish all together, until my actions would no longer have an author.

'You have connected with the creatures, now call them!'

said a voice from far away. This sense – the force I had become, for I no longer seemed to have an identity – merged with the crescendo of noises.

'I… must… pull… back,' said a voice, sounding very much like my own, but it was strained and very, very distant.

The noise built to a deafening pitch. In that moment I existed both inside my body and also in the walls of the chamber, that is the simplest way I can think to describe it. I was entirely confined in my body, I had never felt so completely awake and in touch with every fibre, every bone of my body, yet was at once and the same time outside, existing in the tiny forms of lice, spiders, flies and worms.

Like a rising flood the creatures seeped through the walls, onto the books and onto the floor. Between the flagstones the creeping, crawling horde scuttled and slithered towards me. I recall thinking how horrified I should be, or would be if I had seen this in my normal state. Yet for this new me, this was *not* horrifying, it was glorious. For I was the carpet of black, brown bodies that lay before me. I stretched out my right hand, palm up as though holding an invisible ball and pulled the seething mass into a column. The stone beneath my feet began to loosen as ants, spiders, lice, worms, beetles – every scurrying, creeping creature that lives in the earth – poured into the room, climbing the column, making it taller, giving it shape. And it wasn't just insects and worms. Mice and rats scuttled into the chamber, climbing over the seething carpet of lesser animals. Loer jumped onto the table.

'Are you sure of this?' he said in a shaky voice. The hare's enormous ears wilted and his eyes grew large with fear. I ignored him, focussing all my will on building the column. When it had grown to nearly my own height it began to take shape. A lump grew on top of the thing, becoming a globe, slowly, but surely taking the shape of a head. Stumps appeared where its shoulders were, growing and extending as thousands of insects ran its length and took their place in the form. Within a minute an exact mirror of myself stood before me, stretching out a hand of black and brown insect bodies to meet my own. The longer it stood the more precise its shape became. A gaping hole formed itself into a mouth, two craters became eyes and then, from these sockets the heads of two snakes pushed forth. Their eyes stared back at mine. For a fleeting second I lost control. I could see my 'normal' self standing before me, book in one hand, the other reaching out to touch my new body, the body I now inhabited, for in that second I saw my 'self' with the eyes of the snakes.

I snapped the book shut, was blinded for a second, then thrust firmly and immediately back in my body. The other 'me' collapsed, for it had no form now, it was just a heap of pests, busily making their way back to the earth from whence they had come.

The bird-fish stared at me with its un-blinking eye, its head still cocked. I stared back. There was no need to voice my thoughts, or his, or Loer's. Until that moment I had not known Pendrogeth, now I understood him only too well.

'Three ways of the magi young Master. With this knowledge and these books you must defeat the bringer of evil.'

Chapter 16

An almost full moon sat in the ink of the night sky, painting the island in a blue-white sheen of light. The snow clouds had passed and in their wake had left the island coated with a white crust of snow, frosted and hardened by the wind. The valley of Lamorna was just as beautiful as the day Elsa and I had first seen it, yet could not have been more different. There was no bird song now, just an eerie, pervading silence, broken only by the steady gurgle of the little river winding through the valley to the sea. Trees in full summer foliage, wore coats of ice and snow and from their branches hung icicles where the snow had melted and been re-frozen by the breath of the night.

There was no sign of any life but from the vantage point of the tree tops I could see several paths descending from the cliffs and hills down into the valley. A thin line of black ran down one of these paths; the tell tale sign of many feet walking in single file. I was relieved that the men had kept our rendezvous, I only hoped they had not been followed, surprise after all, was the key to the success of our plan.

As we neared the edge of the wood, we descended to the ground, being careful not to make our presence visible. I reckoned the men were waiting for my appearance so after waiting amongst the trees for a few tense and silent minutes I decided to venture out into the moonlight.

'Wait Master! Your life must not be risked, make yourself known only once we know it is safe to do so.' Before I could object Loer had skipped onto the path and down to the harbour. He sniffed around the tracks, then stood on his hind legs smelling the air.

'I think it is safe,' his voice whispered in my head.

'I'm not so sure,' I replied.

There was single old cottage and a boat house beyond which lay the remnants of an ancient harbour. There was no proper harbour wall, just boulders piled on top of each other to act as a breakwater. Within the wall was a small flotilla of boats: lobster fishers' row-boats, gigs (those many oared boats the Cornish love to race) and fishing boats large enough to carry a single sail mast. But there was no ship. I thought perhaps it had been too much to expect the men to smuggle a ship out of Penzance harbour, right under the nose of Pendrogeth. Where then, were the men and why did I feel so uneasy in the quiet and peace of the moonlit harbour?

The answer came without warning. The boulders on the stony beach hid a host of dark and scaly creatures. In a moment a dortriger was holding Loer by his ears. The hare's hind legs jerked uselessly in the air, searching for ground that was not there. Behind this one dortriger were a dozen or more of the scabrous creatures. Some were laughing, others were smelling the air.

'He is near,' one grunted.

'Fool! Of course he is near. Where there is Familiar there is magi. Now show yourself, he who would rule the Isle.'

'Run Master, run!' Loer's words, I knew, were heard by my ears only.

'I can't,' I replied. I could not leave the hare. His fate and mine were joined.

The dortriger – the same who'd had his face scarred by the bird-fish's talons – came up to the hare.

'Cheated of a meal once, but not twice!' His mouth was wide open, showing two rows of sharp teeth and his long tongue flickered back and forth like a lizard's. The dortriger looked like he might be hungry and I had the distinct impression that he would not be fussy about whether or not his meal was cooked or not, or even if it had been killed before he started eating it.

'I don't wish to rule the Isle,' I said, stepping into the

moonlight. Beneath my cloak, my hands grasped the leather cover of Meredith's satchel. I did not need to read or even touch the books to wake their powers, but I needed them near me and I held determinedly on to the satchel.

'Not rule?' said one.

'No,' I said falteringly, 'but I will not allow Pendrogeth to rule either. He… he's a tyrant.' Their leader thought this hilarious.

'He is a powerful magus and will be good to his subjects. The old master was a tyrant, not least to our kind. Pendrogeth will bring order to this Isle and the land of the living. He is to practice the old magic. At dawn he will make the sacrifice that will bring a new order. These storms and snow, they are signs, the voice of gods. A magus must please the gods, but your master has not! Besides, it matters not what words you speak young magus. For words mean nothing now.' I pulled back my cloak to reveal the satchel. One or two of them laughed, but others shifted nervously, making low grumbles of discontent. Their leader, the dortriger holding Loer by the ears, spoke to reassure his men.

'We are not crows. Yes, we know what you did. You have knowledge of the books but not enough I think. Now, you.' He nodded to the dortriger whose face the bird-fish had marked. 'If you want this hare for your dinner, make haste to Ictis. Sound the alarm.'

This dortriger took a last look at me, his animal eyes connecting with mine, sending a shiver down my spine. He had huge black eyes, an enormous gaping mouth and a wide nose, now streaked with congealed blood. He stretched his mouth open so I could better see the rows of tiny, sharp teeth. He stuck out his tongue, licking the air and letting out a breath of anger and frustration.

'The hare will whet my appetite young magus. You will witness this. Then I shall make a feast of you with my fellows.' There was no doubting the intelligence of these creatures, but they were animals to their core; carnal, base and raw. With a last, rude gesture of his tongue, he lunged off toward the cliff path at a frightening speed. At first he ran like a man, but when he reached the part of the path that steeply ascended to the cliff, he began to scramble on all fours, using his hands and feet to urge him forward. I reckoned he would be in Penzance inside of an hour.

Without thinking my left hand, holding my staff, shot out towards him. A wave of energy ran through me and from my hand. The air shimmered like the reflection on a disturbed pool and the creature was knocked from the path. It tumbled backwards. The braver of the dortriger stepped forwards, but my hand – thrust threateningly forward – was enough to stop them.

'Hargggrrhhhh,' their leader grumbled, fastening his grip on Loer's ears and drawing the hare to his chest. 'You know more of the books than I believed. But you are young in their ways and cannot fight us all. Even the fire would not kill us all. You cannot have learnt that much.' That was why some of them were scared! They believed I had the Book of Fire. Unless I thought and acted quickly they would soon realise that I didn't. Keeping an arm held out, palm facing, to the main body of the dortriger I turned my face to the scar-face, who was now picking himself up, and shaking his head. He was stunned but otherwise unharmed. Starting as a whisper, then a growl and finally a gutteral dialect of all that is animal, the language of the Book of Earth was uttered through my lips, though it came, not from my throat, but from a deep, dark, primeval cave that was at once within me and yet from the bowels of the very earth beneath me.

The dortriger, like an eager dog called by his master, bounded straight back towards me. His countenance of hate and hunger had been replaced by a look of bewilderment, awe, even curiousity. Sure enough, as he neared me, he stooped his shoulders – a show of submission – held his head up and cocked it, as if he was seeing me for the first time and was unsure of what to make of me. As I stared at him, so his features loomed large, my peripheral vision became blurred and his image filled my mind. For a split second – for that was all I could afford – I saw beyond his eyes and into his mind and was able to control it as surely as I had controlled the mice and spiders and lice. He slowly turned his head towards the leader, letting out a low growl. Then he ambled up to him and grabbed Loer. For a terrible moment the two dortriger used Loer as a rope in a tug-o-war, digging their large, sharp claws into his flesh to get a grip. Loer squealed and wriggled desperately, fighting with his hind legs to be free. I thrust my hand forward, meaning to shout: 'Release him' but instead uttering a guttural bark that rang through the crisp night air. The two dortriger dropped the hare, and stared at me, as if in shock.

'Yes Master,' they said in unison. The focus of my attention spread to the other dortriger, the force of my mind spreading over them like a blanket. One by one they fell to their knees.

'You are a worthy master,' said one. The others grunted their approval.

'Magi tricks!' spat the leader looking at Loer, who was now cowering at my feet, licking the blood off his wounds. He had a stronger will than the others, but even he had kneeled upon my orders.

Then suddenly, my senses, which were extended in the very air around me, swung around, alert to the possibility of danger. My staff was poised.

'Wass goin' on?' said Bob. I relaxed, lowering my staff. I had never seen such a welcome sight. For behind Bob was John Tanner, dobbing his ancient cap, and behind him the massive frame of Forkbeard. They led a small army; five score of men and more, armed with guns and swords that glinted in the moonlight.

Forkbeard strode forward at a pace till he was no more than two feet from me.

'Armed to the teeth and ready for action!' he cried pulling a cutlass from his belt.

'Now I know what ye'r thinking lad,' he said in a deep booming voice, pushing me gently aside and moving to the dortriger's leader ''Ow can we, 'oo 'ave not walked the earth for many a moon, do battle with them 'oo is as dead as we. Well all I can say is… ,' he circled the dortriger, and from behind him held his cutlass blade to the dortriger's exposed neck '... they're gonna look pretty funny trying to sink pints at the Navy Tavern... when they ain't got no 'ead!' He threw his head back and roared with laughter, joined by the men who now poured into the harbour from the woods, waving their blades and guns in the air.

''Ow did ye know the lad would be 'ere?' insisted Forkbeard, pressing the blade of his cutlass into the neck of the dortriger. The blade must have been razor sharp even against the thick hide of the earthdweller, for a line of crimson now ran along the metal. The beast looked scared. He knew, and Forkbeard knew, that the pirate might cut his throat for no better reason than because he could.

'We didn't. We and others were sent by Pendrogeth, he has his spies in every bay and on every hill top. We saw him through the trees and sprung a trap,' he hissed.

I pushed the limit of my sight, deep into his mind. He spoke the truth about springing the trap but had exaggerated about Pendrogeth's network of spies. His eyes met mine. He knew I was looking inside him.

'We... are... the... true... inheritors of the Isle,' the dortriger spoke the words venomously. I had to admire his courage. In my own head I spoke these words, projecting them in the same way that I spoke to Loer.

'Then perhaps your will shall be your own, but for now you will be our prisoners.' Then I spoke aloud: 'Put them in the hut. Lock them up.' Though the men would have been happy to cut all the dortriger's throats on the spot, they wordlessly took the prisoners to the boat hut. Rope was used to bind their hands and feet, and the windows and doorway were made fast. Before they were all imprisoned I took one of the sacks they each carried to collect shells and other food. I would need it later.

'We should have killed 'em all. They're the worst kind of scum!' said Forkbeard.

'Best to leave 'em 'ere in any case. Keep 'em from Pendrogeth,' said Bob. 'Here and now they must obey Bill. But it's not their own will. Given half a chance they'd cut our throats as surely as we'd cut theirs. If they got near Pendrogeth again they'd fall under his influence.'

'And what of you John, What about all of you?' I said. It was a difficult question but one that had to be asked. Some of the men avoided my gaze as I looked around the company. John, seeing their reaction, considered his words carefully.

''Tis our will to fight with you Bill. If your magic, and yer own will, is as strong as 'is, e'll not call us to his flag.' More than a hundred pairs of eyes looked toward me, and each man there, in his own way was asking the same question: did I believe it myself? There was a long and awkward silence, which John Tanner rescued me from.

'Counsel!' he said.

Putting the dortriger under guard John, Forkbeard, Bob Trelawney and I split from the main group and discussed our plans whilst the men waited.

'Your sister'll be inside Ictis, of that there is no doubt,' said John, 'my guess is e'll keep 'er there until dawn and then present her in the open courtyard. That's where e'll do the deed.'

'Ictis, the great library – but as much a fortress – and what guards it… no-one knows,' said Bob.

'Do we know anything of what's inside?' I asked.

'We've seen shapes, men or creatures of the elements… we dunno… for they wear hooded robes and 'ave only been seen rarely. What we do know is that the ghosts of men do not enter – and the strange guardians never leave. And even before we reach its walls no doubt Pendrogeth will have its waters guarded also. Should we win, should we find the girl, then…' he turned to me speaking in a matter of fact way '… you'll have to kill 'im. I 'ope yer magic is strong lad.'

But perhaps it would take more than magic. In the light of the full moon I could clearly see our small army; a rabble of miners, brigands, sailors, and every type of sea dog; corsairs from the east, Cornish smugglers and pirates from all the corners of the world.

The men stood, huddled together in small groups rubbing their hands and stamping their feet against the bitter cold of the night. Their faces spoke their minds; they were hopeful, brave certainly, but also afraid. I could see also that they were whispering, their thoughts evaporating in clouds of steam as soon as they escaped from their mouths.

Whilst Bob, John and Forkbeard talked I focussed my mind on the books, drawing out the powers of the Book of Earth. By concentrating on each group in turn I could pick up a little of their conversations:

'For every one of us there'll be ten or more fighting for Pendrogeth.'

'What'll Pendrogeth do us for if we don't win the day?'

''E's a rotten one this Pendrogeth.'

'We've only got John Tanner's word for that.'

'… Oh, would the dawn never came!'

Now is when I was supposed to use the magic. Bob, Forkbeard and John expected it. I was supposed to bend the men to my will as surely as I had controlled the lice and rats and snakes. This was the third way. This was how Meredith had ruled and this was how Pendrogeth was now taking over the island. But if I was indeed the heir, did I have to rule as my uncle had?

Towards the rear of the assembled men was Jethro. He was standing alone, looking nervously from one group to another. Slowly, he took a step back, then another. He was carefully, quietly sinking into the shadow of a tree.

'Where the 'ell d'ya think you're going!' shouted Forkbeard. Several of the men whispered 'shush' as loud as they dared. John Tanner broke away from our counsel, stormed through the men, grabbed Jethro by the scruff of the neck and dragged him to the front of the crowd.

'You've never shirked a fight before now!' said John, practically lifting the scraggly, skinny Jethro off the ground. The men stopped their chatter and watched.

'Pardoning yerself Cap'n I 'ave always been loyal to you

and to the *Seahawk*, but the bounty of this venture ain't the kind I usually fight for!' he smiled apologetically.

'You're no better than the dortriger,' sneered John, but I could see from the men that not all the crowd was unsympathetic to what Jethro had said.

I pulled back the hood that had been keeping my head warm, opened my arms and slowly floated upwards until I was a good three yards in the air.

'Put him under your will Master,' said John.

'Let him go.' I said. There was a murmur of surprise from the men.

'What!' John complained. 'Have you any idea what forces Pendrogeth will have mustered. Our cause is strong but our force is weak Bill. We need every man we can get. Use your magic! Tie him to our flag.'

I spoke loudly, enough to ensure every man would hear me.

'Each man came here by choice. If your choice is now to leave, then go. You will suffer no be punishment should we win and we'll bear you no ill will. But if you go now, bear this in mind. In every tavern in Lyonesse, each man you drink with will know – though it may go unspoken – that you did not fight this night.

The man that joins our band fights for a freedom he already has in his heart, a freedom Pendrogeth's men have lost before the battle begins. He fights because Pendrogeth is a true tyrant, and his descendants – his family in the land of the living – will suffer under the rule of Pendrogeth. This is a weight those who fight this night could never bear.

True, he is a strong magus, true his forces are greater in number. But it is the quality of our band that fills me with pride and hope. Should we win, then honour, courage and valour will be the qualities each of you will be known by. The fewer men to count on, the surer I am of their courage. The fewer we are, the greater the share of bounty. And for such a crew we need a worthy ship!'

Summoning all the powers of the books I called the scattered, broken skeleton of the ship that had brought me to the island, and just as surely as the skeletons of men long dead had become flesh, so the hull of the *Seahawk* rose out of the waters of Lamorna Cove. Its tattered sails fell from its timber frame like a broken web, but in front of our very eyes, and in a matter of moments, the holes filled with canvas till they were sails once more. The mast, all broken and splintered, slowly solidified into the mighty carved trunk it once had been and in minutes a ship lay in the harbour; complete, sturdy, sleek and beautiful as the day its keel first tasted salt water.

The men cheered, waving their cutlasses and pistols in the air. With no further word of encouragement they filed past me, into the small boats of the harbour. They used the row boats as ferries to take the crew of the *Seahawk* to their beloved ship. The rest, for their part, filled the smaller row and sail boats.

I floated over the still water, landing on the bridge of the *Seahawk* with Loer tucked within my cape.

First, we needed wind to take the ship forward. Holding on to the Book of Air with one hand I pushed my other arm forward with my palm facing the sail. The language of air blew from my mouth and filled the sails.

The *Seahawk* skated slowly through the sea to deeper waters, leaving a clean and perfect 'v' shape in our wake.

Though we moved silently I was worried about how visible we were. Within a few minutes we would be able to see Ictis and therefore, would be seen from it. Withdrawing my breath of air, I waited until the ship slowed to a standstill.

The men in the other boats understood clearly what was happening and drew their oars from the water. I beckoned to John.

'The other boats are to attack the mount in a semi-circle under cover of darkness.'

'But how?' I held up my hand.

'Leave that to me. Now listen, when the wind picks up – as it surely will – take the *Seahawk* far out to sea and prepare your men, as though to attack Ictis from the seaward side, charge into the ice as fast as you can and …you have gunpowder?'

'We have cannons and a supply of gunpowder in the hold.'

'Bring it to me; I will dry it with the Book of Air. You must place the gunpowder in small piles on the deck and instruct your men to be ready with their flints. On your order I want the gun powder lit, not enough to blow your men to smithereens but enough for some real fireworks. When the boat is upon the shore the men are to jump from the back of the ship and swim to the mainland. You are to stand upon the bridge and light the remainder of the gun powder then… this is important… when he attacks you leap into the water – Pendrogeth will believe you are me, so you swim to the mainland.'

'But why should 'e think I am you?'

'Take these,' I said. I took the books from the satchel and placed them in the sack I had taken from one of the dortriger prisoners. The satchel I placed around John's shoulders then I gave him Loer, put my cloak on him and gave him my staff. I took the cap from his head, and gave it to one of his crew.

'There, now Pendrogeth will believe you are me.'

'I'm not sure I wanna be you,' said John with panic in his voice.

'You're a decoy.'

'Will it help us?' he said.

'It'll give us the best chance we could have. For now, stay here.' I said.

'Take care Master,' said Loer. I closed my eyes – became lighter than air – and when I opened them was several yards above the deck of the ship. I thrust my staff out and sailed through the air to the top of the cliff. From this vantage point I could see the ship and the boats behind me, and in front, the isle of Ictis.

The island sat still and silent in the bay, still surrounded by a skirting of thick ice. The castle's turrets were frosted with a coat of snow and icicles hung from the parapets and dark windows. Other than thick smoke rising steadily from its chimneys the castle showed no sign of being inhabited. Yet it felt to me that the island itself was watching, waiting. It, or whatever lay within its wall was expecting us.

'Pendrogeth,' I whispered the word aloud.

Looking behind me I could see clouds in the distance. They were whisps of clouds really nothing more, a left over of the storm, yet they would serve my purposes.

Just as before, the air flowed both from within and through me, but – mindful of what the bird-fish had said – this time I expanded my mind beyond the confines of my body and pulled the very air from around me. Opening my eyes I saw the cloud moving swiftly towards and then ahead of me, borne by the wind I had created. Below, the wind ruffled the black and silken waters of the sea. Before long the cloud was across the moon, its shadow drawing over Ictis and the waters of the bay.

I was soon aboard once more, and the *Seahawk* was pulling away from the other boats, heading out to sea, so it could circle in an arc and attack the seaward side of the island. Forkbeard stood on the bow of the ship, watching the last of the boats disappear into the darkness.

'Begging your pardon young magus, but last I 'eard Ictis sat in a block of ice, a yard thick and a mile wide. 'Ow will those boats get beyond it? If they land on it and walk across they'll be sitting ducks…' I held my finger to my lips to quieten him, then picked the Book of Water from the dortriger's sack.

'Lower the sails,' I ordered. Flicking through the book I found the picture of the mermaid; a picture I had seen on first seeing the books in Meredith's study. Holding the book in one hand and with the other raised towards the water I began to speak the language of water.

A pale body shot out of the water. She leapt in the air and with a mighty splash came crashing back into the sea. We had seen a glimpse of her, nothing more, yet in that instant my heart had leapt into my mouth. She was the very embodiment of grace, of power, of beauty.

The very sight of her caused a kind of panic amongst the crew. Some of the men came forward to see her, others shrank from the very sight of her in fear. For a moment there was a struggle between those desperate to get a look at the mermaid – should she surface again – and those who seemed equally keen to stop them.

'Don't look at 'er lads! Don't look at 'er,' cried Forkbeard. He had turned his back on the mermaid and was roughly grabbing sailors by the collar and spinning them round. He had to slap one or two of the men around the face to bring them to their senses.

'But she's so lovely so she is!' complained one man as he fought against Forkbeard. Forkbeard put his enormous frame in front of the man and placed his hands over his eyes.

'Loverly she may be my lad, but deadly as nightshade. Now stop struggling or I'll give you a face so gruesome the roughest port girl in the roughest rum den wouldn't take a look at ye – let alone some sea maiden.'

She surfaced again, this time arcing in the water like a dolphin, so her back and tail shimmered in the water for an instant before diving back into the depths. I ran to the side of the boat, searching for her pale body in the night blackened waters. She was nowhere to be seen.

After waiting for a minute or so I repeated the incantation and this time, as I spoke the words of the language of water I saw what I thought at first was a light in the depths. The light grew larger, forming into hair, a face, eyes – eyes that found my own and pierced them with her gaze. Slowly, her face, then her body became visible as she swam upwards. She did not so much break the surface of the water as shed it like a veil from her body. She sat in the water, her body above the surface, her mighty tail below, moving gently from side to side to keep her buoyant. Her eyes locked onto mine and the words of the incantation stuck in my throat. Seeing a mermaid close up, in the flesh was, I discovered, as different from Ayr's vision as a real woman was from a painting. I was a young man by then, not immune to the charms of a woman, but in my life I had never seen such beauty, nor felt so enthralled. Her body was as sleek and powerful as it was delicate, and it almost shone, so white was her skin. Her hair was the silvery essence of moonlight and framed her oval face, a face so unearthly, so strange, yet utterly, overwhelmingly beautiful that I might easily have abandoned my task there and then and dived into the water, just for a chance to see her closely, just for a chance to kiss those pale lips.

Her words, when she spoke them, were the language of water, but I understood them well enough.

'What is your bidding… Master.' Her voice was mocking, taunting, daring me.

'Bring your kin. They will do me service.'

'There will soon be a new master of Lyonesse – a powerful magus. What if he should command my people? After all, you are just a boy are you not?' she raised one of her eye brows and stuck out her chin. Her laughter echoed like a gurgling stream.

'I… I… ,' though I had summoned her I felt strangely powerless in her presence. 'I'm not,' I said, feeling even younger than my years, I felt blood rush to my cheeks.

'A boy,' she teased, 'sent to do the task of a powerful magus,' she laughed once again. I firmed my grasp of the book and shook my head, as though she were a vision which would disappear if only I could free myself of her hypnotic stare.

'Bring your kind. They will do me service,' I repeated, and returned her stare with as much steely determination as I could muster, 'if only for the sake of one of your own.' There was a long moment in which we stared at each other. 'He's going to kill her at dawn,' I said. She nodded, an almost imperceptible bow of her head, raised her arms above her head and dived.

Not knowing what had passed between us Captain John asked, ''S it safe lad. Has she gone?'

'Keep your heads bowed and your eyes closed. She will return.' A minute later the water erupted with the bodies of more than a hundred merpeople. The men were bearded, handsome and proud. Many of them bore tridents. The maidens were equally strong and each as beautiful as the first.

'Is Lamorna of the Valley Cove amongst you?'

'I am.'

'You served my uncle well, now I must ask you to do my service…and for my sister who is now one of your own.'

'Ask, young magus? If you ask we may do your bidding, but when this dark magus commands us we will be powerless to resist unless… ' I drew deep from the power of the book.

'I command you!' I said. Lamorna of the Valley Cove nodded in approval. As one body, the merpeople bowed their heads.

'Our fleet heads to Ictis, but in their way stands a sheet of ice. Use all your strength and powers to break this ice and clear a way for the boats. Go now, do your work only when the boats reach the ice, yet keep yourselves away from the men, your work must go unseen. Lamorna, I ask that you and some of your kind, do this same service for the *Seahawk*, stay with the boat till then.' Apart from Lamorna and four other mermaids the entire company of merpeople dived and vanished, leaving nothing in their wake but ripples. Lamorna and her friends moved to the bow of the ship where – like dolphins in swim – they would ride the bow wake.

'We're ready to go Captain,' I said to John.

'Take this,' said Forkbeard, handing a large piece of folded black cloth to John.

'I can't do that', said John stepping backwards.

'The order of the world is fell apart John,' said Forkbeard, 'we're all pirates now.' John looked at the cloth for while before nodding gravely.

'Raise the sail,' cried John into the rising wind, 'hoist the Jolly Roger!'

As we moved through the night I watched the flag being hoisted up the mast, its skull and cross bones motif waving in the wind.

Chapter 17

Thanks to the now moon-covered cloud, the night was dark and almost impenetrable to my sight. But with a little help from the Book of Earth I could still just make out the silhouette of Ictis; a dull shadow set between the sea and the tar black sky, surrounded by a skirt of white ice.

There was no sound to be heard but for the wind carrying the *Seahawk* out to sea. The crew and their passengers of pirates and vagabonds did not talk; each man keeping his own private vigil, each pair of eyes trained firmly on the island. None dared to look into the eyes of any other, I think for fear that in another's face they may see a reflection of the dread they held in their own hearts. Forkbeard was the only one to meet my gaze. He smiled and winked as his huge, ring covered hands massaged the handles of his pistols and cutlass. I returned his smile, trying to look confident and brave, though I felt neither,

It was almost a relief, when we heard the first loud cracks as the merpeople began breaking up the ice. As though taking this as a cue Captain John shouted his orders. Men that had stood like statues now ran about the ship, silently busying themselves with ropes and canvas. One sail was lowered, another raised. The ship lurched as it swung round in the water, turning, until Ictis was directly ahead of the ship.

The loud cracking sound of ice breaking was soon joined with gunshot and shouting from both the boat and the island. In the darkness we could see small flashes of red and orange as pistols and rifles were discharged.

I bade a hurried farewell and good luck to Loer, John and the others, then, closing my eyes drew deeply from the Book of Air;

letting the weight fall from my flesh and bones until I felt light enough to fly. As the last traces of solid feeling fell away from my body, I rose into the air.

Keeping a few feet above the water I flew rapidly towards the sounds of the battle, then, when less than a half mile away, I dived into the water, instantly trading the power of Air for that of Water. Beneath the waves I could hear the shouts and cries of men and blasts of gun and cannon, yet they were muffled and distant, never really penetrating the absorbing silence of the sea, which seemed at that very moment like a blanket, which might keep me quiet and safe as long as I chose to keep beneath it.

Ahead I saw first the broken ice, then the hulls of the boats. The merpeople were all around the boats; pushing and pulling them through the broken ice to Ictis. One boat – a large gig – had advanced further than the others and was now static, stubbornly held up by the thickest part of the ice. I circled around the melee of merpeople and boats and surfaced behind the gig. It was empty. As I pulled myself into the boat, the cloud drew from the face of the moon like a curtain and I could see the full horror of our situation.

The first wave of our attack had landed their boat where the ice was thickest, had disembarked and made their way across the ice to the protection of the rocks before the forces of Ictis had fully awoken. They were amongst the rocks now at the base of the castle walls; hidden, but pinned down by the gunfire of Pendrogeth's men and barrage of rocks being hurled by dortriger from the castle walls. The men bravely returned fire as best they could, but the sheer black walls of the castle made for natural bulwarks and parapets, and at their top – and atop all of the inner buildings within the walls – were legions of men and dortriger (it seemed Pendrogeth had opened Ictis to his allies). Hundreds of cannons and rifles jutted out from behind the walls and were being fired without respite.

Those men still in their boats could not run across the ice, for fear of being cut down in a shower of gun shot, yet in their boats they were the proverbial sitting ducks, as cannon and gunshot hailed down on them.

There was a mighty crash as not one but two cannon balls found one of the rowboats, blowing it apart with such force that it fell on the ice and water as a shower of matchstick size splinters. The explosion made mince meat of the four men inside. I had to turn my face from the horror of it, feeling my stomach churn with nausea.

Pendrogeth must have given orders then, for all the gunfire became concentrated on those of our men who had made it to the rocks; providing an apparent respite for those in the boats. But it was an illusion. I was about to shout out to the men, when the sea around us erupted with white froth and spouting water. A mermaid's body was flung high into the air, her body crashing back into the water, as lifeless and limp as a dead fish. The sea bubbled and frothed with some terrible commotion; the boats rocked violently, almost capsizing their crews into the freezing waters.

Pendrogeth had summoned a host of water-creatures, some of which I recalled seeing in the Book of Water when I had first opened its pages. Climbing aboard the boats, or more accurately, trying to pull them into the water, were beings not unlike mermaids, but from the waist down these creatures had the drawn out body and tentacles of giant octopus'. Some of them were fighting – and overpowering – the merpeople. Others were entwining their slimy legs around the limbs of the sailors and plucking their swords and pistols from their hands. Another monster had the body of a man but the face of a fish and in place of hands, giant claws with which he was snapping the blades of swords like twigs. Unless I acted quickly it would be a short and one-sided battle. To make matters worse, the iron portcullis of Ictis was being raised and as though from the mouth of hell itself a pack of wolves was pouring forth, followed by a dozen or more dortriger.

I summoned what I needed from the Book of Water, also drawing deeply from the Book of Earth, filling my being with its animal strengths and senses. And anger.

I sent out blows of pure energy against the enemy not directly engaged in combat, stunning and confusing them. Against those who were fighting the men and merpeople I used the strength of the Book through my bare hands. I jumped onto one poor man, who was being slowly strangled by one of the monsters. I pulled a thick tentacle from the man's neck and then with one violent effort tore it cleanly from the monster's writhing body. The monster screamed, withdrawing into the water, blood gushing from its torso. Next, I jumped to another boat and with a single push, sent the monster with the crab-claw hands back into the water, where two mermen were waiting with tridents to spear him.

Pistols fired, cutlasses cut and thrust, tridents were thrown and plunged into the flesh of the enemy. With all of the merpeople on our side we outnumbered them and with my use of the books I was able to tip the balance of the battle back in our favour – at least temporarily. After a minute or two of fighting (it can't have been more though it seemed like an hour) the ice was stained dark with more of our enemy's blood than our own and those monsters that we had not killed soon disappeared into the waters of the night, chased by merpeople seeking revenge.

We had an instant to act. For as soon as Pendrogeth's men realised what was going on they would surely retrain their fire upon us. The men from the first boat ashore were fighting the wolves and defending themselves from rocks being thrown by the dortriger.

Wolves. These were noble but base animals, who had been given their orders like hunting dogs, and like dogs, were obeying blindly, even though several of their kind were accidentally shot by those who they were so loyally defending. I was sure they would be easy to manipulate, so I drew from the Book of Earth and projected the force of my mind towards them. Their minds were indeed easy to read. These wolves were nothing more or less than guard dogs and Ictis was their territory to defend. I penetrated the mind of the pack leader and forced his attention upon me. When I had it, I emitted a low and guttural growl. I did the same to the dortriger. A challenge.

Like a fish to bait the wolf and dortriger leaders barked at their companions and led the pack across the ice towards us.

The men, not knowing my plan, looked upon the mass of animal bodies as sailors might look upon a mighty – and final – boat crushing wave in a storm; not with fear, but with resignation.

I grabbed a dropped pistol from the floor of the boat and jumped off the boat and onto the ice.

'Come on then,' I shouted and fired the pistol at the foremost of the wolves. The animal whelped and skidded across the ice, leaving a trail of blood behind it. I didn't stop running, nor did I look behind, but I heard the men's war cries and their boots crunching on the snow as they leapt from their boats and began to run across the ice.

The wolves, bereft of their pack leader, were not up to much of a fight, but the dortriger were altogether braver and stronger and they managed to take down some of our number, wrestling them to the ground where they set about trying to bite the exposed flesh of their necks and heads. However, they were a small force and we were quick to help our comrades. Each of the dortriger could take a single man, but not two or three. We soon had the better of them, and were able to make our way to join the men at the rocks, though once Pendrogeth's men realised that their force was not going to hold us back they ceased caring whether they hit dortriger or wolves and fired a fresh volley of gun fire which brought down two of our number before we could reach safety.

Gunfire and rocks pelted down on us, returned occasionally by those brave enough to stick their heads above the parapets of black rock that served as our defences. I was huddled tight behind a rock with one man, a sailor wearing a scruffy overcoat and an old, striped Breton shirt. He was busy reloading his pistol with powder and shot.

'Use yer magic lad, and quick about it,' he said, 'for if ye don't Pendrogeth'll bring another mighty damnation down upon us like them monsters. Or worse.' I ducked as another volley of shot whistled over our heads.

'I can't. Not yet.' I looked into the man's eyes. 'Wait. Trust me.'

A voice which sounded very like Stephen's, cut through the crisp night air, 'From the sea Lord Pendrogeth. They are attacking from the sea. And the boy is with them.'

'Now lads,' I said, 'I'll give you a fighting chance. Scale the walls!'

The attention of the enemy was momentarily diverted to the *Seahawk*, but not all of Ictis's defendants followed Pendrogeth and after a few, mercifully quiet seconds the enemy trained their weapons upon us once more.

But even those few seconds had been enough for our men to begin a serious assault upon Ictis. If the castle could be said to have a weakness at all it was that the walls were so steep and high that once we had started to scale them with the aid of ropes and metal hooks, the enemy could not fire upon us without literally sticking their necks out over the castle walls

I could not give my presence away – it was vital they believed me to be aboard the *Seahawk* – but I could help our cause a little using the books' magic. I climbed around the base of the walls, clambering over the black, craggy rock until I faced a part of the wall that was so steep and tall, no man would try and climb it.

I pulled my power from the Books of Earth and Air, giving me the lightness of a butterfly and the strength and agility of a cat. Though the walls were sheer I found I could attach myself to its marble like surface with ease, and was soon scaling the walls easily. Once at the top of the wall I swung my body over the battlements. There three men were gathered around a pile of musket and pistols, busily reloading them. I blasted them with a wave of energy, knocking them unconscious. Amongst the debris were three small barrels of gun powder. Perfect.

I made a small trail of gun powder and using one of their flints, lit the trail and flung myself off the wall and into Ictis. It wasn't a big explosion but was enough to cause panic among the defenders and provide a chance for our men to scale the walls and face the enemy in hand-to-hand combat.

Inside the mighty outer wall were two circles of inner defences, with streets, houses and other buildings set between them. The cobbled streets seemed to be deserted, with all of Pendrogeth's cohorts occupied with the battle. I ran through the empty streets till I found the second wall and scaled this too. Jumping down on the other side I received a shock. Two men stood on the other side. They wore robes held at the waist by a rope, and hooded cowls over their heads, so it was impossible to see their faces other than their mouths. I braced myself for an attack. But the monks (for that is what they looked like) had their hands clasped in front of them and didn't move them either to defend themselves or search for weapons of any kind. For a tense moment we faced each other.

'We will neither harm nor protect you young magus.' The monk spoke English, but his voice was thick with an eastern accent, the likes of which I had never heard before.

'Who are you?' I asked. By way of an answer the monk slowly held up his hand to me with his palm showing. Even in the dim light of the night I could see that upon his palm was a tattoo. It was of a simple circle, the same as I had once seen on the door in Lyonesse houses, the door that had led to Meredith's library. Then he clasped his hands again and the two of them walked on. I followed their backs with my eyes. They struck up a conversation in a language that was lyrical, soft and exotic. They seemed quite oblivious to the clamour of battle.

I was bemused and intrigued by them, but could not waste any more time. I ran off and soon reached the walls of the castle, walking around the wall until I found myself at the base of a tall tower. Knowing any gates and doors would be guarded I climbed up the outer tower's wall. As it faced the sea, I was sure I would not be seen by any of the enemy.

When half way up I inched around the wall until I could see the battle and most of the castle. I was particularly interested in the tallest, innermost tower, which resembled a massive chimney stack, billowing smoke into the night air.

To get from this tower to the high chimney meant I had to cross some considerable distance. I would have to fly. At least my timing was fortunate for as I flew onto the chimney the second 'attack' was in full flow. Although facing a considerable barrage of cannon ball and gunshot, the men on board bravely returned fire. On the bow were Captain John and Loer, leading the boat's charge into the ice. Fortunately for them the mermaids had broken most of it. Wolves and dortriger were on the very edge of the reef, barking, howling and goading the men of the *Seahawk* as it careered in to them. I saw John swing my staff. Two explosions immediately followed as the men of the *Seahawk* launched their homemade bombs on the unsuspecting dortriger. John Tanner was playing his part well.

'The Book of Fire. He has the Book of Fire,' shouted Pendrogeth's men. In an instant the dark magus was over the battlements and flying towards the *Seahawk*.

'Now John,' I said out loud. Two more bombs were quickly launched; a second later the whole ship was lit up by a series of explosions. In the fierce light I could see John and Loer silhouetted against a wall of fire. The wolves and dortriger fled in panic. There was a mighty final blast as the ship hit the ice. The men behind the safety of Ictis's walls cowered in fear, then slowly they raised their heads, nervously peeking to see what dreadful Fire magic was being unleashed upon them. But in the wake of the blast the men of the *Seahawk* had left behind a burning – but empty – ship.

'Nice work lads,' I said to myself as I climbed over the lip of the chimney.

Hot, black smoke was billowing out of a funnel that was just large enough for my body. If this chimney led where I believed, then to descend down it would require deep and strong magic indeed. I found the Book of Water. I waited long moments until I was not only speaking the language of water, I was becoming its essence. My body weakened, I felt my very being dissolve in the flowing powers of the book, then dove headfirst into the chimney.

Chapter 18

The Book of Water could not protect me all together. Burning smoke filled my senses. The heat burnt my skin, I smelt and tasted the acrid smoke and heard the rush of heat blazing up the chimney. Finally, at the very moment when I could bear it no longer and was about to turn back, I saw the fire below and made a final push against its flames, until I burst through into a large fireplace. From the sheer shock my mind lost its focus. In an instant my clothes were burning. I rolled out of the fire onto a flagstone floor and quickly set about beating the flames from my shirt, jerkin and trousers. It took a few moments for me to recover my senses and gather my wits enough to register my surroundings.

The chamber was the size of a small house and well lit by the fire and several torches hanging from its wall. The roof was of arched stonework and the walls a mix of fashioned, smooth black stone and natural, jagged rock. It looked as though the room had been hewn from the base rock of the island. Above the ceiling I could hear the booming echo of waves crashing into the cliffs of the island. The room had to be below sea level, at the very base of the castle, where its very roots reached into the rock. There were no windows – no surprise as it was so deep within the castle – but more worryingly there didn't appear to be a door either. And there were books, thousands of them, not neatly arranged or shelved like a library or even in my Uncle Meredith's study, but stacked in piles, or scattered over the rocky floor. All of this I took in in a couple of seconds as my eyes quickly scanned the chamber.

I jumped, for standing in the shadows, away from the fire, was a hooded figure. As he stepped into the fire light, I braced myself to fight, reaching for the power of the Book of Earth. But he was clearly of the same order as the monk like figures I had encountered outside the castle walls. He pulled back his hood. He had dark skin and when he spoke, it was with a voice as thick and musky as incense smoke.

'Salutations young magus. My name is Cadmus. Who comes for the Book of Fire?' I didn't answer, but sent my own thoughts outwards to read his mind. I found nothing.

'You cannot read my mind magus. Nor shall you control it.'

'Then you are one of Pendrogeth's.'

'There are those of us who have been on this island always. We cannot be controlled by the magi.'

'You knew Meredith?'

'I was his friend, not his servant… and sometime, his tutor.' He foresaw my next question. 'I and my fellows are from a far off land. A land your people once called Phoenicia.'

'You brought the books to Cornwall,' I said with wonder, 'and these books… ' I indicated the books lying around on the floor, 'you know their ways?'

'Indeed.'

'Where is the Book of Fire?' I asked. Cadmus pointed at the fireplace behind me. The flames were high and fierce, but they did not burn from any fuel. In the heart of the hearth was a book, lying on the stone floor with its pages open.

'Go ahead. It will not burn you, but be careful to keep your hand below the flames,' warned Cadmus. I tentatively put my arm out, tapping the book like you would a hot dish from the oven, merely to see if it were as hot as you had been warned. It was hot, but did not burn. I made to grab the book.

'Wait,' shouted Cadmus 'Make sure you close the book before you take it.' Moving quickly I picked one half of the book and flipped it over, shutting the book closed. The roaring flames vanished instantly leaving no proof of their existence but for a puff of black smoke, which lazily rose up, into the chimney chute.

'You must use the qualities of other elements to contain the power of Fire. If you fail in this it may destroy you… as well as anything that is in its path. It has the power of creation, yet in order to create you must destroy. It is this power for which the Book is known and used most often.'

'You were a friend of Meredith Cadmus. I ask you in his name, will you help me now?'

'The King is unthroned, his seat is empty. I may serve, by my will, whomever becomes such a one. Until then I could no more help you than I could Pendrogeth. Yes, I know of him. He has possession of this citadel, he has discovered many of its secrets, but he has not found this chamber.'

'Do you know what he is planning to do when the dawn comes.' Cadmus nodded.

'It is the old magic. If he succeeds in this he will be master of Lyonesse.'

'And in the land of the living?'

'If he is crowned he shall have full reign, and will pass between that land and this place at will, with all the forces of Lyonesse at his call.'

'How do I get out of here?'

'You must find the door using the books... and wit, and wisdom, and courage. This was your uncles' will – no-one shall take the book without use of such faculties and qualities.'

He withdrew into the shadows, pulling the cowl of his robes back over his head he said:

'What keeps you from the door is...

darker than moonless midnight
as powerful as the gods
more evil than all the demons of hell.

I felt beads of sweat form on my brow and my breath quicken. The stone walls were silent and still, yet whatever blocked – or guarded – the door sounded like it had to be dangerous. I couldn't see anything blocking my way other than solid stone... yet... the stone! The stone itself was blacker than any substance I had ever seen. It was dark and strong. Darker than moonless midnight? Perhaps. But more powerful than the gods? And – according to the riddle – more evil than all the demons of hell? Something did not ring true.

Cautiously, tentatively, I reached for the Book of Fire. Perhaps when I had mastered this book too I would be able to source its powers at will, yet in that moment I was afraid to try. I gingerly picked it up from the sack I carried, half expecting it to burn my fingers. But it did not. Its cover was of old, dry leather, not dissimilar from the Book of Earth. But instead of that book's animal instincts and urges I sensed not with my mind, but within my mind, something quite intangible and indefinable, yet undeniably there; something pure and terrible, that was neither emotion nor thought nor anything physically real. Something that was at once calm yet strong – like the heart of a flame, and I sensed that, just like the heart of a candles' flame, this feeling, this essence could, with encouragement, grow and transform into a raging all consuming fire.

Cadmus had told me to use the books, as well as wit and wisdom and courage. Book or books I thought? Why not this one book on its own? As with all the others I tried to focus its powers. For a target I chose the furthermost wall. I focussed within my mind the pure energy of the book, but no flames shot forth from my out held arm, no column of red and yellow heat erupted from the book as I anticipated. Perhaps I needed to open its pages? Keeping my face turned away I opened the book ever so slightly. Like a vent on a raging oven, flames leapt out of the book as well as the most piercing light. It was as though all hell was contained in the book and by opening its covers just a sliver I was giving hope and vent to all the hungry fires that burned there, and which poured forth from its pages, eager to destroy, to consume. I closed the book before the flames forced me to drop it.

So how, I wondered, could I harness its powers – which I undoubtedly felt within me – without opening the book? Then I realised. The fire, Cadmus had said, was to be contained by the other elements (and in a sense had not the book itself been contained by the other elements being encased by the earth and covered by sea and air?). I had to use them to control its force. Keeping a grip on the book I forced my attention on one of the torches on the wall and simultaneously used the force of Air to blow the flame. A great tongue of fire shot from the torch to where I focussed it on the far wall, instantly lighting the entire chamber in a yellow and orange glow. So, this was how I could use it; at all times containing and manipulating its powers with the other elements, just as a fire is fuelled with wood or peat, dowsed by water or fed by air, being both controlled and shaped by other elements.

I turned, alarmed by a loud clanking sound echoing from the fireplace. They must have noticed that the chimney had stopped smoking and become suspicious. Somebody – or thing – was loudly making its way down the chimney. I would have to be quick or face whatever Pendrogeth was sending to hunt me. I performed the trick with the flame, sending it around the arches and corners of the chamber until the flame hit a spot where, instead of bouncing off the wall it simply passed through it as though the wall were nothing at all. Then it hit me. Nothing at all. Had Cadmus not said I would need wit, as well as wisdom and courage to try and face something so powerful and evil? I had found the doorway in a far corner of the chamber, and what was guarding it?

Nothing. Nothing is darker than moonless midnight, nothing is more powerful than the gods and nothing could be more evil than all the demons of hell.

Utilising all the powers of the book together I pushed my mind to the door and pulled at its form with my mind. It fell apart as easily as a sandcastle, dried and blown apart by shore winds.

Taking a torch I passed through the portal. I found myself in a corridor of carved steps. I took my chances going up but soon discovered that the stairway led to another chamber, this one more of a natural cavern from which led a myriad of stairways and tunnels hewn from the rock. As in the chamber, I could hear the sea, only now it seemed to be around as well as above me; the sounds of waves crashing on the ice bound shore boomed and echoed through the chamber, mixed with the rain-like sound of pebbles being dragged by the swell across the reef bed of the sea. I chose a stairway that led steeply upwards but had travelled only a few yards when I discovered to my dismay that the stairway didn't lead upwards very far at all. After a few yards it led down into another cavern which, like the one I had just left, had numerous pathways and corridors leading from it.

I followed another path, and found another cavern, then another, and gradually found myself being drawn deeper and deeper into a maze; for that is what it surely was. The further I travelled the more disoriented I became, with the echoes of the sea all around; booming and rushing through the tunnels so it was difficult to tell if the source was above, below or all around me. Before going any further I stopped for a while to consider my options. Above the sea I could hear the wind. It had picked up and was moaning and howling through the walls of Ictis, and above that sound, very faintly I could hear crying. Using the Book of Earth I focussed my hearing. I ran down one tunnel, it grew weaker. I ran back, down another, then another until I found one where I could hear the crying more clearly. This passage led to a cave, just like all the others (or for all I knew one I had already visited), only here the crying was quite distinct... and close. It was a desperate kind of weeping; the steady whimpering and sniffing of a girl who had been crying for a long time but who was so miserable she was unable to stem the flow of tears.

'Elsa! Elsa, Elsa, Elsa, Elsa.' The sound of her name echoed back to me from the deep bowels of Ictis. The crying stopped. 'Elsa,' I repeated.

'Bill?' came the reply, hopeful yet disbelieving.

'Elsa, dear heart it's me, Bill.'

'Wh... where are you?'

'I don't know, lost in a maze of tunnels. Don't shout, I can hear you clearly and I don't want you to give the game away. Where are you?'

'In a cage, suspended at the roof of a massive cave. The only way out is above. There's a trap door there.'

'Is it guarded?'

'Yes, I think so. The men look in once in a while.'

'Right, keep crying, or singing or something, anything, just make a noise I can follow.' Elsa, started singing a ditty, but in such a way that it sounded a like a feeble attempt to keep her spirits up. She always was a good little actress, I thought to myself.

Using my acute hearing I followed the sound of her song and after a while discovered a cavern much larger than the rest, and above me, suspended in the air was a cage, and in the corner of that cage, curled up into a little ball and pressed against the bars, was the most welcome sight I had ever seen.

'Elsa,' I whispered.

'Bill, Oh Bill. I'm so glad to see you. Lord Pendrogeth put me here. You wouldn't believe what he can do… '

'Trust me, I would. You were right about Meredith being a magician… '

'Pendrogeth says he's dead, drowned in the storm, but I can't believe it Bill I just can't.'

'I don't know Elsa. I don't know what to believe. Now listen. I've got Meredith's books and can do… and, oh hell, there's no time to explain. Now look Elsa, I don't want you to be scared.'

'Of what?' she said. I could see her hands holding the bars of the cage and behind them, her wide eyes peering at me. I steadily floated up into the air until I was level with her. I should have known my sister better. She wasn't the least bit scared. But she was impressed.

'Blimey! How d'you do that?' her eyes were wide as saucers, and still had the translucent quality of a mermaid's gaze. Elsa looked tired and her clothes, freckled face and sandy hair were dirty. But she was unharmed.

'Listen. There's a whole army of men out there doing

battle with Pendrogeth and his lot and whilst they're keeping them busy I've come to rescue you.' I floated to the top of the cage and squeezing myself between the top of the cavern and the cage, landed gently on the cage floor. I put the torch down so I could hug Elsa.

'We've got to be brave now Elsa. Are you ready?' Above us I could hear the sound of footsteps on stone and the clanking of chains.

'As I'll ever be.'

'Then stand back.' I took the Book of Fire from the small sack and picked up the still flaming torch.

A tongue of fire burst forth from the torch I carried, turning the trap door into ashes in an instant.

Without giving whatever enemy I was to face a moment to recover I flew through the floor of a dungeon. Two men were running towards the only doorway, but I quickly conjured a gust of wind to slam it shut before they could escape.

The two men cowered in a corner, not attempting to hide their fear of the Fire. One of them must have been unlocking the trap door when the flames had burnt through – for his hair and beard were heavily singed.

'Don't kill us,' they pleaded, 'take the girl, take her.' Keeping a careful eye on them I helped Elsa out of the cage and ordered the men to take her place. In a corner of the dungeon was a heavy oak table and chairs. The men's dinners were on the table along with a deck of cards and a jug of ale. We upturned the table and dragged it across the still smoking hole to ensure the 'guards' could not cause us any further trouble, at least for a while.

'Follow me,' I said, cautiously. There was no one behind the door, nor any sign of life in the long corridor in which we found ourselves, or in the spiral stairway to which it led. Slowly, carefully we ascended the stairs and as we climbed higher felt cold, fresher air on our faces. 'We have to be above sea level now,' I said. Sure enough, after a time we passed a window looking out on the sea. I could see that the night sky now had a grey complexion to it; a dull bearing that meant dawn could not be long in coming. We climbed the steps for an age, and by the time we had reached their top I reckoned that we had to be in the upper most levels of the castle. A heavy door barred our way.

Behind the door I could now hear gunshot and cries, but they were occasional and sparse, not the sounds and fury of the heat of battle. Had our side won the day I wondered, or was Pendrogeth at that very moment sealing his victory over our meagre army? Keeping Elsa safely back I pushed the door open.

But there was no one there.

Beyond was a large room, with high stained glass windows and oak panelling on the walls, in the centre of which was a large round table, surrounded by a dozen or so high back chairs, one of which was grander and larger than the others. At the far end of the room were two doors, one open, another shut. Grabbing Elsa by the hand I rushed to the open door. It opened on to a small open - air courtyard.

Yet again, I braced myself for an enemy that wasn't there. Straining to listen I searched the night air for signs. But there was no gunfire now, no cries of battle, just the howling of the wind through the castle. And even as I listened to the wind for any sounds it might mask, so it began to fade as the first threads of light filtered into the sky.

A blanket of silence descended on Ictis.

At the end of the courtyard was a high, wooden gate, framed with ornately carved silver. It opened silently.

Beyond it was a larger courtyard, also open to the elements.

From there I could see most of the island; its distant moors still draped with snow and ice, its shore now awakening in blue and turquoise as the dawn's rays lit up the sky. We walked towards the gate. Far below the castle, the tide had retreated, far enough for the distance between Ictis and the isle of Lyonesse to be exposed. A large crowd of people had gathered there, all their eyes trained on the courtyard.

And in the court, another crowd, mostly of Pendrogeth's men. But Anthony was there, as well as Dr Gonzales, passengers and the crew of the *Seahawk*. So was John Tanner, and Bob Trelawney and Forkbeard. They were tied with chains and rope and had been forced to kneel in front of a stone altar. Next to them, holding a whip each, were the loathsome Stephen and Trinkle the jester. The Phoenicians were there too, stood on the edge of the court, keeping their distance from the prisoners and their captors.

Upon seeing us the crowd parted like a peeling wave. In their midst stood Pendrogeth, dressed in his black robes and standing on the altar. His arms were outstretched and his face was set east towards the rising sun. As the sun lit up his deathly white face he turned to face me.

'Are you ready for death boy?'

Chapter 19

I put myself in front of Elsa.

'Oh, do not worry about your sister young magus. The bait has served its purpose,' he said scornfully, 'if the quarry is too quick for the hunt then a trap will do the job just as well.' He turned to speak to the whole assembly of Ictis, raising his arms into the air and shouting his cold, hard words over the gathered crowd.

'Where there was order there is chaos, where there was calm and peace we have turmoil and tempest, where there was peace we have war... brought upon us by this young pretender and the rabble he leads.' Pendrogeth pointed at me, his hand, like his voice, trembling with rage. From the crowd came a cheer of approval, though I noticed Forkbeard spat on the ground and pushed against the chains that bound him.

'The old magic requires... demands... a sacrifice. In defeat he must offer his blood, in defeat he must offer his heart. Only then shall the dark forces be appeased. Only then shall order be restored.' The crowd thanked him with cries of approval. He turned his attentions to me, and just as I had once projected my own mind into that of the dortriger, so his dead, grey-yellow eyes pierced the walls of my soul; a cold, sick intrusion that filled my heart with dread, yet I could not tear my eyes away from his gaze any more than I could ignore the ice tinged words of his thoughts as they rang in my head.

'It will be easier for you, and for those whom you profess to love, if you come willingly...,' he left a pause, waiting to see what I would do or say.

I was able, with no small effort of will, to turn away from

his gaze. All eyes were upon me – some amused, some scornful, some desperate, some pitying.

Elsa's hand slipped into mine. She had not heard Pendrogeth's words, but she spoke as though she had read the confusion in my mind.

'What would Meredith do?' she whispered, giving my hand a squeeze.

'I know you don't have it boy. Your show back there was just a ploy wasn't it?' his words sounded inside my mind.

My eyes met his. Our minds locked together.

The smug sneer dropped from his face, as it dawned on him that the Book of Fire was indeed my possession.

He knew he could not afford to wait; he rose into the air, muttering an incantation. I too, flew into the air, easily dodging the blasts of energy that shot out of his staff. I counted with some blasts of my own, then, holding the torch in one hand and with the Book of Fire in the other sent a huge tongue of flame at him. For a brief moment he struggled against the flames, escaping only by flying high into the air with this robes ablaze. But his mastery of the books was at least as good as my own, and from the air around him he conjured a wall of ice and snow to temper the Fire's force.

He sent wave after wave of energy at me – of air, water and ice, but I nimbly dodged each of them, or protected myself with a shield of fire. This bout continued for some time, with neither one of us hurting the other or even breaking the variety of shields we forged from the elements to protect ourselves. There were gasps of amazement and shock from the crowd, as we got further embroiled in the duel, with jeers and boos, or cheers of support when either of us momentarily gained the upper hand.

'I tire of these games,' shouted Pendrogeth eventually and from the folds of his robes he took one of his books. He rose high into the air, twenty, thirty, forty yards, all the time swooping and ducking so that I could not reach him whilst he read his incantation. It was more a song than a thing of speech. But of what language? A whisper of air, sang through the dawn air. But this wasn't the only 'voice' singing the song. The high notes in the air were matched by a guttural growl rumbling through the black rock beneath our feet.

We all of us, the hooded Phoenicians, the dortriger, Trinkle and Stephen, the ghosts of men and women made flesh – all watched in awe struck horror as the walls and high turrets of black Ictis began to shimmer and tremble. The whole castle shook in the grip of Pendrogeth's force. Pieces of the highest walls began to break apart. Several people held up their arms to protect themselves from the imminent collapse of the walls and there were cries of protest and pleas for protection.

But the 'rock' did not fall upon our heads as the crowd feared. As chunks of black stone broke free from the walls of Ictis, they reformed and shape-shifted, becoming dark flying creatures from the blackest midnight nightmare; bats, eagles, crows, snakes with wings. They swirled around Pendrogeth, clouding the blue, dawn sky, turning day back into night; filling the clear air with dreadful, croaking, vicious calls.

I flew over their heads and straight into the dark cloud, sending a blast of flame straight at them. The sheer force scattered them widely. From below, came a heart-warming cheer.

'Get 'em Bill,' Elsa urged me on. But the flames had not hurt the monsters, merely confused them for a brief moment. A strong, howling blast of air had the same effect; holding them back for a second but causing no harm.

I realised I could not fight them off forever, for the flying creatures were slowly surrounding me; as I sent an elemental force in front or above me so they gathered behind and below, until I was held in the centre of the swarm. They lingered, awaiting instruction from their master.

Close up I could get a good look at them; crows with beady, glinting eyes, eagles of jet black, eagerly flexing talons that looked as though they might tear through sheer rock; winged snakes with hungry fangs and forked tongues that flickered back and forth in their pitch dark, eager mouths.

If ever there was a time to unleash the powers of the Book of Fire it was then. I reached into my sack and found the tome as the creatures began their attack once again, feeling their beaks, claws and mouths ripping at me. I dropped the torch and opened the book, holding it firmly open in both my hands.

Thought, sense, emotion, knowledge, instinct. They were all burnt from my mind. All I could see, all that I *was*, was a white heat, pure and empty.

As though from a distant world I heard my voice above the raging flame. I was screaming. After a few seconds my sight returned. My clothes had been evaporated by the heat and my body was aflame. You see, I was not on fire, I was fire. My body pulsated red, orange, yellow, white, the heat running through my flesh and burning the air around me. My scream was not the pain of my flesh (though I felt that too and it was beyond agony). I screamed because my very soul was being incinerated.

Like a flaming comet I crashed to the ground, all vestiges of strength, all illusions of control gone. Yet I could not close the book, not until I had done what I needed to. I held the book towards the rising sun, offering it to the source of its power and hoped – prayed – for help.

Like a river of fire, the powers of the book flowed into the rising sun, the roar of its flames easily drowning the screams of the crowd.

I followed the flames with my eyes, staring straight into the sun.

I heard the dragons before I saw them, their screeching, piercing cries as loud as the roar of the book's flames. They flew gracefully out of the sun, as though it were an egg which hatched a terrible spawn, made of its own pure qualities and as they came closer I could see that the beasts did not have the scales of myth and legend, but like my flesh had a colour and texture of fire.

My own conjured flames had not touched the monsters called by Pendrogeth and forged from the very rock of the island. But the dragon's breath was an altogether different force; like coals in a furnace the creatures' black skin, scales and feathers, glowed red and yellow and orange in the heat, causing them to scream and writhe in agony before turning grey, and then, when their screams stopped, ash-white. The swarm, as much in a frenzy of panic as the human crowd, broke into small clouds of creatures, frantically flying this way and that, zigzagging through the sky to escape the dragons. Yet steadily and surely, the dragons followed the flying horde through the sky, breathing their flames wherever the creatures fled. And when the dragon's had finished with them, they froze in the air momentarily before dissolving into ashes, which fell upon Ictis like a dusting of light snow.

As the sky cleared the cheers of the *Seahawk* 's men grew louder, and though my skin and soul burned I dared not close the book for fear I would forfeit the victory. I could not stop before I knew Pendrogeth and all his dark forces were defeated. But where was my enemy? As the dragon's cleared the sky they searched in vain for the master of the creatures that had fought.

'The Book of Fire, give it to me now,' demanded Pendrogeth. He stood on the altar. At his feet, bound in rope and chain, and held down by dortriger, was Anthony. In Pendrogeth's hand he held a large ceremonial dagger, and in a frozen moment – as time slowed down – I noticed the inlaid precious stones and ornate carving of the metalwork glinting in the sunlight. It, was pushed up against Anthonys' throat.

Above us the dragon's flew in circles, angrily screeching and screaming.

'Unlike these ghosts of men, your uncle still lives, but I shall draw the blade across his neck and you shall watch him die. First him, then the girl, then all the living passengers. You may have the Book of Fire boy, but how many shall we kill before you win the day?' I looked around. Pendrogeth's men, and dortriger, had a hold of all of them – including Elsa. They could and would, be killed very quickly. The dragons could not very well fight the enemy with their human shields.

I closed the book and dropped it on the floor. As I let go if it the flames left my body and evaporated into the sky. I collapsed, utterly devoid of feeling or sensation other than numb pain and an aching sense of sorrow. The fire had taken the essence of me, leaving nothing but a naked husk. I felt near to death, unable to move and barely able to breath, but I could still see – just – and through a dark fog watched as a sick grin spread over Pendrogeth's face. With his foot he roughly pushed Anthony from the altar.

'You are lucky Tregenza, I shall need you when we return to Penwith,' said Pendrogeth. Though I had precious little sensation left I was dimly aware of being held and of a wet teardrop falling on my brow.

'Bill, Oh Bill, you could not have done more,' said Elsa.

'Fetch the sacrificial robes,' said Pendrogeth's voice. With no moment of respite to think, or fully take in what was happening to me, I was torn from Elsa by unseen hands and dragged across the stone floor.

'Leave him alone you pigs,' said Elsa.

My naked, near lifeless body was picked off the ground and I was roughly forced into a white gown. Then I was thrown onto the altar. My head lolled backwards so I was looking into the sky. The dragons had ceased their screaming and were circling ever closer to the ground.

'Now they shall obey me, and when the deed is done. You shall be their carrion.' Pendrogeth was leaning over me, that same sickening sneer of victory on his face. Only this time he had a deadly calm in his eyes and in his voice, for now he knew there was no escape, no chance of reprieve. He could afford to relish the moment.

As his men bound me to the altar he held the knife aloft. It glinted with the sun's reflection, poised and ready to plunge into my chest. I was dimly aware that I was about to die and that my last sensations would be of Pendrogeth tearing my heart from my chest.

I could hear the words of his incantation, and see clouds racing across the sky. In the distance I heard the rumble of gathering thunder. I did not know where the books were, my mind could not reach them. I could not bear to look at Pendrogeth so turned my head, only to see a worse sight; Forkbeard, Anthony, Elsa, John and Bob Trelawney, each of them broken by despair. Around them the crowd began to sway and sing:

> *keep the blessed harvest growing*
> *may our cup be o'er flowing*
> *catch be full and harvest plenty*
> *nets and barns be never empty*

Among the crowd was a boy. He neither sung nor rocked in time with the music, but stood amongst them as still as a scarecrow in a field of wind blown wheat.

I knew the boy. He had visited me in his dreams.

'Loer,' I whispered. His thoughts echoed in my mind like the tide in a distant sea cave. His sad, beautiful eyes spoke to my own.

'Master, you have called all the powers but one. A power not of the Sun, nor of the Sky, nor Sea, nor Earth, but all of these in their essences combined. I speak of that which makes them fast, of that which holds them and in this place commands them.'

Pendrogeth grabbed my chin and forced me to face him. He readied himself for the murder. In that moment I made my calling. Pendrogeth did not move. It took a moment for him to realise that he could not. He was as a statue. Frozen still.

I heard the sound of laughter, a soft and gentle, ringing laughter and in the crystal clear dawn light could see the light, ethereal hands that held him. Ayr and her kind were all around, and through and in the air itself. As Ayr floated above me, she began to sing.

To this day the memory of her song makes the hair on my neck stand up and fills me with longing. Not because I recall its words or melody – for it was the kind of song that the moment you heard it you knew you would no more remember than you would ever hope of hearing it again – but because it was the very essence of beauty and grace, nothing more or less, and all of us, every single one, stopped breathing, stopped being, and listened in thrall to her song.

When the song was finished she did something so strange, so utterly bizarre that I almost laughed from disbelief. She barked. Like a dog. All the air spirits began to bark and howl and the air sounded with invisible hooves and paws on stone, and the 'taroot, taroot' of a hunting horn. Pendrogeth was released from his bonds. He held his arms up against an invisible assailant and at the same time, rather comically fumbled inside his robes for his books.

But he did not find them. And it wasn't just him. All the crowd, other than our family or those who were our friends, ran and cowered and beat their arms in the air to fight off unseen attackers.

'Now Nimrod, now Storm, get 'im Thunder, round on 'em,' ordered a voice above the clammer of barks and deafening thunder of the hunter's hooves on the black stone.

The enemy were steadily pushed, herded and hounded onto the very edge of the courtyard until they threatened to topple over onto the battlements below. The sounds of the hunt dissolved slowly till all that could be heard once again was the slow whistle of the morning wind. Seemingly out of thin air two large and hairy hounds appeared in front of the crowd. They growled and raised their heckles whenever one of the crowd so much as moved. All the ropes and chains that bound us were gone and as one Elsa, Anthony and the others ran to me. Elsa threw her arms around me. Helping hands pulled me to my feet and patted my back and head.

'Well done lad,' said John, his voice trembling with emotion.

'Ye'r strong in the ways of the magi!' said Bob.

'But it wasn't me,' I began to explain.

'Yer Uncle Meredith would be proud,' said Forkbeard.

'That I am… and more,' said a voice.

Behind us, at the top of the courtyard stood Meredith. He was dressed, simply as ever, in his old leather jerkin, plain white, collarless shirt and canvas trousers. Over his shoulder was slung his leather satchel, in his hand he held a staff. Meredith opened his arms. Elsa rushed to him. With his arm around her shoulders he strolled towards us.

'We thought you were… dead,' Elsa said between bursts of joyful crying.

'Oh my lovely girl,' he said, holding her close, 'everything shall be made clear,' and with those words he laid a kiss her on her crown and gently pushed her from him. Then he turned Pendrogeth. Though bereft of his books, he still held the sacrificial dagger and despite Meredith's growling hounds he moved as though to attack. Meredith neither made a move to run nor to use his powers. Instead he simply repeated a phrase I had heard him use once before. He said again the first words I had ever heard him speak, that day on the moor when we had first arrived in Cornwall.

'You can't kill that which cannot die.' There was a gasp of horror. Pendrogeth stopped still. 'Nor that which is already dead,' he added. Meredith spoke directly to Pendrogeth, who returned his steady gaze with cold, grey hatred. The truth of Meredith's words found their target as surely as an arrow. The dagger fell to the floor, clattering loudly on the stone floor.

'Dead?' I whispered. Meredith climbed on to the stone altar. The dogs relaxed and all of us, friend and foe alike gathered round to hear him. His voice was strong, and sang with grace and majesty.

'Yes, dead. I am Sakrifis for Lyonesse and one its own. For now I am subject here… as well as master. I drowned in a tempest, forged by my hand and the powers I call to my employment… ,' there was an audible gasp, ''Twas I that conjured wind, called storm, commanded seas. 'Twas my anger given body and flesh enough to tear the skies apart and rent a hole between the land of the living and this place. 'Twas I that brought the *Seahawk* to these shores. And I shall tell you why. For here I could vanquish mine enemies and bring those traitors in my own house to book.' Meredith looked directly at Stephen, who withered under his gaze.

But he also passed his eyes over Anthony and Dr Gonzales who dared not look him in the face. 'Now the sacrifice is made, the young magus has served his apprenticeship, the battle is won. This masque my friends is played out, only the epilogue remains.' He looked to those amongst us who had been Pendrogeth's prisoners. 'You who live still and who mocked and taunted me at the Feast of Lyonesse. I believe the terror of this storm was punishment enough. You shall return to the mainland. Those passengers of the *Seahawk* not assembled here lie around these shores and even now, my faithful spirits who laid them down to slumber, are waking them and preparing them for their journey home.' (I was minded of the bodies I had found on the beach, who had been alive though unconscious). 'Now,' he spoke directly to Forkbeard, John Tanner and the men of the *Seahawk*. 'Most loyal fellows, whose deeds in life were not always pure, as spirits of Lyonesse you have redeemed yourself of past sins. You have given me service of your own will and shall soon be free, for your time 'twixt one life and another is now done, and Ayr… ' Ayr flew down from the sky until she hovered in the air in front of Meredith. 'I promised you freedom once… '

'Sire, we creatures and spirits; mermaids of the sea, dragons of the sun, dortriger of the earth and spirits of the Air, we are servants of the elements in truth, yet tied to magus and master; enslaved… by the books… what of us?' Ayr's voice trembled as she spoke. She sounded nervous, even afraid.

'Light spirit, your service to the magi is almost done, you shall be released, but you must do me one last deed,' his voice darkened, 'bring before me four men of sin.'

Forced by unseen hands Anthony, Dr Gonzales, Stephen and Pendrogeth were dragged in front of Meredith and made to kneel before him. Standing in front of them he had true majesty, but at one and the same time had an air of the despot about him. The smile on his face told of his ease with the darker side of his powers.

'I am Master of Lyonesse, Lord of this Island, King of this

realm, whose powers you are not capable of imagining but yet… but yet… 'He moved on them swiftly, placing himself inches from Anthony. 'You brother! You would usurp this order and sell the birthright on which we have stood for a thousand years?'

'I… had to do something. Testing times…'

'Testing?' he said with contempt. 'What is loyalty? What use fealty, if they mean nothing in the hearts of weak men when times are "testing"?' Meredith leant forward and grabbed poor Anthony by the hair, pulling his head forward so he could speak directly into his ear. 'Brother, I did not need your faith when we were strong,' he whispered. He left a pause for Anthony to reply. But his silence spoke of his shame. Meredith moved his attention to Dr Gonzales.

'A doctor, who would declare my mind unfit and use such diagnosis to rob me of my heritage. How do you find me now 'healer'?' Next he moved to Stephen, using his large rough hand to force Stephen's chin upwards so that he was forced to look at Meredith.

'Well, traitor, have you had wine enough to drown your shame?' then he spoke as though to himself. 'Strange, that I did not see the spy in my own house. Strange that one such as you should be the key to my undoing.'

Finally he faced Pendrogeth, who, unlike the others, did not attempt to turn from Meredith's scrutiny. He said no English words to his foe but keeping his eyes upon him, spoke the language of air. The atmosphere tightened as we waited for the spell to take effect. Ayr floated above them. She looked terrified.

'What spirit,' said Meredith, 'will you hesitate?'

'Please Master,' she said, and from her eyes tears fell that sparkled in the air like diamonds, 'if the price of freedom is such deeds I would remain a slave.'

'Why do you hesitate when I command you?' said Meredith, quietly and calmly. There was a long silence. He was not going to ask a second time. The atmosphere, which had been so full of joy, now thickened with tension. Meredith kept his eyes trained on Pendrogeth. Ayr barely whispered her reply.

'Pity... Sire.'

'Pity! Should they not burn under the sun where there is no shadow? Should they not sometime be locked in the black bowels of the earth, or from time to time feel the winter winds gravest chill, or in a fathomless sea suffer drowning a thousand times?' Meredith looked to Ayr, who, suspended in the air, let her tears fall freely.

He raised his staff as though to strike, not Pendrogeth, but the very spirit who had been his most loyal and trusted servant. She did not flinch, but raised her face and stared straight back at him. Her teary eyes glared with defiance. She was almost daring him. But as he looked upon her the anger melted from his eyes. He sat down on the altar with his head in his hands. It was a long moment before he spoke again.

'... And shall you who are nothing but air shed tears out of a pity I do not feel? Shall you who are the essence of my own breath, be more compassionate?' He stood up grabbed the staff with both hands and with one violent movement brought it down upon his knee, breaking it cleanly in two. Throwing the broken pieces away he turned to the crowd.

'Your service to my kind is done,' his voice boomed over the courtyard. With no more than a flick of his wrist the greater part of the crowd simply vanished. There was no sound of thunder, no slow dissolving of their physical forms into transparent wraith like spirits, no protestation or pleas, no sign of the magical forces which wrought the change. It is simply that one moment they were there, the next it was as though they had never existed.

'You who remain, men of the *Seahawk* and their friends. You shall have the duty of returning your passengers safely to the shores of Penwith. The sea shall wash the memory of this place as tides wash footprints from the sand. Now go, and thereafter, do not return but sail for Albion, where you shall meet your kin.'

John Tanner looked curious and was about to open his mouth to question Meredith, but Meredith just smiled and nodded and Bob and Forkbeard and John Tanner also vanished into thin air, followed quickly by Anthony, Dr Gonzales, Cadmus, the Phoenicians and others. Only Pendrogeth, Meredith, Elsa and I still remained from the crowd of people that had filled the court. Loer was at my side (now once again in the form of a hare). The dortriger shuffled nervously. Above us the dragons and spirits of Air circled silently.

'Your desire 'Lord' Pendrogeth was to rule over this realm. This shall be granted. But mind this. That you will have not one human subject and all the houses, harbour and boats – every item built by human hand in wood and rock and metal, was but a ghost also and shall now, having served my purpose, dissolve in the morning light. This island, in its natural form shall remain and be given over to the dortriger, for it is their domain by nature, as will the sea be provided to the merpeople and the sky to Ayr and all her kind. These dragons shall return to the Sun from where they were unleashed. All their wills are now their own.' He smiled at the dortriger who were already whooping and dancing. They descended on Pendrogeth and dragged him away. Next he turned his attentions to Ayr.

'Flighty spirit. You are free,' he whispered. Ayr and her kind melted into the light of the rising sun. 'At my bidding she protected you throughout your adventures. In the cave, in the ice, even when you first flew. We were always with you lad, in one way or another.' I hugged him, for I knew the end was near now and I would not see him again.

'What about you Uncle Meredith? Will you come home with us?' asked Elsa, joining me in holding on to him, though it was a weak plea, and I knew she dreaded his reply.

'Do not mourn for me child. I am Sakrifis and like all such, my sacrifice is indeed a birth of kinds, a beginning as well as an end.'

'But what… but where…?' He gently pushed us away.

'In the roots of barley and wheat that shall now grow in the valley; in the turquoise depths that will soon teem with fish; in the wind that whistles o'er the stone walls on the moors. I will fly aboard the wings of the owl by night and ride the sunlight to the earth at break of day… and finally do the task I had set myself, for now I understand how it shall be done. Remember this,' he looked at Loer with a knowing smile and repeated to us the riddle of the *Seahawk*. When he had finished he said:

'Now, Bill you have served your apprenticeship well, but with good fortune you will never need these books again,' he patted the satchel.

'What will you do with them?' I asked.

'They shall be lost to you, but should you ever need them again, they will find you. Now, the time has come for us to leave this place.'

'But will we ever… ,' he shook his head.

'We must say farewell. I leave it to you to remember what has passed and to use your knowledge wisely. I trust you with my legacy.'

'But, but you can come back,' said Elsa, her voice quickening with panic, 'you're a magician, a powerful magician, you can bring the dead to life.' He put a finger to her lips, then placed his hands on my shoulders.

'You shall remember Bill, for if ever you need the books again it is important that you recall what you have learnt of their ways. You will find it hard enough to believe your own memory and they shall tell you this is all a dream… and they will be right… '

'A dream,' I said.

'Now, the souls of men, the walls and chimney of house and inn, the towers and halls of Ictis… memories… ghosts… all… will dissolve, and leave no trace, for they are nothing but the essence of a dream, dreamt in a life…'

Everything around me; the black stone of Ictis, the bright dawn sky, the whisper of the wind – became shrouded in darkness and silence, till my only waking sense was of Meredith's voice and his face, floating in an unfathomable void. Though his eyes were constant, his features began to change, slowly at first then with frightening speed. He was the boatman who rowed me to the *Seahawk* at the Festival of Lyonesse, he was the old man who teased Pendrogeth outside the cave, he was the bird-fish, he was Cadmus the Pheoenician, he was Loer, he was his hound.

'… that begins and ends…' He was gone.

'… with a sleep…'

An abyss. That is the only way I can explain it. And the deeper into this abyss I fell the more I wanted to be a part of it. I would gladly have gone into that abyss then, sunk in a fathomless ocean like a ship which, having fought against the storm, lets the waves wash over it, and surrenders to the long, slow pull of the deep, sinking and sinking until it is no more troubled by wind and waves but can rest in the silent void. Forever.

It was not dark, for I had no sight to see the darkness. It did not last an eternity any more or less than it lasted a split second, for there was no time to measure. It was not a place I can describe for there was no 'there' there. It was nothing.

My first inkling that I was returning was when I became dimly aware of having limbs, limbs that I could move and feel, and in the distance a round pale, blue orb, that shimmered like a reflection.

I felt a coldness creeping over my skin and a pressure inside my chest, gentle at first, but as I sensed more cold and the blue orb became ever larger and closer, this pressure grew, becoming a heavy desperate force. I opened my mouth to breath but instead took a lung of cold, shocking water.

The blue globe was the sun, seen through many feet of water. It was high above me, too high. Then it was obscured by… a face. Elsa's face. Her mouth was open. She was breathing. She pulled at me with her hands, lifting my arms over hers. With a powerful stroke, she swum upwards, bearing us both to the surface. Hands dragged my limp, soaked body over the rail of a boat.Elsa was helped aboard too. I was sick.

Voices, shouts, the cries of gulls, the glow of sun on my water-frozen cheeks.

'We've found 'em,' shouted a voice, a man's voice. My blurred vision rocked like a stormy sea, slowly balancing itself. Mr Penrose's brown face loomed in and out of focus. There was another figure behind him. A woman. A familiar face, though it took me a few seconds to place her. It was Miss Ariel, her wide open mouth grinning as she pulled at the oars.

'Don't worry,' she said. 'You're safe now.'

Chapter 20

A blanket was quickly placed around my shoulders.

'You've got the luck of the devil!' For a split second I thought I was back in Lyonesse. The voice was Ayr's. I stood up in the boat, making it rock, and was forcefully pushed back down by Mr Penrose.

'But who... where? Ayr,' I said, looking at Miss Ariel. It was then that I realised the most remarkable thing; that their voices were almost identical and Miss Ariels' open, kind face and beautiful blue eyes were quite like those of Ayr's. 'A spirit of the air. That's what you said – that day at the Festival.'

'A what lad?' said Mr Penrose.

'Bill, we thought you were dead. Everyone else came ashore ages ago,' said Miss Ariel.

'Everyone?'

'Now, we've got to get you somewhere warm and dry,' said Miss Ariel in a matter of fact voice. But the lines in her forehead told of her worry and she wouldn't look me in the face. I threw the blanket aside.

'Everyone?' I repeated. Miss Ariel looked out to sea for a time, I think to steady her nerves before she spoke.

'All are accounted for apart from Lord Pendrogeth and... I'm afraid no one has yet seen or found your uncle Meredith. Bill, Elsa, it is a miracle that we found you alive after all this time. I am not at all sure that your uncle has been so lucky.' She seemed quite shocked when I smiled.

'Oh no,' I said, 'he's not coming back.'

'Back?' she said, 'I know this must be a terrible shock... '

she carried on talking, groping for the right words, words to either explain or to comfort, but which she knew would do neither. Elsa looked shocked, almost unable to comprehend what was being told to her.

I picked up the blanket and pulled it around me, steadying my gaze on the waving, still storm rocked, seas. Before long we had come ashore.

'Best get you home immediately' said Mr Penrose, 'Dr Gonzales'll need to get a look at you both, though 'e has barely recovered from the ordeal himself.'

'But we can't go to Lyonesse House yet. What about Uncle Meredith. We might find him still. Everyone else has survived,' said Elsa. I put my arm around her.

'Elsa, he's not coming back,' I said.

'What do you know about it? I'm just a young girl and I survived. You don't know anything.' I felt her pain then, and for the time being left her alone.

'What happened Mr Penrose?' I said as we climbed into the small, pony-led trap that would take us to Lyonesse House.

'Can't you remember lad? Your boat went down in a storm – the likes of which… '

'I know, but when, which day?' He arched his eyebrows in surprise.

'Why yesterday of course. You'd never 'ave survived more'n one night in them waters. 'Tis a miracle that anyone survived for so long.'

So the time that had passed in Lyonesse was no time at all, I thought. I had arrived on its shores in the morning following my night adrift in the storm. According to Mr Penrose, that was now.

'When were the others found?'

'Well, yesterday and last night was not safe for any boat and none dared put to sea for fear of losing more souls. This morn at dawn the relatives lined the shore, 'specting nothing more than the corpses of their kin to be washed up. Yet 'twas not to be. Some was found swimming far out to sea, others were washed up on rocks and sand, unconscious but still alive.

There was nothing natural 'bout that tempest, and nothing natural 'bout how the folk aboard that boat came to shore alive and well, when they should be dead and gone in the storm… like the lost souls of Lyonesse.'

'Tell me Mr Penrose. Do you believe in that old myth of Lyonesse. Lost souls and ghost islands?'

'Lyonesse? Dunno. I know I can't explain what happened this last day. The only thing I know for sure is that most who say they are sure of 'ow things are, or why they are, are often the most ignorant folk I meet. Argh, I reckon there's more to this world than most can dream of lad. Who knows what is possible.'

When we reached the house Anthony and Dr Gonzales were there to greet us. When he saw us Anthony faltered and had to be helped to stay upright by Dr Gonzales. As he did not ask, I assumed word had reached him that Meredith had not been found.

It was rather awkward after we had climbed down from the trap. We stood in front of the doctor and our uncle, listening to the steady clip-clop and trundling wheels of Mr Penrose's pony and trap slowly melt into the summer sounds of birdsong and a gentle breeze brushing across the treetops.

Anthony spoke first.

'My dear boy. I feel such mixed emotions. I am so glad that you and your sister have survived what must have been a terrible night in the water, yet so very, very sorry that events have led us to our current state. I fear Meredith has not survived the storm… and if it hadn't been for yesterday's appalling events. If only I had stopped them… ' Anthony faltered, struggling to fight back tears. 'But I tell you one thing – I shall respect his wishes. If the bank foreclose on us so be it, but I shall not sell.' And then he shed tears of pride and anger as well as sadness.

'That won't happen,' I said.

'My boy I am afraid it will. It's too late you see. Even if the

crops recovered and the boats came in full every day for month…
it is too late.'

'No,' I insisted. 'It isn't.'

'Isn't it?' he said, more gently. I looked deep into my
uncle's eyes and for brief moment the sorrow left his face and he
looked as though he were somehow comforted by my words,
though he did not know why, or how.

'You've had an ordeal. It might be best to get some rest,'
said Dr Gonzales

'But don't any of you remember?' I said, 'Lyonesse?'
Anthony looked at me with concern.

'To your rooms now, both of you. We shall talk further
when you have rested.'

We were left to sleep, though there was no chance of it and
as soon as their footsteps were heard on the stairway Elsa tiptoed
in to my room.

'What were you talking about Bill? Lyonesse? What have I
missed?'

'You? Not much, you were in the middle of it.' Elsa could
no more hide her feelings than her mood but for once I could not
read her eyes. She was smiling.

'What do you remember of the storm Elsa? Nothing right?
Well there's a reason for that. And remember the hare that first
day, when John Tanner – I mean Meredith's man, the mute –
picked us up, and we saw Meredith bring that hare back from the
dead… and the dolphins at Sennen that day, the kite, the
mermaid. You believed it all didn't you and I – the fool I was – I
didn't. But you did. Remember? And the water, how do you think
you survived in the water? You're a weak swimmer but you
practically rescued me didn't you? There's a reason for that too.
Look, I know this is going to be a lot to take in but… we, all of us,
we've been somewhere you can barely begin to imagine.'

'Bill,' she whispered, slipping her hand into mine and
squeezing, 'If you say its true I believe you.'

'You remember.'

'No… I don't remember anything, you'll have to tell me. I mean I remember the ship sinking, but the next thing I can recall is coming up in the water with you… except I was pulling you up and it was easy, and I was… ,' suddenly she looked scared, '… breathing.' She put a trembling hand to her mouth, then ran her fingers down her face and on to her throat, she was shaking her head.

'Look in the mirror Elsa, look at your eyes. I think you might be… ' The door was opened slowly and Anthony's head appeared. He clearly expected me to be asleep.

'I thought as much. You ought to be resting. I know it's difficult, but please try.'

'Perhaps I should give them something,' said Dr Gonzales, striding into the room, his carpetbag already open.

'There's no need, really. We're fine. I was just going to tell Elsa… Look, all I ask is that you listen to me. Hear my tale. It's important as there isn't much time.'

'Tale, what tale?'

'Please!' Anthony looked exasperated, but he sighed and nodded.

'Go back to your room child,' he said to Elsa.

'No Uncle, please let Elsa stay, she needs to hear this too.' Anthony came and sat on the bed with Elsa. Dr Gonzales stood awkwardly for a while before deciding that it was best to humour me. He dragged a chair in from another room. When he sat in it, he pulled a pipe, matches and a bag of tobacco from his bag.

'Go on then young man, say what it is you have to say,' he said filling the pipe.

> *Racing, jumping, running fast*
> *In shadow it shall be found*
> *In mid-summer moon, deeply cast*
> *Yet sleeping gently in the ground*
> *Who was the first but now is last*
> *Will lead the way by quarry of stone…*

I meant to finish the riddle but was interrupted by Elsa.

'The face of the future shall become the past
And then the treasure trove's your own.'

she said, seeming surprised by her own words.

'How do I know that?' she said.

They didn't quite look on me, or Elsa, as though we had lost all our senses. In fact Anthony and the doctor tried to hide what they must have thought, with concerned, kind eyes.

'And 'erm, what does that mean young man? Elsa?' said Dr Gonzales.

'I… I don't know, I've never heard it before,' said Elsa.

'What it means is… , well it's a riddle. There was once a terrible storm at Lamorna that sank a smugglers' ship whilst it was being chased by a Customs' frigate… '

'The *Seahawk*,' said Anthony, 'that old legend.'

'Yes, the riddle was told by the only survivor to his rescuers, and it is believed that if deciphered it can lead the riddle solver to the treasure. '*In midsummer moon, deeply cast,*' well it is the mid summer moon now and '*sleeping gently in the ground*' has to mean buried or hidden, '*quarry of stone*' must refer to the stone quarry near Lamorna.'

'Well I can see your logic Bill. But what about the rest of the riddle?'

'I don't know but I do know that Meredith, or his servant, was searching for that treasure the last few days before the Festival, at Lamorna Cove.'

'Is that how you know this riddle, did Meredith tell you? How do you know – or think you know – this Bill?' asked Anthony, screwing his eyes tight in concentration.

'I want to tell you the whole story, I do, but you'd never believe me. But please trust me enough to believe that something happened that day when Elsa and I got lost in the caves, something that leads me to think the treasure *is* there, but it can only be found now during the midsummer moon when the tides are at their lowest, and the entrance to the cave is open. Don't you see? We have to go there, now, before the tides flood the entrance!'

'I repeat Bill. How do you know this?' Anthony was not going to let me off the hook. 'I want the truth now Bill and will know it if you try and fool me,' he pointed a finger at me.

'Very well then… ' I told them the whole story, the dreams, the discovery of Meredith's library, Pendrogeth at the museum in St. Ives, and then everything from the time when the ship went down, to mine and Elsa's sorrowful parting with Meredith. The only part I missed out, was Elsa's 'changing.' I never stopped to think how ridiculous or incredible my story sounded, nor worried that I was telling them a tale in which they had each played a part but of which they had no memory. When I had finished they looked at me with eyes of wonder, not knowing what to make of me, or my incredible tale.

'Uncle Anthony. The day of the Festi…Yesterday, when we boarded the ship, did you notice its name?' I asked.

'I cannot say as I did,' said Anthony, screwing up his forehead, trying to remember.

'It was the *Seahawk*, and its crew lost souls – from the island of Lyonesse.' I said.

'All that saltwater has turned your mind boy. Who filled your head with these old legends? Mr Penrose?' said the doctor.

'All have been accounted I was told, excepting Pendrogeth and Uncle Meredith. Well what about the captain and crew of the ship? I'll bet no-one has reported a single one of them missing?' My eyes searched those of Uncle Anthony and Dr Gonzales. They exchanged a look. Dr Gonzales arched his eyebrows and shrugged. '… And what of your night in the water Uncle?' I continued, 'what about when the ship went down? If your own account is so different to my own tell me what happened. But I'll bet you can't.'

'Well that is straightforward enough,' Dr Gonzales started, 'the storm had been raging for quite a time, I do remember, quite a time and then…and then, well, the ship sank didn't it…I mean it must have… and then the water… ' he searched for words to describe a memory that didn't exist.

'And you Uncle Anthony?'

'Well…well I'll be… Do you know, I can barely remember the sinking of the ship nor any of it, not until I was ashore not long after dawn. I thought my mind must have blotted out the terrible experience, but… '

'And that is what happened,' said Dr Gonzales, taking control of himself once he had got over the surprise of realising he had no recollection of the events, 'must have happened, to most of us I expect. But not to Bill. You see lad, according to your tale you lost Elsa in the water. Well in a time of great stress and probably in a semi-conscious state your mind has conjured up this story. You are acutely aware of the financial stress on the Estate and in your mind you have made a demon of Lord Pendrogeth, partly because of his attempt to take over the Estate and partly because of the dreadful events at the Festival. Also, according to your uncle you nearly lost your sister once, in the caves at Lamorna. In the sea it appears you lost her again, and your mind has forged this delusion, at least in part to cope with the stress and guilt. Most of what you have told in your story can be traced to your experiences here in Penwith. Miss Ariel for example has been transformed into this 'Ayr' spirit in your tale. The hare, you say, appeared in your dreams – more than once – and did you not say you donned the disguise of a hare at the Festival? I'll give you another example. The legendary Isle of Ictis, did you not say that you had seen Miss Ariel's painting of it some days before?'

'Yes.'

'And was the citadel you visited in your dream not *exactly* the same as in the painting?'

'I… I… don't know,' I stammered. But he was right. The Ictis of Lyonesse was the same as Miss Ariel's painting.

'And the caves you allege to have travelled through, they were formed from your memory of your day at Lamorna Cove. And your sister has no recollection of this 'library' you found in this very house?' I thought to rush downstairs, to go to our late grandmother's room, to see if the library where we had first discovered the books was still there. But as soon as I had the thought, I realised that it wouldn't be. It had been Meredith's portal to Lyonesse. That door would now be closed.

'I don't wish to upset you Bill, merely to put pay to a dangerous fantasy,' said Dr Gonzales. 'A very powerful fantasy too, to be so detailed, so remembered but… ' said Dr Gonzales, leaving a silence for us to fill with our own conclusions. 'Just a dream my boy,' said Dr Gonzales, 'Eh Anthony… er Anthony?' Our uncle was still looking into my eyes intently.

'I'll tell you something I do know and it pains me to admit it but… I don't feel sad for the loss of Meredith. I should do, but I don't. It's as though he's gone… yet hasn't and… I'm sure of it… '

'Shock,' said Dr Gonzales, 'simple as that. Now I think we all need some rest '

'No,' said Elsa, speaking directly to Anthony, for she knew she would get nowhere with the doctor. 'We have to go and find the treasure.'

'Children I have nearly lost you twice, I am most certainly not going to entertain the idea of you, or anyone, chasing around those damn caves,' said Anthony, but he sounded unconvinced by his own reason.

'Please Uncle Anthony,' I said.

'Dr Gonzales?' said Anthony, looking to the doctor.

'Well, Anthony,' he said, tapping his pipe on his chin, 'it may surprise you to hear that I think such a search can actually do no harm. It will put an end to these fantasies whereas if we do not do this…. I fear you will never hear the last of it.' Elsa let go of my hand and bounced off the bed like a coiled spring. She gave Dr Gonzales a kiss.

'I can be changed in two ticks,' she cried running to the door. Anthony stood up immediately, hands on hips.

'Not a chance young lady. The doctor and Mr Penrose will

accompany Bill to Lamorna Cove this afternoon. You will stay here… with me.'

It was late in the afternoon by the time we reached Lamorna Cove. Mr Penrose (the Mr Penrose who attended the gardens of Lyonesse) took us there in his pony and trap.

Our arrival aroused the interest of Miss Ariel. She came straight to us from her cottage and hugged me.

'I am so sorry for the loss of your uncle. Such dreadful events. Mr Penrose, Doctor… '

The doctor darted his eyes away to indicate that they should talk privately. Whilst we waited I tried to catch what they were saying and picked up that if Meredith's body were not found (as I was sure it would not be), then within a week a memorial service would be held, as was the custom when men of Penwith were lost at sea.

The doctor also explained to Miss Ariel the nature of our visit to Lamorna. She was quickly enlisted to join our adventure.

'The cave from which you children were rescued, by your uncle's servant, could you find it again?' she said.

'I expect so,' I replied.

'Mr Penrose we are anticipating exceptionally low tides are we not?'

'Look, here's me nephew Jimmy Penrose, he'll know for sure.'

A boat big enough for six men and two sets of oars, was being slowly rowed to the shore. Only two men were aboard though, and they were struggling to get the boat in to the dock, where another pair of fishermen waited to help land the catch and secure the boat up the slipway. It held a cargo of nets and crates. The crates were brimming with fish.

'How's it Jimmy?' said Miss Ariel.

'Catch is good, we just left a team o' men from round Mousehole way, nets are proper full, like the fish 'ave been waiting for this moment these last few months. Must be something to do with that terrible storm.'

'It is,' I said.

'Jimmy, when is low tide?'

'That'll be 'bout half an hour Miss.'

'Jimmy,' said Miss Ariel, practising her most winning smile. Her white teeth shone from her brown face and her blue eyes sparkled. 'Could you 'erm, lend us your boat a while, and if you would pilot it too I'd be doubly grateful.' Jimmy tried not to grin too obviously.

'Begging pardon Miss, but this 'ere team is still employed by the Tregenza family, not like most, and as you can see me and the boys is a little busy with the best catch we've 'ad in many a month.'

'It's okay Jimmy Penrose, it is on Anthony Tregenza's business that we need the boat,' said Dr Gonzales.

'Right you are sir. In that case, I shall welcome you aboard as soon as these fish is landed.' Miss Ariel disappeared with one of the men. In silence we all helped the men lift the crates of still writhing fish from the boat. When the task was done Miss Ariel re-appeared bearing two miner's lamps.

'Where to then?' said Jimmy. Dr Gonzales, Mr Penrose and Miss Ariel looked to me for instruction.

'There,' I said, pointing to the distant headland.

As we approached the cave we could clearly see the entrance exposed by the low tide. The senior Mr Penrose, the doctor and I all took off our shoes and stripped to our trousers. We jumped into the water, and then, bearing the lamps and some matches that were handed to us, swam the few yards into the cave entrance. Once in, with the lamps lit, we could see just how large and complex the cave system was; several passages led from the main chamber, but it was easy to see which Elsa and I had taken – only one was big enough to enter without either crouching or climbing.

'Mind your footing,' Mr Penrose's words echoed through

the cave. The three of us walked in single file, keeping one hand on the cave wall, which was slimy with algae and encrusted with limpets, testifying to the fact that the cave was usually submerged in water.

'Be careful,' I whispered, 'it descends rather sharply,' Mr Penrose and the doctor and I climbed steeply down, ten yards or more. Here the passageway split into three. We chose the one that lay directly ahead. From my memory of mine and Elsa's adventure this seemed the most likely route.

As we explored the cave's deeper reaches, the eerie orange light of the lamps showed that the passage split into two more than once, but after a few false turns we found the chamber we sought.

'Well I never!' said Mr Penrose. In the dancing orange light thrown by the lamp we could see white bones. A full skeleton of a man lay on the floor.

'You know that pirates would often cover their buried treasure with the body of a man, in part to keep prying eyes from looking any further, but also so as the dead man's ghost could guard the treasure against anyone who sought to find it,' said Dr Gonzales. I kept a wary eye on the bones as Mr Penrose turned the skeleton over with his foot. But there was no trove there. No box. No chest. We searched the highs and lows of the chamber. There was nowhere to dig, for the floor of the cave was of solid rock, nor was there a nook or cranny where the treasure might have been stashed, nor a pile of rocks beneath which the treasure might be buried. In silence we searched the other passages and chambers, but each was as barren as another. Eventually, after an hour or so, Mr Penrose voiced the inevitable.

'Listen lad. We've been 'ere a while. The tide'll rise soon and to be honest it'd take hours, maybe even days to explore these caves properly.'

'But the treasure is here. It has to be.' I said. He placed a heavy hand on my shoulder.

'Come on lad. Best find our way back.' Dr Gonzales took no satisfaction from having been proved right, but I think he was relieved, believing the experience would put me back in my right senses, even though I might look – and feel – quite foolish for a long time.

When we arrived back at the house Anthony and Elsa were waiting outside (no doubt Elsa had kept vigil at my bedroom window, waiting for our re-appearance). I don't know if Anthony expected us to return anything other than empty handed, but Elsa had been more hopeful and as we approached, the pony trap slowly clip-clopping down the track, it was heartbreaking to see the disappointment on her face.

'Right then, now this business is over I had best get back to the affairs of the Estate,' said Anthony, rather awkwardly. 'Your mother shall have to be informed, not only of our sad loss but also of the preparations that we will have to make regarding the house and Estate. Mr Penrose, I understand Stephen was also safely returned this morning?'

'He was sir, but 'e 'as not been seen since.'

'Well as he is not present I fully expect he is in The Turk's Head supping be… '

'No sir. On coming ashore he was awful shook up and apparently swore there and then on the first Bible 'e could find – and with witnesses – that 'e would never touch a drop of anything stonger'n tea no more, not till 'is dying day.'

'Well, in any case he is not here. Never mind, I shall prepare supper myself, but if you don't mind children I won't join you. As I have said there are affairs to attend to.'

'You said you would not sell,' said Elsa, almost accusing him.

'And I won't, but I have held the bank off these last few days on assurance that we had a buyer. When they discover that we are not selling, the wheels of debt recovery will be set in motion.' For the sake of Elsa he held back from using the word 'bankrupt'.'

After our supper Elsa and I sat in her room watching the

sunset of the late evening. During the afternoon the few remaining clouds had been blown away by the final breath of the storm, leaving a becalmed sea and a clear sky. A reflection of the sun glinted brightly on the mirror waters and the cliffs, heather and gorse burnt with the orange fire of a late summer's eve. It felt strange to be in the presence of such beauty when my heart was so heavy.

'Do you still believe me? After all I didn't find the treasure did I?' She ignored my question.

'What were you going to tell me, earlier, before you told us about Lyonesse. You said I'd changed.'

'You were rescued by mermaids Elsa, in the storm, but you paid a price. You see, they took you for one… of their own.' She laughed. A scornful laugh, a scared laugh. 'Look in the mirror, look at your eyes,' I said. She walked to the wardrobe and stood in front of it. She stared at her own reflection as though it were a real face, reaching slowly out to touch the glass. Then she turned to me, and I could see the pale green of her eyes had almost turned white. She seemed a stranger to me then. Without another word she slowly walked to her room.

Chapter 21

When I decided I was not going to sleep I went to the window. The moon was full and bright, painting every detail of the landscape with its ghostly glow. I breathed deeply of the night air, standing there for a while before I returned to my bed.

'William… ,' it was no more than a distant whisper in the still night, so quiet, I doubted whether I had heard anything at all. I stopped still, frozen to the spot.

'Wiiiillliiiaamm.'

I slowly turned. There on the grass were Meredith's hounds. They were running in circles around a statue. Or was it? It was a hare, frozen still, but around him, his shadow played, running and leaping and jumping and wrestling with the dogs. In the distance I could hear a hunting horn. And as I stared at the lawn, and then at the moon, and back at the dogs and the hare, the hairs on the back of my neck began to rise and a delicious shiver raced up my spine.

'Of course! Of course,' I spoke out loud, 'the quarry of stone.'

Elsa had slipped in to my room without me noticing. She was standing right beside me.

'Do you see them?' I asked. She gazed upon them for a time, then slowly turned to me.

'This is no dream,' she said.

'This is no dream,' I echoed. 'The quarry of stone Elsa, the tor up on the moor and the stone circle where we saw Meredith the day we arrived, when he brought that hare back to life. The tor next to the stone circle. It looks like a hare from the sky; I saw it from Miss Ariel's plan. I was wrong about the treasure being in the cave at Lamorna. It's on the moor. I was wrong about the tides too, but I think it's something to do with the moon and if I don't go now I'll never get another chance. Are you coming?' She looked at the lawn. The hare and the dogs had gone.

'There's no way you're going alone!' Elsa disappeared to her room to dress and I did likewise. We met in the hallway and ever so carefully, and painfully slowly, found our way through the silent house, down the stairs, and out through the front door without a sound. Once outside we made our way to the small garden hut in which Mr Penrose kept his scythes, forks and other equipment. I found a spade and slung it over my shoulder. It was all we would need. Then we set off on our quest.

A perfect circle of a moon sat in the dark ocean of the sky. Its complexion was of the palest gold, shining on the land like a second sun, turning the landscape into a ghost of the day; a pale reflection, where every silver-blue detail of field and moor and woods was bright and alive, yet every feature was echoed by dark and silent shadow. There was no wind, nor sign of any life, not even the call of owl, nor scurrying of rabbits, nor the distant bark of a fox. Though we were far from the house Elsa still whispered:

'It is like the whole world is sleeping, even the land and the animals, and only you and I are real, only you and I are awake.'

She was right. I couldn't even hear the distant whisper of the shore, which was usually an ever-present song in those parts. In the wake of the storm it seemed even the restless sea had chosen to sleep. It was a long walk, an hour or more, during which we barely spoke.

Eventually we came across the stones. It was easy enough to find them. The road led straight past them, high on the moor, over the brow of the highest hill. The stones were quite eerie, highlighted in the spectral glow of the moon and though they did not have the form of anything that had once lived, they seemed unnervingly like statues, watching us as we began to explore the circle.

But where to look? Next to the stone circle was the tor,

with the small cave where we had seen Meridith lay the hare. I looked at the tor and at its shadow. I had to admit to myself that from the ground it didn't look anything like a hare though from the sky – in Miss Ariel's plane – I remembered the tor had looked very much like a crouching hare. Even if the treasure were here, I thought, it could be in any number of places; inside the small cave, behind one of the stones, or in the centre of the large circle within the stones, where the grass had been shorn down to the earth by rabbits. We stood in the stone circle for quite a time, absorbing the atmosphere and thinking about where to look.

'What time is it?' said Elsa, breaking the silence. I picked out my pocket watch.

'Ten minutes to midnight,' I replied.

I noticed then that as the moon made its arc through the sky, the shadow of the tor, which had been quite indistinct, now seemed something like the outline of a crouching hare.

'Elsa, look,' I said, grabbing her arm and pointing to the shadow. Slowly, very slowly as the moon climbed to its zenith, the shadow gradually shifted its shape, elongating and stretching, as if it were a live hare, slowly sitting up and unfurling its long ears and limbs. It took a good ten minutes, but eventually the shadow of the tor precisely resembled a hare sitting on its haunches, its ears erect and its noble head in profile. I looked at my watch. At precisely midnight, the moon shone through a fissure in the tor's gnarled rock, sending a beam of moonlight directly on to the shadow-head of the hare. As the shadow-head passed over a rock on the ground, the moonbeam hit the rock, transforming it into a dazzling, oval eye.

In my mind's ear I could hear Meredith reciting the riddle of the treasure,

> *Racing, jumping, running fast*
> *In shadow it shall be found*
> *In midsummer moon, deeply cast*
> *Yet sleeping gently in the ground*
> *Who was the first but now is last*

Will lead the way by quarry of stone
The face of the future shall become the past
And then the treasure trove's your own

We watched in wonder, unable to move until the shadow had moved on and was once more an undefined mass of darkness. Then we ran to the 'eye'.

The stone was deep set, surrounded by a skirt of long grass that the rabbits had, curiously, left alone. I had to dig around it before we could lift it. Underneath was a damp patch of earth, patterned by worms and lice that wriggled and scurried into the shelter of the grass.

'Go on,' urged Elsa, digging her elbow into my side. The spade crunched into the ground as I booted it in. A foot or so down, the spade went in a final time, but this time there was no crunch of earth scraping against the spade but instead, a dull thud.

We dropped to our knees and with eager fingers scraped away the dirt. By coincidence – though it felt like a blessing – the shadow was chased around the rock by the moon at that moment, and the moon's light flooded the hole. At the bottom I could see a strip of metal, holding panels of wood. It was the lid of a chest.

For a second we looked at each other in amazement before setting at the digging in a frenzy. Before long we had the chest out of the hole and on the ground. It was small, perhaps a foot long by ten inches wide and six deep. But big enough, we knew. There was no lock. With trembling, mud stained fingers I opened the lid.

Diamonds, rubies, pearls, sapphires, moonstones, cat's eyes, turquoise, emeralds… every kind and size and hue of precious stone tinkled and crackled as I dug into them and held a small handful up to the moonlight. There were small stones, large stones, some round and smooth, others cut into perfect symmetrical patterns with myriads of faces that glinted and sparkled like frost in sunlight. Carefully I turned my hand over and let them fall like a precious rain back into the chest. I closed the lid slowly and let out a long breath. Then we whooped and hugged and danced and crowed and shrieked and sung to the moon.

Uncle Anthony was surprised to see us already up when he came down to breakfast. He looked terrible, his black suit crumpled and his hair dishevelled in a way that we had been more used to seeing on Meredith.

'Children – you could not sleep?'

'We've got breakfast for you,' said Elsa, 'it's in the dining room.' Anthony smelled the air, looking at us suspiciously. Nevertheless, he allowed Elsa to take him by the hand. At the head of the table we had placed the small chest, now cleaned of the earth in which it had sat for so many years.

'What is this?' he asked. He was not amused. We could see by his frown that he did not think this was the time for games or riddles.

'Open it,' I said, 'but before you do Uncle Anthony, please believe me when I say that every word of what I have told you is true, and that Meredith is with us now and always… and that this is his legacy, just as he wished.'

Anthony looked at the chest, then at me, and at Elsa. He opened the chest. In the morning light, the stones were infinitely brighter than in the night, picking up the light of the room and magnifying it a thousand times, lighting Anthony's face in a glow of magic.

'Good Lord,' he said.

'It's the treasure of the *Seahawk*,' I said.

'Good Lord,' he repeated, then he stood up, opening his arms. We all three held each other for a long time. No word was spoken. We all knew what this meant.

When Anthony had gathered his wits, he took another look at the stones and allowed himself a smile, the like of which I had rarely seen since we had arrived in Cornwall. Then he rushed to the cellar, returning with a bottle of wine and three glasses. He poured a full glass for himself, a smaller one for me, and a drop for Elsa, mixed with water. He raised his glass and we followed suit.

'To Meredith Tregenza,' he said.

'To Meredith,' we echoed, and drank the wine.

It ended as it had begun, on the platform of the train station at Penzance, on a hot and cloudless day.

Our mother was with us, having come down to Cornwall, both to attend Meredith's memorial service and to accompany us home. During her few days at Lyonesse House she had gathered up a few possessions of Meredith's and also some of our late grandmother's, so taking all of our boxes and bags onto the train was going to be quite a task. However, we had no need of porters, as a small farewell party had come to the station to bid us goodbye. Anthony was there of course. So was his servant Stephen (who had gone under quite a transformation since returning to the house – as well as being both contrite and sober, he now seemed quite particularly nice and loyal and hard working, though Dr Gonzales, had had to give him aids for sleeping as Stephen was having the most terrible nightmares concerning 'monsters' and 'barrels of wine'). The good Dr Gonzales was there also. He was an executor of Meredith's will and was helping Anthony with the will and the affairs of the Estate. In this capacity, and as a friend of the family, he had been a daily visitor to the house since the day after the Festival of Lyonesse.

Two of the Mr Penrose's were also present, one had been our uncles' gardener, the other had been the captain of one of the Tregenzas' fishing boats. Please note, I say 'had,' for in our uncle's will he had divided the Estate quite considerably, and had provided most of the boats and land of the Estate to various wings of the Penrose clan and to other men and families who had never defected to Pendrogeth, nor ever shown Meredith ill will. Hence Mr Penrose the gardener was now the proud farmer of a small holding of some thirty acres, and Mr Penrose the fishermen was now both captain and equally proud owner of two fishing boats.

Anthony (and the name of Tregenza) had retained Lyonesse House and a modest adjacent farm. The treasure had been enough to pay off the debts, but it had not been so much that Anthony could have held the whole Estate together, even if he had wanted to. Not only had Anthony not objected, I think he had been relieved.

Miss Ariel was present too. Her debt to my uncles had been written off and the plane she so loved was now her own.

'Come on,' said Miss Ariel, lugging a box off the cart, 'if we don't get you and this luggage on the train soon you'll jolly well miss it.' These words made my heart ache, for I truly dreaded getting on the train and would have been more than happy to miss it. For in spite of the recent memorial service, the mood of our small party was in keeping with the bright and cheerful day and we might just as well have been setting off for a picnic. The sun was over the eastern hills by an hour or more and it shone down on the cool, blue waters of the bay, making me wish that we were at that moment finishing a long breakfast and preparing for a walk on the moors, a visit to the market or a day exploring some unknown cove or beach.

'What will you do now Miss Ariel?' I said as she passed luggage for me to take aboard the train.

'Well, I'll continue to fly to the Scilly's, I expect there'll be other work for me too and… do you know, I don't really know. I've been so keen to pay off the cost of the plane I suppose I've never really thought beyond that. It's a strange thing Bill. Wanting your freedom and getting it aren't the same thing. But don't worry, I'll be fine. Now you make sure you don't forget all about us you two,' she said wagging a friendly finger in our faces.

'And you mustn't forget us either,' said Elsa. Then she looked out to sea and spoke, it seemed, almost to herself 'I promise we'll come back as soon as we're able.'

'Not much chance o' forgetting you two is there now?' said Mr Penrose the farmer. 'Why, 'tis to you two, that we owes our fortune.' The porter blew a whistle. 'Now get on that train and give us your leave. There's crops and stock need tending to and fish thass needing to be caught and much other work to be done besides. For there *is* a treasure, 'pon the hill and under the sea. There is diamonds that have to be found anew each day,' he laughed, 'it is what yer uncle Meredith wished for us.'

As I prepared to board the train I looked upon the bay, its turquoise waters bright with the promise of the day, and smelt the fresh salt air and one last time felt the Cornish sun upon my face. In the distance I could see men working the fields and upon the bay, boats setting out for the day's fishing.

'Yes Mr Penrose, I am sure it is,' I said.

'Goodbye… ' said Dr Gonzales, patting our heads and shoulders, '… and, I'm sorry.'

'What for?' I said.

'Meredith…' He faltered, then took a deep breath. The others were busy saying goodbye or loading baggage on to the train. Elsa was distracted by Miss Ariel. He talked to me alone, 'You don't know this Bill, but the truth… the truth, is that we almost did him a great disservice, and if it hadn't been for the storm… well I think we might have blackened our souls with deeds we might have regretted. In a funny way the storm saved us from that path… ' I smiled and hugged him.

'Fare thee well lad and lass,' said the Penroses, turning me round and shaking me roughly by the hand.

'Goodbye,' said Stephen, bowing.

'Safe journey to you all. I love you all dearly, and come back soon.' Anthony shouted as the train began to pull away.

We waved until we could see them no longer and settled in for our long journey home. Elsa and I sat on different sides of the carriage, each of us looking out of the window. Elsa stared into the distant sea, savouring every last glimpse of the diamond blues and emerald greens, watching the gulls circling over the distant fishing boats, losing herself for precious moments in the sparkling, sun blessed depths. For my part, I gazed upon the distant, carpeted moors of gorse and heather and was mesmerised by the golden crops, rolling and waving in the gentle breeze.

After a time, we passed the last of the moors and could see the sea no more.

Epilogue

bi,

So dear heart, my tale is ended.

From the high hill of my old age I have gazed at the distant past, divested myself of its memories and you, for better or worse, are now the bearer, both of what has passed and what will be.

This is a blessing and a curse, for I pass to you not only our secrets, but also a great and terrible responsibility. As I stated before, the fate of Lyonesse House – and so much more – is in your hands.

So go now, with the memory of my adventures still fresh in your mind, and go alone, to Penwith. Take the key contained with this letter. Make the journey down to Cornwall, tonight, by train. At Penzance Station take a taxi to the gates of Lyonesse House, I have left a set of directions for you to give to the driver.

The gates to the Estate are iron and will seemingly be rusted solid. But for you they will open, trust me in this. Walk through the green and quiet woods, go waist deep in the grass and knotted weeds, to the old and empty house. Don't be shocked, nor made curious by its run down façade, broken windows and ivy covered walls. Keep to your task. With the key, open the front door.

When you are inside you will pause, unsettled by being alone in the dark and the silence of this near ruin of a house. The summer songs of the birds and the whisper of the distant shore will seem a world away. Yet hold your nerve.

On the ground floor, near the old servants' quarters, you will find a room. To the back of the room you will find a cupboard, and on its door a circle. Open it. There you will find a subterranean passageway and at its end, a room. A library.

Somewhere within the library, perhaps on the table or hanging from the door, you may discover a leather satchel. Inside the satchel you will find four old, leather bound books, identical in appearance but for the faint inscriptions borne on their covers: 'Dowr,' 'Ayr,' 'Dor', 'Tan.'

Use them wisely Abi, for as Meredith once said to me, it is possible to do great harm with such books, as well as good.

Myth and Legend

The poet Ted Hughes once said that the south west of England was 'un-exorcised'.

Perhaps more than any other place in the British Isles, Cornwall has maintained a rich heritage of myth and legend. Tales abound of missing sailors being lost to the charms of mermaids, of ghost ships that appear from the mists, and of hidden treasure guarded by the ghosts of pirates. When these myths are combined with the seafaring traditions, Celtic history and dramatic landscape of Cornwall, it is easy to see why legend has endured, and why visitor and resident alike are still so fascinated by Cornwall's legacy of supernatural and fantastic tales.

Many Cornish legends, some customs and a smattering of history are included in the story (indeed, they are crucial to the plot). Here, I have outlined those stories and legends, which inspired me to write *Storm of the Magi*. These are just a taste of the many Cornish myths and folk-tales that exist. There are plenty more for you to discover.

Lyonesse

Cornish Legend

Lyonesse is said to have existed in pre-Christian Cornwall as an area of land bridging western Cornwall and the isles of Scilly. Legend has it that Lyonesse was a seat of civilisation and culture, all of which was lost when it suddenly, and inexplicably, sank beneath the waves sometime in the Dark Ages. It is said that the bells of Lyonesse can still be heard ringing from the deep – a haunting reminder of Cornwall's very own Atlantis.

In the book

Lyonesse was once the name of the southwest tip of Cornwall (now Penwith). It is Cornwall as it once was, when magical forces held sway and mermaids and sea serpents swam in its coastal waters. It exists now as a ghost of a time and place long since passed, a 'lost' island, no earthly navigator could find, peopled by the ghosts of pirates and elemental spirits. It is home for those souls whose mortal bodies were lost at sea, or trapped in mines, whose bodies were never found and subject to Christian burial. When ghosts, mermaids and sea serpents appear in Cornwall, it is from Lyonesse that they are called.

Isle of Ictis

Cornish Legend

Ictis, the City of Books. The Phoenicians and other ancient civilisations are said to have come to Cornwall, visiting an island where they traded for tin. Records of this trade go back as far as the 4th century BC. Ictis was the Roman name for the island. Perhaps it earned its other title (City of Books) because the various civilisations that came to Cornwall imparted knowledge; of astrology, astronomy, mathematics and alchemy; books of magic and science, for then there was no such distinction between them. St Michael's Mount near Penzance has been cited as the most probable location of Ictis.

In the book

Ictis, is the capital of Lyonesse, a labyrinthine, fortified library situated on an island off the coast of the mainland. Here the magical forces of the magis' books (see below) are at their strongest.

Festival of Lyonesse

Cornish Legend

Pagan festivals were once a vital part of the community calendar (indeed, they were the calendar!). Customs involving dance and drama, rites of fertility and even sacrifice were practised to mark the passing of the seasons, to induce fertility and to appease and contain the forces of nature to ensure good harvests. Such festivals held great social, religious and agricultural significance.

Many of these customs have long since disappeared, absorbed into the Christian calendar of events, banned, or simply forgotten. Yet in Cornwall, perhaps more than any other place in the British Isles, they remain in some semblance of their ancient form and are an important part of the calendar to this day. Good examples are Padstow's Mayday, Mazey day in Penzance and the Lafrowda day of St. Just.

In the book
The midsummer Festival of Lyonesse harks back to the days before Christianity and science were in the ascendant. In those times the ruler of Lyonesse would make a sacrifice on the summer solstice to the pagan gods. The purpose of this practise was to ensure good harvest and full fishing nets. Though the sacrifice was usually an animal, if the crops were weak or the fishnets empty, a human sacrifice would be made.

At the modern day festival a 'King' is chosen by the local people, to symbolically rule over the community and forces of nature. He performs a mock sacrifice; the burning of a straw effigy. Many still believe that this ritual and the role of the Festival King are essential to securing a successful harvest.

The Magi and their Books

Cornish Legend
Precious little is known about Celtic religion and even less about its priests, the Druids. Much of their lore and custom were closely guarded secrets, even within their own society. When magic was perceived to be a very real power, the line between 'magus' and 'ruler' was blurred and those who practised magic were feared and respected.

In the book
The magi are directly descended from the Order of Druid Kings who once ruled Cornwall, an Order whose mission was to maintain balance between the Elemental forces of Nature and the Society of mankind. They continue to practise their secret arts, wielding power over forces natural and unnatural. They can call or

quell a storm, bring ghosts into our world or even bring the dead back to life.

The source of their powers are ancient books, provided by the magi who travelled to Cornwall when the Phoenicians and other great civilisations came to Cornwall trading for tin. The most powerful of these are the books of Earth, Air, Fire and Water. The book explores what the Celtic Druids might have made of the knowledge imparted to them by the eastern civilisations that visited Cornwall.

The magi's magic is based on their core belief: that everything that exists is composed of the base elements: earth, air, fire and water. The Spirit though, is constant and may exist in many guises, each a different form and mix of the four base elements. Hence a ghost may appear as flesh and bone if willed to do so by a magus, or the spirit of a human may re-appear in the body of an animal. People, animals, plants, even inanimate objects can be subject to the will of a magus, his skill lying in the artful manipulation of the elements through the use of the books.

Treasure and Ghost Ships

Cornish Legend

Tales of wrecking, smuggling and piracy are common in Cornwall. Not surprisingly, buried or hidden treasure is a common factor in these tales, as are legends of pirate ghosts, or ships that appear in the mists that roll in from the Atlantic. It has been suggested that many of the ghost stories accompanying tales of treasure were dreamt up by the smugglers and pirates themselves, as a way of keeping prying hands and eyes away from their booty.

In the book

A horde of treasure is believed to be hidden in a cave in or near the cove of Lamorna. It once belonged to an infamous smuggler called John Tanner, Captain of the *Seahawk*, whose boat and crew were famous for outrunning the ships of HM Customs.

The magus Meredith resurrects the ship and its crew to carry the living to the ghost island of Lyonesse.

Mermaids

Cornish legend

Numerous Cornish villages and towns have their own tale of a mermaid, usually of a sailor losing his heart to a 'siren of the deep.' The most famous example is the mermaid of Zennor (if you visit the church there you can see a carving of her image).

Why is the mermaid such a popular and enduring figure in myth? I think it says something about our love of the ocean, and also of men's fear of the 'danger' of alluring beauty.

In the book

Like all the mythic beings of Lyonesse, the mermaids can be called to the service of the magus Meredith, and this is how we first see a mermaid; being summoned to rescue dolphins from the nets of fishermen. Later on, we see the merpeople called by the apprentice magus Bill, but with considerably less confidence! For he nearly succumbs to the seductive powers that mermaids famously have over men. Theirs is a power that can be harnessed by the magi, but which is ultimately – like the sea – impossible to tame.